TRUST FALL

If you want to read my other books or keep up with new releases, check out my website—
Author Lyndsay Marie
www.AuthorLyndsayMarie.com

or visit me on Amazon
https://www.amazon.com/author/lyndsaymarie

This book is for Amber, my book-bestie! I couldn't have done this without you!

ONE
Jameson

"What the hell do you mean he got away?" I bit out.

This was the second time in less than a week that one of Kane's idiot men had almost gotten inside my casino. It was bad enough they even made it onto the property, much less halfway down the corridor and practically out onto the gaming floor.

Okay, maybe not quite that far, but it still felt too close for comfort.

The line fell silent.

With the telephone clutched in a death grip pressed against my ear, I gazed up at Ivan. I watched him as he sat there just as casually as could be across from me with a dumbfounded *don't ask me* look plastered on his face.

"Answer me," I demanded with a huff. My words were directed at Chris, Emerald Haze's general operations manager. Ivan knew I was talking to him, too.

Lyndsay Marie

"Yeah, James," he breathed defeatedly. "I'm here. I don't—I don't fucking know how. He ran out and got away from us before we could catch up to him. Leon took a pop at him, but the guy slipped through the woods on the south side."

"Unbelievable. Did anyone see or hear Leon shoot?"

"Not that I'm aware of. He used his silencer. Again, I'm so sorry. I know we fucked up."

"You think? I've got Kane's men creeping and crawling around this place like flies on horse shit, and *you*, of all people, almost welcomed them in with open arms and a cup of tea."

I'd given all my men one simple order: stop anyone who isn't supposed to be here in their tracks and stop them at all costs—it didn't matter where or how.

That's it.

That's all they had to do these days. I didn't think that was too much to ask for.

"Y'all have one job. One. Fucking. Job, Chris. Do I need to start doing this shit myself?" I wouldn't. But I was getting close to it.

"No," he sighed. "Again, I'm sorry."

"Sorry doesn't fix it. Bullets do." Even though a bullet was what had gotten me into this clusterfuck in the first place.

As much as I hated death and dying, I'd long accepted that killing was a necessary evil in this business. Sometimes that meant kill or be killed. We all had enemies in this industry, and unfortunately, my dad's had been

8

passed down to me. Kane was only going to hold off for so long before saying *fuck it* and ripping off the proverbial Band-Aid.

I had less than a week before said ripping occurred.

I massaged my forehead in an attempt to ward off an impending migraine, then let out a slow, deep breath, trying to calm my nerves and collect my thoughts before opening my mouth to speak—an art I'd yet to perfect.

"Is everyone else okay?" I asked because even when my guys messed up, which wasn't very often, I still cared about them. The last thing I wanted was for anyone else to get hurt or end up dead.

One was already enough.

"Yeah, we're all good," Chris reassured. "Everyone's fine."

"Good. Don't let them that close again."

"Yes, ma'am."

"Thank you. Now, get back to work." I slammed the phone down on the receiver, ending the call.

I already knew everyone thought I was a t-total bitch, but a job like this wasn't meant for the soft and weak. I'd spent the majority of my life being conditioned for this role—to be callous and coldhearted.

I wasn't about to let them prove me wrong now.

"James." Ivan rubbed the back of his neck.

"What?"

"Go easy on our guys. You know we're all feeling the pressure here, right?"

Lyndsay Marie

"There won't be any more *guys* left to feel the pressure if my crew lets any more of these assholes get away. At this point, I want to see bodies stacked up to the goddamned sky. I don't even give a shit where we dispose of them anymore. Throw them out in Kane's parking lot. Let his patrons use them as speed bumps for all I care."

I plopped down onto my executive leather office chair and pulled up the security cameras that covered the exterior perimeter of the property. I did a quick scan of the south side of the property, where the perp had been chased.

Nothing.

The sun was shining, and the grass was brown but still had a smattering of green coloring left to it here and there. Trees had lost most of their leaves.

It was as though he'd never been here.

"These guys are getting entirely too close for my comfort." They'd mostly stayed away from me until recently. Now, they were popping up left and right. None had gotten as close as the one today, and he'd somehow managed to make it all the way through the front door.

In their defense, it was getting harder and harder to spot these guys. They'd come in through the main entrance, and if not for my keen-eyed surveillance crew or the extensive research IT did on Kane and his circus, we'd be none the wiser as to who they were or their intentions.

But my men? Oh, they knew.

"I agree. That's why I keep telling you we need help."

10

I stared Ivan down through squinted eyes. "No. We do not. We can handle this ourselves."

"Yes, we do, and no, we cannot. James. You're—" He paused, scrubbing his hands down his face. He was clearly just as sick of my shit as everyone else around here. "You're in way over your head, and forgive me for what I'm about to say, but you're hardheaded as fuck. I know that's not what you wanna hear, but it's—"

I held up my hand to stop him. "Save it. I already know what you're going to say. You, of all people, know how damn near impossible it is to find someone—anyone— we can trust. You're not just gonna pull some Joe Blow off the streets of Tunica or Memphis and expect him to do what you or any of us do. That's what Kane does, and he's sloppy for doing it."

"I don't disagree, but please, hear me out."

I closed my eyes, waiting to hear what he had to say, even though I didn't want to hear another word about needing help.

"I might know someone."

"Might? What do you mean you *might* know someone?" Ivan *might* know someone? This was news to me.

"Okay, okay." He waved his hands dismissively. "Relax. I *know* a guy. Better?"

"No, not at all." There was a substantial difference between just knowing someone and having them readily available to put their life at risk. Those were two completely different things. "Look, Ivan. I've got Kane's men crawling up my ass, the Haunted Hearts Gala coming up this weekend, which means I've got less than a week left to either kill or be killed, and you're sitting here *now* telling me you know someone who's readily available at your disposal, who can come in and do your job?"

"Yes?"

"Your whole-ass job?" I asked flatly because I was not entertained by his proclamation.

"That's exactly what I'm saying."

"Christ. And why am I just now finding out about this *friend*?"

"I have my reasons."

"Me not ending up dead is a damned good reason to tell me who this person is and why you've held out on me."

"I think now's a good time to, you know, call him…before it's too late."

"Hell, at this point, we might as well put a target on all of our foreheads and walk over to Kane's place and get this shit over with. 'Cause right now, our margin of error is close to zero. Actually, it is zero."

"No shit, James. Why do you think I'm sitting here practically begging you to give me a chance? Let me bring my guy in."

My guy. I couldn't for the life of me think of a single soul Ivan knew that I didn't who could easily waltz in here and take over for him. Someone who didn't need to be trained. I was also very well aware I didn't have a choice at this point.

I swallowed the lump in my throat. "Do you trust him?"

"With my life."

I leaned back, matching his posture. "And mine?"

"Yours too, obviously. Look. I'm getting too old for this shit. I can't look after you like I used to; you know that. We've played it safe for a long time, but Kane isn't gonna stop until he gets what he wants, and right now, it's you. I couldn't live with myself if anything ever happened to you. God knows your dad would come back from his grave and finish me off if I did."

A smirk tugged at the corner of my mouth at the sentiment. "Yeah, he probably would."

"If you let bring him here to essentially take my place for a few days, I'm of better use to you out there than I am in here, ya know?"

Unfortunately, he was right.

"Fine. Tell me more. How long have you known this *friend* of yours, and why am I just now hearing about him?"

"He's been...unavailable, we'll say. But he's loyal, and I've known him practically his entire life."

I rolled my eyes. "His? Not yours? He already sounds too young." Not that I had much room to talk. As far as I knew, I was the youngest leader in the industry.

"Well, he's probably close to your age, if I ventured to guess. Maybe a few years older. I'm no spring chicken, as you can tell. I'm going to have to be replaced eventually. This could be a way to transition someone else into this role."

"Great. So, a youngish, egotistical, testosterone-fueled prick?"

"Jesus, James." Ivan tilted his head from side to side, cracking his neck. "You've got issues. You know that?" He shook his head. "You need someone younger than me and someone who knows what the fuck he's doing who can keep up with the demands of the job."

"You mean my demands?"

"Exactly. I can't guarantee your safety or mine anymore, and that scares the shit out of me. Look at what happened today."

I sighed. "I get it. I do. But you know how I feel about outsiders."

Ivan was one of the very few people I truly trusted. He'd worked for my dad since I was in diapers. There were even pictures floating around somewhere of him feeding me a bottle.

Now, because of some sick twist in fate, he worked directly for me. That alone probably aged him an extra ten years.

"Look how long it took my dad to assemble this team. Why should I trust you to just bring in some guy you've been keeping in your back pocket for a rainy day?"

"It's not like that. I would never withhold valuable information from you."

"Sure as hell feels like you already did."

"There's just some things you're gonna have to learn on your own about this business. This guy? I know he's got

14

what it takes. He's also my last resort. Otherwise, I got nothin'."

Fuck. "If you can at least guarantee me he isn't some punk-ass kid who's going to stand in my way or screw around and get me killed, then he *might* be worth talking to. But I make no promises."

He held up his hands. "No worries. I haven't talked to him in a while. Knowing the nature of his work, I don't even know if he's still alive."

I slouched, sinking further into my chair, feeling like I'd just had my ass beat at this point. I looked over and studied my laptop screen, scanning the cameras across the parking lot and back loading dock, then down into the wooded area of the south property line one more time. Things seemed normal enough…for now.

"Fine. Find out if he's alive and willing to work. Get him here so we can chat. The sooner, the better."

"I'll call him before lunch and have him here by this afternoon. How's that sound?"

"Sounds like I hope it's not already too late."

Lyndsay Marie

One year.

Well, almost.

Three hundred and fifty-five days, to be exact.

Not that I'd been counting…well, maybe I had been just a little. Except I wasn't crossing days off the calendar to some important life event or counting down to an upcoming fun-filled date. Not even close.

"Refill?" my waitress asked, holding up a stainless-steel carafe.

I glanced down at my nearly empty cup. It wasn't like I had shit else to do, but a third cup of coffee seemed like a bad idea. Even for me.

"Uh, no, thanks. I'm good for now."

"Can I get you anything else?" Her tone was borderline impatient. I'd been taking up this table for at least two hours.

I flicked my gaze to the worn-out silver name tag pinned to her left upper chest. Not that I needed to. I'd been in this restaurant at least four days a week for the last eleven and a half months. I knew her work schedule.

"No, thanks, Nancy. I'm good for now."

She placed my check face down on the table. "Until next time."

Little did either of us know there wouldn't be a next time.

I'd discovered this little coffee shop/diner during my first week in Nashville. It was within walking distance of where I'd be living for the foreseeable future, and it had free Wi-Fi. There was the added bonus of being located on one of the busiest streets in the city and the best place to watch unsuspecting patrons come and go about their morning routine. Mostly, it was hungover businessmen discussing the stock market or the latest sports stats, stay-at-home moms coming in from their morning yoga class, chatting about their shitty marriages and kids' latest milestones over a vanilla soy latte, and college kids studying for various degrees they'd probably never use in hopes they'd make an actual difference in the world someday.

These people were oblivious.

It's been said that the average person will cross paths with thirty-six murderers in their lifetime. Thirty-six. That's a lot. Yet not a single person here was any the wiser that a man who probably had more blood on his hands than their local general surgeon would essentially be sitting less than ten feet from them at any given moment of their mundane morning.

Lyndsay Marie

These people have no idea just how above average they are.

I pulled a crisp twenty from my wallet and laid it on top of the handwritten check. I didn't need to look. My order was always the same. The total had never changed.

As I stood to leave, I felt my phone vibrate against my thigh. I pulled it out, and the name IVAN flashed across the screen.

I swiped the green Answer button and held the speaker against my ear as I sat back down and waited. I hadn't seen or heard from him in almost a year, but I knew he hadn't changed and never would. One thing about Ivan was he always had to have the first and last word. Today would be no different.

I stared out the picture window at the rain-covered street. The rain had finally stopped after what seemed like too goddamned long, but the evidence of it remained. Cars passed, throwing rainwater onto the sidewalks. Patrons rushed back and forth, hugging close to the building, trying to avoid being splashed from all directions.

After what felt like a lifetime, a familiar voice finally broke through the speaker. "Hey. You answered. I'm surprised."

I waited for a few seconds to respond. "I'm good. Thanks for asking. How can I help you?"

He let out an awkward laugh. "What makes you think I'm calling for help?"

"Because you're not calling to wish me a late happy birthday." I had no idea what Ivan was about to throw at me, but my best guess was it wasn't good, and I wasn't going to like it.

"Fair. And you're right. I've, uh, got a bit of a situation on my hands."

The last time he presented me with a *situation*, shit did not end well for a lot of people.

"Yeah?"

"Yeah. I need your help. There. I said it. Happy?"

"At no point does your admission to needing my help give me butterflies. I'm still pretty fucking salty about the last time you needed my help."

"Well, there's nothing I can do about it now. I've moved on from that, and so should you."

"I'm listening."

He sighed into the phone. "If you're wondering, the answer is no. This isn't like *that*. This job is…different. I need to hire you for your protective services."

I scoffed. Couldn't wait to see what kind of offer he was about to present. "And you can't get someone else to do it?"

"I would if I could, but you know how it is in this business. As much as I hate to admit, you're still the best man I got on roster. Really, you're the only man who can handle this." I could hear the frustration in his voice. It sounded more like he was at the end of his rope and was either about to let go or hang himself with it.

"That's not very reassuring." Ivan had a lot of men at his disposal. To think I was the only person he knew who could handle *this*, whatever the fuck that meant, didn't give

19

me much hope for whatever clusterfuck he'd gotten himself into this time.

"No shit. How you think I feel? Things have been getting a little more…convoluted, we'll say. I need someone reliable, someone I can trust. Ya know?"

Everything about this conversation so far reeked of absolute disaster. I only knew this because I knew Ivan. He had a knack for getting himself into situations he couldn't get out of alone. Not to mention, he'd called me because he couldn't trust anyone else on his crew, and that wasn't very reassuring.

But as shitty as he'd made my life once before, I didn't think it could get much worse. "I guess tell me where and when."

"Yesterday woulda been great, but in reality, I need you by tonight."

"Ivan. You can't be serious."

"Unfortunately, I am. I'm on a schedule tighter than a camel's ass in a sandstorm."

"Where would you like me by tonight?"

He paused for a few seconds, then answered. "Here." His response was barely an audible mumble, like he didn't have the balls to even tell me.

"Here? As in Emerald Haze here?"

"Yeah. That'd be the one."

Seeing as how I'd left that place, sending me back to Mississippi sounded like a really stupid fucking idea. Even for him.

"Are you serious, Ivan?" I lowered my tone so the guy sitting at the table directly across from me hopefully wouldn't hear me about to lose my shit. He briefly glanced up at me over the newspaper in his hands before seemingly going back to reading as if he hadn't just been eavesdropping. "You want me back there, knowing how you sent me away? Are you sure that's a good idea?"

Emerald Haze was the last place I wanted or needed to go. Putting me back to work there sounded like a bigger pain in the ass than the way he'd gotten rid of me the first time.

"Dead serious. This is where I need you, unfortunately. If I had any other choice, we wouldn't be having this conversation. Sorry to inconvenience your daily latte routine."

"Dick."

"I've been called worse. But all things considered, you and I are still the only two who really know what happened. And we're gonna keep it that way."

"God damn, Ivan. I somehow find that hard to believe."

"Trust me. If anyone else knew, don't you think there'd be a witch hunt for you by now?"

Okay, I had to give him that. If Ivan had only called me only as a last resort, some serious shit was about to go down, or already had, and he couldn't fix it.

"I can't fucking believe this," I mumbled under my breath.

Lyndsay Marie

"How you think I feel? I'm chasing my tail around here, and I don't like it. Things are getting out of control. I can already feel another ulcer growing."

"I don't know, Ivan. This sounds—"

"Look, I know this isn't the most convenient—"

"It never is," I deadpanned, cutting him off. We'd had a sort of symbiotic relationship—I did their dirty work, almost no questions asked; they compensated me very well. The better I became at my job, the more they realized just how much they needed me. I guess to my benefit, I was of better use to them alive than dead.

"I'll at least make it worth your time."

"How's that? 'Cause I'm quite enjoying my quiet mornings and caramel lattes."

"I'll double your pay from last time."

"That's a lot of money." And not at all the offer I'd expected. He'd paid me enough for my last job I didn't need to work. Not for him or anyone else. At this point, I was just doing it out of sheer boredom. *Hush money is a beautiful thing.*

"Yes, it is."

"Why so much?"

"Because this won't be easy."

"Has it ever been?" The question was rhetorical. How this particular job could be any harder than the last one was beyond me. "What makes this one so difficult?"

"Because." He paused. "This one is different."

"Different? Different than what? Execution? Extortion? Because I recall very distinctly, once upon a time ago, you treated me like your bitch boy and threatened me with my life if I didn't comply. That's the only reason I agreed to last time. It got me the fuck away from that place."

I glanced around the coffee shop. It was still packed, but morning patrons had stopped pouring in and were down to a slow trickle. I was sure the guy ten feet away was getting an earful.

"Yeah, well, lucky for you, your role will be changing. Though things could be a bit more difficult, depending on how you look at it."

I held my phone against my ear with my shoulder and scrubbed my hands down my face. My scruffy beard against my palms reminded me how badly I needed to shave.

The thought of going back to Emerald Haze for any reason made my stomach turn. But if shit was about to hit the fan, the stakes were much higher than Ivan's pea brain could even fathom. It wasn't his life I gave a fuck about.

"I don't think anything I do could possibly be any worse than the last hit. How long's this gonna take? Any idea?"

"Let's get through this weekend. How's that sound?"

"Sounds really fucking expensive." There was no way Ivan was going to pay me that much money for a few days' worth of work without it costing me something just as valuable in return. "What's this going to cost me?"

"Potentially, your life."

THREE
Jameson

"When's this guy going to be here?" It'd been less than an entire business day since Ivan had somehow convinced me that it was a good idea to let him bring in outside help, and by some miracle, he'd have him here by this afternoon, provided the guy was still alive. Ivan's ability to produce help this fast and the confidence he had in this random man gave me an uneasy feeling.

I snuck a glance at him. He sat in his usual spot whenever he was in my office—an antique, emerald-green leather chair with tarnished brass studs and hand-carved wood accents on the armrests. He had his legs crossed, casually resting one over the other, and was probably playing Mario Kart on his phone. All I could do was pace back and forth across the floor behind my desk, burning a trail in the carpet.

"Relax," he said with a shit-eating grin. "He's here."

"He's here?" I stopped short. "Already?" Already. I didn't know why I was so surprised that Ivan had delivered on his promise. After our conversation this morning, Ivan stepped out of my office to call the guy, and within ten minutes, he assured me this guy would be here before dinner tonight. "Where is he?"

"Jesus Christ, you need to relax." He stood up and pocketed his phone. "He's in the lobby. You want me to bring him up here, or you wanna come down and meet him?"

"Um, just put him in the Diamond Suite. I'll meet y'all over there in a few. I've got a few things I need to check on first."

He gave me a look like he knew I was full of shit. I didn't have anything to do but pull myself together.

"Sure. I'll text you when he's settled."

"Thanks. Stick Jordan at the door, would you?"

"Roger that."

Ivan made his exit. As soon as the door closed, I flung my laptop open and pulled up the security camera feed. I clicked through the different views until I found the one I was looking for.

A few minutes passed, and Ivan eventually appeared on the screen. I watched as he greeted our guest. He approached him like an old friend, and I suppose he was to some degree if Ivan trusted him enough to ask him for help. He scanned him up and down before giving him a pat on the shoulder.

Lyndsay Marie

I zoomed in to get a better look, but the guy had his back to the camera. I stared him down from behind as they walked toward the hotel towers.

Nice ass should have been the last thing that came to mind, but the man was built like a beast. He towered over Ivan by at least a half a foot, and judging by his broad shoulders, bulky upper arms that were hugged deliciously tight by the sleeves of his button-down shirt, and his narrow waist cinched by a leather belt, I could only assume he worked out regularly. Because no man walked around naturally looking that good.

He must've ridden in on a bike. He had a matte-black motorcycle helmet in his grip, hanging at his side.

I switched between camera views as Ivan led him across the main casino floor past the card tables, through the dining area, and over to the elevator lobby near the nickel and penny slot machines. Security gave them a nod as they walked through the corridor.

The two stood side by side, chitchatting like old friends who hadn't seen each other in a while. When the elevator finally arrived, I caught a better view of our *guest's* face.

My stomach dropped to the floor.

"No fucking way," I cursed out loud to myself as recognition hit me like a ton of bricks to the chest. His face might've been masked by a week's worth of facial hair, but I knew that jawline from anyone. "That son of a bitch."

I was going to kill Ivan…and then his *friend*.

Every image, every pushed-down memory I'd ever had of him burned into my brain, every second from the day we met until the day he'd disappeared from my life when I needed him the most, and every single intimate fucking moment in between resurfaced in a split second of a flash of a profile view.

"Two can play this game," I mumbled. I pulled up the workers' contract with the NDA, made a few quick changes, then printed the documents out. Envelope in hand, I stormed out of my office, slamming the door shut, blowing right past Jordan.

He pushed himself off the wall. "Everything okay, ma'am?"

"Peachy."

He kept up with me as I opted to take the stairs, trying not to slip and fall on my ass in the process. I made my way across the casino floor faster than I ever had. Considering I was wearing heels, I was impressed with my ability to move at such speed and not sprain my ankle or faceplant the floor.

Jordan stood silently beside me as I jammed my override key into the lock, taking us straight to the penthouse floor of the hotel tower.

When we came to a stop, I stepped off first and continued my trek to the guest suite. Just as I raised my hand to knock, the door opened. Ivan was on his way out, both he and his *friend* laughing. They didn't have a fucking clue I was even here.

"Are you two done having fun yet?" I asked Tweedle Dumb and Tweedle Dumber. I shot a look back at Jordan. "You can go now. Thank you."

27

"Yes, ma'am," he replied, then left.

When I looked back at Ivan and *Roman Motherfucking Stone*, the blood drained from his face, confirming every single one of my suspicions. My sudden presence processed in their pea brains—he and Ivan both looked like they'd just seen a ghost and shit their pants in response.

"Funny how fast the laughter ceases when I'm around."

Ivan cleared his throat. "Ja—Jameson, you remember—"

"How could I possibly forget?" I cut in with a forced smile, looking up at Roman as he towered behind Ivan.

Roman folded his bulky, muscle-clad arms across his chest. *Stop gawking.* A distraction like him was the last thing I needed at the moment.

He looked anywhere but at me and mumbled what sounded something like "Jesus fucking Christ" under his breath.

"Surprised to see me?" I asked Roman.

As I waited for him to respond, I narrowed my eyes and gave Ivan a death stare. He knew he'd fucked up. Hell, I had fucked up by not listening to my gut and digging deeper and asking him more about his connections. Instead, I'd put what little faith I had left in anyone and given him full control over this situation.

"Listen, James. I told you to trust me. So just hear me out, okay?"

"I *did* trust you. I did hear out, and this is what you bring me?" I pointed to Roman. "A dead guy? You both owe me a really big fucking explanation. *Big*!"

"Shit," Ivan mumbled as he scrubbed his hands down his face. *What? Didn't think that far ahead?* "He's not— he's not dead."

"No shit, Sherlock...not yet."

"Nobody said he was dead," Ivan affirmed.

"We'll talk about this later," I told Ivan. Then, I glared at Roman. "Well, where the hell have you been?"

I hadn't spoken to or seen Roman in almost a year. None of us had, not that I knew of. All I knew was that he was here one day, gone the next. Anyone who knew anything about his whereabouts had remained tight-lipped about him ever since. I tried calling him and sent him text after text. I got nothing. We all assumed he was dead. That was just how things worked around here. When people fell off, it wasn't because they'd decided to up and quit for a different job somewhere else. It was because they'd been gotten rid of. I never expected him to be one of those people.

Now here he was, standing less than four feet in front of me like he'd never left in the first place.

"It's complicated," Ivan responded with an apprehensive tone.

"Good thing I didn't ask you. Where. Have. You. Been?" I demanded.

I knew the risks of the job and the risks that came with being with a man like Roman. It wasn't uncommon for men like him to be here one day, gone the next. He'd been with us for a lot of years. Our business needed him more than not. He'd become an asset. I'd never expected him to be one of them, and apparently, he hadn't.

Roman's chest rose, and his nostrils flared as he sucked in a deep breath before slowly letting it out. "Like Ivan said, it's complicated."

"Then somebody start fucking explaining. I don't have all goddamned day."

Roman cleared his throat. "Ivan asked for my help. That's what I'm here to do."

I poked Ivan in the chest with the corner of the manila envelope. "My life is on the line. I trusted you to bring someone in to protect me, and *this* is who you call?"

"Wait, wait, wait a damned minute," Roman cut in as he stepped forward. He tapped Ivan on the shoulder as Ivan stood between us, rubbing the bridge of his nose. "You're paying me to protect *her*? You told me *you* needed my help."

"I do need your help," Ivan said, holding up his arms toward me as he slipped his way out of the war zone and stood off to the side, leaving nothing but air and opportunity between me and Roman. "With her."

Tears stung behind my eyes, but I refused to let them fall. Not now. *Not ever* again. I promised myself a long time ago that I'd never shed one single tear over another goddamned man. "You know what? Fuck the both of you."

"No way, Ivan," Roman stated, throwing his hands in the air. "I'm not babysitting James. Find someone else."

"Listen, James, I swear I'll explain," Ivan had the balls to pipe up.

"Then you'd better fucking start because if *this* is who you expect to protect me, you both had best be on you're A game, or I'll make sure neither of you lives to see your next birthday." I looked up at Roman. "Yours isn't too far off."

"You don't get a choi—" Ivan started.

I cut in. "What's wrong with me? Not what you expected?"

Our gazes met. It was the first time we'd locked eyes in what felt like a lifetime. A very, *very* small shred of me wanted to break down, throw myself into his arms and have a long, overdue cry. I wanted to tell him about all the shit I'd been through, how badly I'd missed him, how much I missed us.

Thankfully, anger took over, outweighing my vulnerability.

"Not at all," Roman said. "Seems like Ivan left out the part about *who* it was that needed my help. I just assumed it was him."

"Assuming was your first mistake. It seems like he left a lot of relevant parts out. So sorry to disappoint you."

He tilted his head ever so slightly. "I'm not disappointed," he said with a tone that felt like it had some underlying softness to it. "Just surprised...and a little confused. That's all."

Aren't we all?

Ivan lit up a cigarette right there in the middle of the hallway like he owned the place. I swatted it out of his hand and stepped on it, smashing the whole thing into the carpet.

Lyndsay Marie

"What the hell, James? I'm dying here. Y'all are killing me."

"You're killing yourself with those things. Take it outside."

"Fine." He threw his hands in the air. "I'm going to the docks. I'll be back in a few. Y'all handle this on your own." He looked at Roman and grinned. "She's all yours, kid." Then, he bent down and picked up his squashed cigarette, stuffed in his front pocket, and walked away.

"Bastard," I mumbled.

Once Ivan was out of sight, Roman spoke first. "What the hell is going on?"

"Why don't you tell me. Hmm? Y'all seem to know a hell of a lot more than I do."

"It would seem so."

"I thought you were dead," I whisper-yelled. "Let's start there, then we'll come back to why you're here."

He briefly closed his eyes. "Assuming was your first mistake," he said, mocking me. "And honestly, I don't fucking know what's going on anymore."

"Where have you been? Hmm? You at least know that much." I gave him a moment to collect his thoughts, see if he was going to tell me. He didn't. "Roman. I called you; I texted you—at least a thousand times. You never once responded. Hell, you didn't even open my texts. Every message I've ever sent was left delivered and unread."

He took a slow, deep breath in and gazed down at the floor. "It's just," he started, "it's business."

"Business? Huh. Interesting. That's how you saw us? Business?"

"What? No. But how else do you want me to look at it? I'm just a pawn used to carry out tasks in a game I can't fucking win. I was given a job, and I did exactly what I was told to do. Again and again."

"Right. So, in the span of less than forty-eight hours, I lose the two closest people to me in my entire life, only to find out after months of mourning, one of you didn't actually die? And it's just business to you? No, Roman," I seethed, "this is *very* fucking personal."

He let out a huff. "I don't know what to tell you. If you don't like my answer, then find somebody else to do this."

"Believe me, I wish like hell I could. If Ivan had told me he was bringing you here to protect me, you wouldn't be standing here right now. But we both know you're the only one who can do this."

"I do, and I hate it. Did you ever think that maybe you're not cut out for this kind of work?" He stepped forward, standing less than a foot away, never once taking his eyes off mine. It was like he lured me in and held me with a single stare. I wanted to punch him and kiss him— because, yes, we'd once had *that* kind of relationship. Apparently, I still found him sinfully attractive, even though he'd been resurrected from the dead. That was until he opened his mouth to speak again. "This is a man's job."

My intrusive thoughts won.

Lyndsay Marie

"You sexist pig." I reared back, and with as much force as I had, I swung my arm around to slap him across the face. It was long overdue.

His hand reached up out of nowhere, grabbing me by the wrist before I could make contact. He jerked me forward, causing me to stumble straight into him.

"I meant," he spoke in a low tone, "this isn't a job for *you*." The way his words rolled through his chest sent chills down my spine.

I could feel each rise and fall of his chest as it pressed against mine. Power radiated off every square inch of him. Hell, it practically seeped through every pore of his body. Then, I made the mistake of taking a deep breath, causing his cologne to invade my senses. Whatever he was wearing made him smell so damned delectable. *That* pissed me off even more.

"I've been training for this job for half my life, Roman. Rest assured, I can handle it. But if we're going to be stuck together, I'll make every minute of your time here a living hell."

"I'm looking forward to it, but you're taking your misplaced anger out on the wrong person." He dropped my arm, and I took a step back, putting space between us.

I massaged my wrist where his fingers had been. "Then who should I take it out on?"

Just then, Ivan walked up. "Y'all two get everything worked out here?"

Roman stared Ivan down as he approached. I would have given up this entire casino to know what was going through his mind at the moment.

"He'll do," I tossed over my shoulder. We all knew if anyone could keep me alive, it was Roman. Hard as it was to admit, hiring Roman to protect me was the smartest thing Ivan had probably ever done in his life and subsequently the dumbest. Because I wanted to know where the hell he'd been.

I'd already wasted enough of my time. I held out the manila envelope clutched in my grip. "Everything you need to know about your *new role* is outlined here. You'll need to sign the contract and separate NDA."

"Seriously? You want me to sign another contract and an NDA?" He arched an eyebrow. "I'm already on payroll."

"New day, new rules. Besides, I can't risk anything at this point. Even with you."

He took the envelope from my hand, rubbing it between his fingers. "It's awfully thin."

"That's because all the bullshit has been cut out. So you shouldn't have any trouble understanding it. I'm giving you exactly twelve hours to read it over. Make sure we agree on everything and have a *very* clear understanding."

He gave me a suspicious look.

"I'll be back in the morning."

"That's like five in the morning," Roman protested.

"Is that a problem?"

He shrugged. "Don't you want to sleep in?"

Lyndsay Marie

I almost laughed in Roman's face. Ivan let out a grunt from somewhere behind me. He'd experienced his fair share of waking up before the sun. Now, it was someone else's turn.

"This is a 24/7 operation. I can sleep when I'm dead…and hopefully, that doesn't happen on your watch."

FOUR
Roman

Ivan had warned me that this job was going to suck ass, more or less. *He couldn't have been more right.* After Jameson turned over a list of my duties and expectations, she and Ivan left me to my own devices for the night.

I combed over the NDA. It was all very basic verbiage, though there was one part that stuck out and looked like Jameson had typed it up herself. There was no way in hell the family lawyer would have made mention of some of the shit on here.

Knowing James would be back at the ass crack of dawn, I crawled into bed by ten. Something told me that sleep would be a luxury around here. I spent most of the night tossing and turning, rolling around like a gas station hot dog. All I could do was lie there, trying to figure out how things had gotten so out of hand that Ivan would risk bringing me back. Even worse, knowing what was at stake.

Then there was Jameson. Even though Ivan had more than assured me he and I were still the only two people who knew about where I'd been and why, there was no way in hell James wouldn't ask a million and one questions when given the chance. How was I supposed to explain to someone who'd once been my best friend behind closed doors, a woman who I'd secretly loved with every fiber of my being, why I had just vanished without a trace? And now, I was back with even less of an explanation about where I'd been. The one thing I knew for sure was there was no way in hell she could ever find out why I'd left in the first place.

Ever.

Now here I was, almost a full year later, back in north Mississippi, holed up in the Diamond Suite at the very place that almost destroyed me. A part of me wished I'd never taken Ivan's phone call.

I'd barely closed my eyes before my alarm went off. The last thing I wanted was to be late.

No sooner than I'd stepped out of the shower, dripping wet with a towel wrapped around my waist, than there was a knock on the door. I assumed it was Jameson, given her punctuality.

"Here goes nothing," I grumbled out loud to myself, only half knowing what I was getting myself into.

I swiped the envelope off the bedside table and headed toward the door. When I flung it open, Jameson stood in the hallway, hands on her hips. Her lips were pressed tight as her gaze darted up and down the length of my freshly showered body. She sucked in a deep breath through her nose.

"You're early." I spoke with a mildly cocky tone and half smirk, knowing damn well I'd just caught her eye-fucking me. Then again, I couldn't help but do the same to her.

She was dressed for business in a white, semi-sheer silk blouse, navy blue pencil skirt, nude-colored heels that were way too high for this job, and legs for goddamned days.

Fuck.

"As I expect you to be as well," she stated bluntly. "You don't look ready at all."

Ivan wasn't far behind, looking run-down and ragged, like he needed a few days' worth of sleep himself. *So, is this what I have to look forward to?* Jameson had probably ripped him out of bed hours ago with her high-gloss black talons. I almost felt bad for the guy…almost.

"I slept great. Thanks for asking."

"I didn't. Get dressed. I need to get to work."

"I still have time," I teased as I waved the envelope.

She gave me a no-more-bullshit, pointed look. "You have two minutes, Stone."

"Boy, I tell you, with a mouth like yours, this hardly seems worth the money putting my life on the line and all if this the kind of attitude you're gonna have with me."

"And with an ego like yours, it's going to be hard not to kill you myself and just risk it on my own."

Wow. She was feeling extra spicy today. "I was joking."

"I wasn't. There's no joking either."

"That wasn't in your contract."

She scoffed. "Feel free to add it."

"Shit, you drive a tough bargain, you know that? I don't know if this is even worth half a million."

Her eyes went wide, and her jaw practically hit the floor. *Uh-oh.* "*Half a million*? As in dollars?" she squeaked out. "Who in the hell is paying you five hundred grand to do this?" She looked back at Ivan. He did a choke-cough thing. "You? You son of a bitch."

He shrugged. "I figured it was worth it. I mean, look what he's gotta put up with."

"Rob is going to kill me, Ivan! Does he know about this?"

"Of course he knows. He does the books. Who do you think approved it?"

She covered her face as she let out a half grunt, half moan into the palms of her hands.

My lungs burned from holding in a laugh and keeping a straight face.

"You know what? Fuck the both of you. Ivan, I'll deal with you later." She glared at me through squinted eyes. "I swear to god, Roman Stone, if you so much as step out of line one time—*One. Time.*—I am going to make your life a living hell."

"You already do. I've no doubt you'll keep up the good work."

She glanced down at the dainty gold watch on her wrist. "I have shit to do. Go get dressed; I'll send someone from security to come get you. You're already late." She snatched the envelope out of my hand, spun around on her heels, and stormed away. Ivan took off after her, trailing not far behind.

"Thanks a lot, Ivan," I called out down the hall.

He tossed his middle finger over his shoulder before he rounded the corner and disappeared.

Lyndsay Marie

I could have easily given Roman five more minutes to get dressed and take over from here, but what I really needed to do was get the hell away from him so I could collect my thoughts and pull myself together. Because right now, I loathed how mouthwatering he looked. Roman was already deliciously distracting as it was. Now, he looked like he'd put in more work on his body to get into even better shape. *A little time away has been good for him.* Then, he had the audacity to answer the door fresh out of the shower in a damned towel, the rest of his exposed skin dripping wet. I could have licked every rogue drop of water off his chest.

How sad was it that all I could think about was what it would feel like to have him fuck the stress out of me.

I sighed at the thought. That was then; this was now. *Let it go.*

Him working for me was going to be a big problem. I'd already made the mistake of falling for him once; I was going to have to do everything in my power to make damned sure that didn't happen again. I was going to have to work overtime to keep my defenses up against him. That would be the only way not to fall for *anything* about him because *everything* about him was all too easy to fall for—cocky attitude, dark sense of humor, steadfast dedication to the important people in his life. All of it.

This is why you made that rule, James, I reminded myself.

Ivan and I exited into the hotel lobby, my heels echoing against the marble floors as I stomped ahead of him.

"I should fire you," I hissed under my breath, looking back at him.

He let out a soft chuckle. *Smug bastard.* "Me? What'd I do?"

I stopped short and turned around, causing him to run into me with an *oof.* I gave his shoulders a hard shove. "You know good and damned well what you've done. Where has he been?" I asked, with bitterness in my tone. "Hm? Where the hell has Roman been? Because *not dead* is blatantly obvious, and you've known the entire time?"

"James. I do—"

I poked my fingernail into his chest, shutting him up.

"Ow, shit," he said, rubbing the spot where I'd poked him. "That hurt."

"Good. But don't you dare stand there like the sneaky little prick that you are and tell me you don't fucking know,

43

Lyndsay Marie

Ivan. I will rip your balls off and gift them to your wife for Christmas embalmed in a mason jar from the kitchen."

My tone grew louder the angrier I got as I tried to process how in the span of less than a day, my entire world had been flipped on its head, and I had to question everything I thought I knew about my life. I felt like a fucking snow globe in the hands of a toddler on the run.

I'd spent the past year mourning the loss of the only two men I'd loved. First, I watched helplessly as my dad died on the living room floor of our family home, and the very next day, I learned that Roman, the only person I wanted to confide in, was now gone, too.

"First off," he started, dragging me out of my thoughts, "you need to keep your volume down. It's too damned early, and guests are gonna hear you. The last thing Chris needs to deal with before six o'clock in the morning is complaints of some crazy lady losing her shit in the hotel lobby." He reached out and gripped my arms, glancing around for wayward patrons or anyone who might be within earshot. He dropped his head and shook it, then looked back up at me. "And you're right. I do know where he's been. But I'm sorry—you know this kind of work, it requires a certain level of…confidentiality. Right now, I can't say anything."

I wanted to tell him *fuck you and your confidentiality*. I was running this show now. But I didn't have the energy to argue with him, knowing he wouldn't give me the answers I wanted. I knew then I was going to have to find out on my own. Unfortunately, as much as Ivan pissed me off and kept my blood pressure through the roof, he'd yet to steer me wrong—minus that one tiny detail that he'd

44

brought a man back from the dead, and now I had to deal with having Roman Stone as my bodyguard.

My shoulders slouched in his grip. "You're right," I said, feeling defeated yet not ready to throw in the towel. "But going forward, I know everything."

"Promise." He gave my arms a squeeze before letting go and pulling one of his phones out.

"Everything, Ivan. I mean it."

"I swear. Everything. I gotta go. You got ears?"

I patted my hip where my phone was tucked inside my skirt. "Always."

"Call me if you need me."

"Yeah. Sure." He left me standing helplessly, fuming from everything.

It was still early, but I figured Chris would probably be here by the time I made it to his office. He worked almost as much as I did. I wondered if he sometimes slept in his office, too.

I said good morning to the hotel front desk staff as I passed by, and no sooner did I start the trek through the casino than I ran into Kelly.

"Good grief. What are you doing here already?" I asked her. "This is early, even for you."

She huffed, blowing wayward strands of hair out of her face.

Kelly had been an integral part of Emerald Haze and our operations for at least a decade. She'd started out as a cocktail waitress when she was dating one of our maintenance men. They met in her hometown, got engaged, then moved to this part of the country because it was where he was from. Then, he got caught having an affair with another cocktail waitress. Kelly dumped him but ended up staying because she liked her job. After a few years of being on staff and getting to know her, she took a promotion to events coordinator and eventually became one of us.

"Trying to finalize things for this weekend, get all my ducks in a row…or at least out of the middle of traffic. You know the drill…'cause at this point, I'm one fuckup away from walking out into traffic myself."

"Don't do that. You're doing a great job, and I like having you around.."

"Thanks, James."

"Seriously. Let me know if you need anything." I started to walk away but paused. "Oh, really quick before I run off. Do you know if Chris is here yet?"

"I haven't seen him, but you never know with him. He practically sleeps in his office."

"Yeah, I know the feeling. I've gotta run back up to my office, but if you see him before I do, tell him I need to talk to him for a minute."

She readjusted the stack of files cradled in her arm. "Uh-oh. Sounds serious. Wink-wink." She nudged me with her elbow.

"It's *not* like that." *Anymore.*

Yes, Chris and I had what I would consider a brief fling a few months ago. Operative word—had. That was all water under the bridge. Desperate times called for desperate measures, and when you hadn't had good dick, or any dick for that matter, in a very long time, you did what you had to do.

Unfortunately, I was vulnerable; he was available. We both took advantage of a convenient situation. The only reason Kelly even knew about us was because she'd walked in on us making out in a supply closet, of all places. I had no choice but to come clean to her about it 'cause how else do you explain sucking face with an insubordinate? It wasn't like I was performing any lifesaving measures.

Besides, if Chris and I were going to get caught by anyone, Kelly was the only person I could trust with that kind of info. Regardless, I called things off with Chris later that day out of fear of the sheer messiness our being together could create in a work environment.

"Sure. If you say so. Unless there's something you aren't telling me." She glared at me suspiciously through squinted eyes.

I threw my hands up. "There's nothing going on with him." *Not anymore.*

"Mmm-hmm. If you say so."

"Nothing. Promise."

"Okay, well, I just worry about you. If you need anything or you wanna chat, you know how to find me."

"Thanks, Kelly. I appreciate your concern, but rest assured, everything between me and him is strictly business."

Whether Chris and I ended things a week or a month ago, I had a feeling things were about to get very, very messy.

Lyndsay Marie

I grabbed my room key card and wallet off the nightstand and tucked them into my back pocket just as someone knocked on the door. I had no idea who James had sent to escort me, but at least they'd shown up as promised, not too long after James and Ivan had left.

A tall, lanky man not much shorter than me stood in the middle of the hallway when I opened the door. He was dressed in uniform—white button-down shirt with the Emerald Haze logo embroidered on the left chest, the name JORDAN embroidered in all caps just below that, black slacks that had probably never been ironed, and scuffed black dress shoes.

This guy worked for security? No wonder Ivan felt like he had to risk bringing me back here. He looked fucking useless except for going on coffee runs. If this was any insight as to what I had to work with, we really were all royally fucked.

"Ready?" he asked in a slow Southern drawl as he tossed a set of keys into the air, catching them with the other hand.

"And you are…?"

"Jordan." He tipped his head to the side. "I's asked to take you to Miss Hazentree."

This was the first time I'd seen Jordan, and I'd done a lot of work for Elliott and Ivan over the years. Though, he could've been moved over from the downtown warehouse.

"Roman." I stuck my arm out to be friendly, shake his hand. He just stood there. He glanced down at my outstretched arm, then back up at me without a word. I dropped my arm. *Okaaay then.* "So, you new here?"

"Nah."

This conversation was clearly going nowhere. "Alright then. Where to?"

"Other side up on the top floor." He turned and started walking away.

"Guess you want me to follow you?" I mumbled to myself, pulling the door shut behind me. "Lead the way." Even though I could have gotten around this place with my eyes closed.

We made our way through the employee/maintenance-only areas, weaving our way through back hallways and places reserved for deliveries. At one point, I did have him make a quick pit stop on the way. The closer we got to Jameson, the less and less I wanted to

Lyndsay Marie

be here. The thought of walking into that room gave me an uneasy feeling and stirred up memories I'd long suppressed. Not because I was afraid of her, though I probably should have been to some degree. I just didn't have a fucking clue what I'd gotten myself into or what to expect out of any of this situation. And I'd been up against a lot darker, dirtier key players in the industry.

Jordan rapped his knuckles on the door when we arrived.

Looking around, I noticed the entire top floor had been deserted; it seemed like Jameson was the only life left up here. Cameras were still in place, so that was somewhat reassuring. It looked like more had been added since the last time I was up here.

"Miss?" he said into the wooden door. "We're here."

"Come in," she announced from the other side.

A lock released, and Jordan opened the door, walking in first without a word.

"Took the two of you long enough." Jameson glared at us over the top of her laptop screen.

"Sorry, boss," Jordan replied, tilting his head toward me. "*Someone* had to stop for coffee and a cupcake."

Asshole. "It was a blueberry muffin." I brushed my hands down the front of my shirt, flinging off any wayward crumbs that might have fallen. "The healthiest option on your grab-and-go buffet."

She looked at me. "Thank you. You can go," she told him without taking her eyes off mine.

"Want me to hang around outside?" he asked.

50

"No. Thank you. We'll be fine. I'll call you if I need you."

"Yes, ma'am." Jordan backed out, pulling the door closed, causing the space to go eerily silent. If not for the sound of my breath passing through my nostrils, you could've easily heard a fly fart.

This was the first time Jameson and I had been completely alone since being reunited, and it did *not* feel good.

"Have a seat." She waved her hand toward the empty leather chair in front of me.

"I feel like I'm at the principal's office," I half mumbled. I loosened the collar around my neck and sat down directly across from her.

It'd barely been a year since I'd seen her, but it felt like decades. She looked exhausted, but not the kind of exhaustion a person felt when sleep-deprived. This was the kind of fatigue you felt when your soul needed rest. Yet, she was every bit as beautiful as she'd always been.

The whole *look but don't touch* clause I knew she'd added to the NDA of her own accord made sense now. It was going to take the self-control of a professionally trained K-9 to keep my hands off her.

"Coffee?" she asked.

"No, thanks." I raised my paper cup. "We stopped and got some on the way."

"I wasn't offering. Is that really what took you so long to get here?"

"Nope. I ate breakfast, too." That made her scoff. "That Jordan guy doesn't say a whole lot, does he?"

She shuffled some papers on her desk, stacked and secured them with a paperclip, then dropped them into a drawer beside her. "He's not paid to talk."

"It was just an observation. So, how do you want to go about doing all of this?"

"I'm not entirely sure yet. This was all very unexpected. Ivan kind of blindsided me." She closed her laptop and leaned back, folding her arms across her chest.

"Tell me about it," I deadpanned.

One minute, I was enjoying my coffee and morning routine at Nancy's Diner on Broadway Street. The next thing I knew, I was on my bike, rolling 110, headed west.

"This is kind of weird for me," she spoke softly. "I'm not even sure where to start. I feel like I'm so far behind, and now this." She waved her hand in my direction. My presence most definitely threw a wrench in her week.

"I know what you mean." The last thing I wanted was to make shit even more uncomfortable for her and myself. The last time I did work here, I was essentially Ivan's bitch boy. Now, less than a year later, he wanted me to be Jameson's bodyguard. "Well, do you want me to just follow you around everywhere? Shoot anyone who crosses your path or looks at your ass?"

"More or less. Except I don't need you shooting anyone. Not unless it's absolutely necessary."

"What about me?"

"What about you?"

"Can I look at your ass?" She already knew I wasn't going to *not* look.

She rolled her eyes.

"Okay, fine. I'll scrub that off my list of duties."

"You don't need to look at my ass, and I don't need you to go *everywhere* I go."

I arched an eyebrow. "Like the bathroom?"

"Specifically, the bathroom. And if I'm inside of here"—she pointed her finger downward—"I'm fine. You don't need to sit around watching me work. When I need to go anywhere, as soon as you get a phone, I'll reach out and let you know. In the meantime, I'll either have you with me, or I'll get Ivan or someone else to stand in place."

"Got it. Do you want me to feed you and tell you you're pretty?" I smirked, trying to lighten the mood or, at the very least, get some semblance of a smile out of her. The air was too damned thick with tension.

"Don't be so fucking ridiculous. I can feed myself."

"So just tell you you're pretty?"

"Roman." She dropped her head into her hands and rubbed her temples.

"Okay, okay. I'm sorry. I'll stop." Clearly, she'd lost her personality somewhere along the way.

"Whatever it is you're trying to do here, it isn't working. We're not about to pick up where we left off like old friends. We are *not* friends. You have a job to do, and I need you to be focused on the task at hand, not out here trying to get nominated for class clown."

Ouch. That stung. I knew she'd be pissed off at me, and I didn't blame her. I just didn't think I'd actually be hurt. "I'm not trying to get nominated for shit. You're the one with the stick up your ass. I was just trying to lighten the mood a little."

"Well, don't. I'm so fucking stressed-out right now. You have no idea."

I needed to know whatever was going on that suddenly required my presence, and that information needed to come straight from her mouth because I knew I wouldn't get the truth from anyone else around here.

"Then give me an idea. What am I doing here? Why does Ivan seem to think I'm the only person who can help you?"

"Because you are. That's how bad this is."

"Then start talking. What am I going up against?" The only reason Ivan had used me or kept me around was because he knew I'd get the job done and done right. I could make people disappear off the map without a trace. Now he needed me to protect Jameson? None of this sat right with me.

She looked up at the ceiling for a moment, contemplating. "Remember Kane?"

"Of course." Everybody in this industry knew Kane. Elliott had once been Kane's biggest rivalry and an even bigger pain in the ass. Elliott always liked to try to stay one step ahead of Kane. If he'd heard of something Kane wanted to get into, whether it be weapons, museum artifacts, or alcohol, Elliott would try to get to it first, just to fuck with him. Kane was also known to be very unstable and unpredictable. There wasn't much that man wouldn't do to a person if he thought he'd been betrayed in some kind of way. "What's Kane got to do with you?"

"He's been coming after me."

And there it is. Fuck. The last thing I wanted to hear and probably my biggest fear. "Are you sure?"

"Oh, I'm pretty positive."

"I don't mean to sound like a prick, but why? What in the hell did you do?"

"Me? Why do I have to be the one who did something?"

"You're kidding." I raised an eyebrow. "Kane only reacts when he's been provoked. That's a fact."

She flicked a paperclip across her desk. "He thinks I stole one of his boats." Her tone was barely audible.

"Why does he think that? Did you?"

"No…?"

"No? Is that a question? You don't know if you did?"

"I didn't exactly steal one…"

"James. Talk."

She let out a sigh, and I knew whatever she was about to tell me was going to piss me off. "I sank it."

I looked up to the ceiling, sucking in a long, deep breath. "You've got to be kidding me. Why in the hell would you do that?"

"Because," she said as she picked at her fingernail, "a few months ago, he killed one of my men."

"So?"

"What do you mean *so*? He killed one of our security crew, for no good fucking reason."

"Oh, I guaranteed Kane had his reasons, one of those being you sunk his shit into the Mississippi River. What happened?"

She sighed. "Kane had a boat come up missing. I don't know if he ever found it, but he thought I was the one who'd taken it. So, I guess to send me some kind of message, he had one of my men killed. Briggs was making rounds, patrolling the perimeter on a golf cart. Surveillance lost him on the radio and cameras. So they went out and backtracked his last known route. They found him just off the trail, slouched over the steering wheel with a hole in his head."

Kane had a lot of men working for him. Probably a lot more than Jameson or Elliott ever did, and definitely more feral. Mainly because Kane didn't give a fuck who he hired. If they didn't comply or perform to his standards, they'd just disappear and never be missed. As far as Kane was concerned, the people he hired were as disposable as the trash his casino produced.

"So you sunk one of his cargo boats?"

"I did. He wasn't about to kill one of my men in retaliation for something I didn't do in the first place."

"It—fuck. It doesn't matter. You should've just left it alone. Let Kane get his revenge, wrong as he was, and moved on. Now he's after you? Why? What did you do?"

"Nothing!" she practically shouted at me. "Another one of his boats came up missing. He's still accusing me of taking them."

"Do you have a death wish?"

"Roman! I didn't do it! I don't know who did, but I don't have time to find out. I'm just trying to host this gala and move on with my life."

I shook my head in disbelief. "Is there anything else?"

"No. Not yet."

"Not yet? You mean not ever." I had no doubt in my mind that Kane would take out anyone if he thought they'd crossed the wrong line. Diverting or sinking one of his boats definitely crossed that line, even if he had killed one of her men first.

"We've tried to tell him we don't want or need his shit, but you know how he is." Her voice trailed off.

"Yeah, I do, unfortunately. So you didn't take his missing boat or have anything to do with it?"

"No. Not at all."

I shook my head. Somebody here knew something. "Well, I guess it doesn't matter. He thinks you did, and he's on a fucking rampage now. You know he isn't going to stop until he gets what he wants."

"No shit. I'm well aware."

"So what's he want?"

"Me."

"Ever since we announced the Haunted Hearts Gala, Kane's threats have been more and more frequent. But if it makes you feel any better, it was a small boat that I sunk, and he was able to retrieve everything."

I knew that wouldn't make a difference to Roman; he knew more about Kane than I ever did. I knew enough to know I was in way over my head, though I'd never actually admit that to him.

"So far, none of what you've told me has made me feel any better."

If he didn't like what I'd already told him, he most definitely was not going to like this next part. "He also said he wants to meet up and have an in-person chat."

"He what?" He jerked his head up. "How do you know that? Did you talk to him?"

"Yeah. He called me. The day after I sank his boat to get back at him for killing Briggs. He said he thought it was about time he and I got together for a little one-on-one."

"Did you already set up this meeting?"

"No. Not yet. It's not exactly high on my priority list."

"We might just need to move it up there."

I watched as Roman took a long sip of his coffee; his hand practically wrapped around the entire cup. Watching him and his every move stirred up memories of what those hands used to feel like gripping my body, pinning me down. The way his fingers curled and dug into my flesh. My body responded to the way we'd once moved together.

It had been way too long and at the same time not nearly long enough since we'd been together. The best thing for me to keep a straight head and clear mind around Roman had always been to simply stay away...which had rarely ever worked out. No matter how many times I'd told myself in the past he and I needed to lie low—we could not be caught together—inevitably, we found our way back to each other.

Given the context of our current conversation, I had zero business thinking about being pinned beneath him.

"Jameson." He snapped his fingers. "Did you hear anything I just said?"

I shook myself back to reality. "What? Yes, I heard you."

"Then what did I just say?" he asked.

Lyndsay Marie

I cleared my throat because, shit. I hadn't been listening. I'd been lost in thought about all the what-ifs and had-beens.

"That's what I thought," he hummed. He wasn't buying my bullshit.

"I'm sorry. I just—I've got a lot going on. I think things are finally catching up to me. Between Kane, the fundraiser, now you coming back from the grave—" I gave him one of those looks, the kind that sent a message without saying *we'll talk about this later*. "—it's hard to stay focused sometimes."

He held my gaze. I swear if I didn't know any better, I could feel him physically reading my thoughts. Right now, that was not a good thing.

He continued. "I said I'm going to need a few things from you."

I arched an eyebrow. "Like…?"

"First and foremost," he said, clasping his hands together, "I need a gun."

"I can do that."

"I'm also going to need a burner phone on your network."

"Noted. Anything else?"

He smirked. "Master keys. Ones that will open every door on the property—*all of them*."

"This is where you lost me. You're only here to keep me alive through the gala. Nothing less, nothing *more*." Emphasis on the *more* because I needed to remind him and myself that he was only here for work. Because being this close to him again was all too tempting. "You can have a gun and a phone. You don't need keys to anything."

"You want me to do my job? Then that's what it's going to take. I don't think that's asking for a whole lot, considering. Based on everything you just told me, you don't have much of a choice. If I'm going to protect you, I need access to you."

I closed my eyes. I couldn't believe this was happening. Why, of all people, me? Why, of all people, *him*? *Is there not anybody else who could do this job?*

"Fine. I'll see what I can do."

"Thank you." When I opened my eyes, I caught him staring, the slightest hint of a smirk tugging at the corner of his soft, full, dark pink lips. "See, that wasn't so hard, now, was it?"

"Everything about you is hard." My mouth snapped closed just as fast as the words escaped.

"You have no idea," he mumbled under his breath.

I completely ignored his comment. No way I was touching that one—figuratively or literally.

"I've got a question for you," I said, tilting my head.

"Fire away."

"Where've you been for the last year?"

"I was working."

"Working? That's it? Just working?"

"Yup. Just working."

"Interesting. Because Ivan told me you were dead." Those weren't his exact words, but death had been implied.

"You'll have to take that up with him."

"I did. He won't talk."

He shrugged as if to say, *tough shit.* "I don't know what to tell you. He gave me a job, and I did it. We had a deal. If that changes, I'm sure you'll be the first to know."

"You mean like him bringing you back here to play bodyguard, or babysitter, as you called it? You mean first to know like that?"

He pressed his lips together. I guess our past didn't matter. Roman didn't want to talk? Fine. I knew his weaknesses. *Two could play this game.*

If he wanted to withhold information from me, then I'd coerce it out of him. It wasn't a want but a need at this point.

I stood up and rounded my desk. He watched in silence as I propped up against the edge of my desk in front of him and rested my foot on the seat of the chair in the space between his legs. His eyes wandered from my face down to my chest, to the space between my legs. This position gave him a clear line of sight up my skirt—enough of a view for his imagination to run wild but not enough for him to actually see anything.

He propped his hands in front of his mouth, his index finger covering his lips.

"See something you like?" I asked nonchalantly as I inspected my nails like I didn't know what I was doing.

He casually raised his shoulder. "I've seen better."

"Liar." I slid my foot forward, pressing the bottom of it into his crotch. He didn't flinch.

Heat pooled between my legs at the sight of him sitting there, laid-back, just as casually as if he were watching a football game on TV in the comfort of his own home.

He reached down, grabbed my ankle, and rubbed the bottom of my foot against his crotch. Even through my shoe, I could feel he was already rock hard.

I gripped the edge of my desk for support. Shit. *Don't let him win this.*

"Where've you been?" I asked again softly.

He glanced up at me through his long, dark lashes. "I already told you—working." The pad of his thumb lazily slid back and forth over my bare skin on the inside of my ankle.

"Hmm. It's a shame. We used to be close. Very, *very* close, remember? We used to tell each other everything. You seem to have forgotten."

He skimmed his hand up the back of my calf, stopping just behind the back of my knee. "I remember everything about us—about *you.*"

His hand continued to roam upward to the inside of my thigh. Just as he reached beneath the hem of my skirt, I snapped my legs closed and stood up.

"Nice try, but you did forget one thing. I'm the one in charge now, and the only place you're putting your hand is between me and a bullet."

"I'd like to think I'm not going to have to do that—not for you or anyone else."

"You will if you have to."

Lyndsay Marie

"Not at all sounds even better."

"You're insufferable."

When I turned to walk away, Roman's arm wrapped around my waist and, in one swift move, had me bent over my desk, his chest pressed to my back as he pinned me down against my desk from behind.

He grabbed a fistful of my hair and gently tugged my head back, exposing my neck. The last time he had me in this position, he was inside me.

"Let's get one thing straight. I don't give a fuck who's in charge anymore. When I tell you I remember everything, I mean *everything*. Every dip and curve of your body, the way you taste, how your tight, wet pussy feels gripped around my cock. Oh, I remember all of it. I've been there…done *that*. Don't *you* ever forget it." His words were soft, his breath warm against my ear as he spoke.

Oh, this is so bad.

I used my desk as leverage, pushing my ass into his hard cock, nudging him back just enough to give myself some room to spin around and face him. "If you're not going to tell me where you've been, then we are done here."

He stepped forward, pushing me back into my desk until I had nowhere else to go. He caged me in with his arms on either side of me, pinning me with his gaze like a predator to its prey.

"Yeah," he challenged. "Something tells me we're just getting started."

EIGHT
Jameson

I'd never been so goddamned irritated with someone in my entire life. I was the horniest I'd been since I could remember and could have very easily caved in to him. *God knows I wanted to*. But even more than that, I needed to keep a level head because he had information that I needed, and I wasn't going to get any of it with him balls-deep inside of me.

Reluctantly, I shoved his chest, pushing him back, and got the hell away from him. My original plan of attempting to half-assed seduce any kind of information out of him had majorly backfired, no thanks to my lack of oxygenated brain cells because all of my blood flow had been rerouted elsewhere.

"*We* are not just getting started. There is no *we*. There's you, and there's me, and you're only here to do a job," I reminded him and myself. Roman squared his shoulders as he took a step back. *Good.* The best place for him was as far away from me as possible. "You know what? Why don't you go see Ivan—he should be in his office or somewhere. He's around. I'll send him a text and tell him you're on your way. He'll get you whatever you need."

"What about you? I can't just leave you here by yourself."

"I've got some things I need to wrap up here, then we'll regroup and come up with a solid game plan."

He folded his arms across his puffed-out chest. "I don't think I'm supposed to leave you unattended."

I rolled my eyes with a huff. This was ridiculous. "I'll be fine. What's another hour?"

The thing about having known someone for as long as I'd known Roman meant I knew all the buttons to press to get him going…defiance being one of them.

He narrowed his eyes, his gaze practically pierced through me. "A *lot* can happen in an hour."

"Not in here." My dad's office was probably the safest place on the entire property.

He shook his head. "No fucking way, James. I can't leave you. Not according to the contract I signed."

Shit. He wasn't wrong. I did have it in his contract that once he took over, he wasn't to leave my side until this was over.

"Lucky you, I wrote the contract, and I'm telling you it's fine. I'll be fine. I'll get Jordan to stand post."

He squinted his eyes. "If you say so, but this is the last time I'll leave you unattended. I take this *job* very seriously. Enjoy your freedom while you still have it."

He turned and left without another word.

As soon as the door closed and latched shut, I pulled up the camera feed to the hallway outside of my office, watching him as he walked down the hall toward the elevator. He poked his head into some of the vacant office spaces before disappearing.

There's nothing there, nosey.

Seeing Roman in person after all this time, when I never expected to see him at all, ever again, stirred up a flurry of mixed emotions—ones that I was sure I'd buried deep enough they weren't at risk of resurfacing. Keeping my feelings at bay was so much easier when I thought he was dead.

Spinning a pen between my fingers, I stared out the window into the clear blue sky. The storm that had lingered over us for the last couple of days had finally passed. This was the first time I'd been able to see the sun from my office in almost a week. The outside world was still cold, wet, and littered with dead leaves and organic debris, evidence of last fall, and the South was on the outer fringes of fall.

I couldn't remember the last time I'd gone outside out of pure enjoyment. The only time I ever seemed to leave the four walls of this godforsaken building anymore was to walk to and from a golf cart or a car, going from one building on the property to another.

I'd finally come to the realization that it would be a very long time before I'd ever be able to leave my self-made prison. At least not until the man who'd started all of this was face down in a swamp.

I glanced at my watch and realized I still hadn't heard from Chris. So I typed out a quick text to him.

Me: You here? Need to see you.

A few minutes later, he replied.

Chris: Yup. Sorry. Got your message from Kelly. Been busy. Want me in your office? *winky face*.

Me: No. I'll come there. Sit tight.

I gave my hair and face a quick check in the mirror, making a half-hearted attempt to pull myself together. The last thing I wanted was to look like I'd just been bent over my desk, praying for some form of sexual gratification, and not just left sexually frustrated. Not that what I looked like really mattered in the grand scheme of things. Chris and I weren't a thing anymore, not that I'd ever considered us a *thing*, more like we *had* a thing. He'd certainly seen me in worse shape.

Chris and I had always maintained a professional relationship...mostly. He'd been the assistant general manager, just behind Ivan, for the last couple of years. In the weeks following my dad's murder, not only did he step up as the acting GM, but he became my go-to person when I needed comfort. He was someone to talk to, a shoulder to lean on.

Once upon a time ago, that person would have been Roman. *He* used to be my escape…until the day he'd disappeared off the face of the Earth, and I'd been left to believe he'd been killed, too.

It didn't take long for things to heat up between us. *Rock bottom is a lonely place to be.* Since he was technically my subordinate, we had to keep things very casual and even more hush-hush. The sneaking around was all fun and games until the day Kelly walked in on us in the middle of a hot and heavy make-out session in an office supply closet, no less. I ended things with Chris that afternoon.

Kind of…almost.

Let's just say that I'd had my share of moments of weakness since then, and he never turned me down. Chris and I, on rare occasions, found ourselves tangled together in between the sheets a time or two over the last few weeks until I finally called things off officially, though he wasn't ready to let go just yet.

His door was ajar when I arrived at his office.

"Jameson." He smiled as I stepped into his office. "Come on in. Close the door."

I shut the door, knowing I probably should have left it open. I didn't plan on being here that long, and we definitely did not need privacy.

He rounded his desk, walking straight toward me with his arms outstretched for a hug. "How are you?"

I took a step back, trying to evade his embrace. For starters, my head was pounding, and I felt like I hadn't slept in years. Second, he and I weren't close like that anymore. I wasn't sure we ever were. His overly friendly demeanor had me feeling extremely uncomfortable.

"I'm fine. This won't take long. I just wanted to talk to you about this weekend."

His eyebrows scrunched together. "What's wrong? You look…stressed. But more than usual." He reached out to touch my cheek.

I turned my head away. "It's nothing. Just a rough start to the morning. You know how it is around here sometimes."

He wrapped his arms around me and pulled me into him. Familiar as his touch was, it didn't feel the same, and shitty as it was to even think about, he didn't feel like Roman.

"I do know how it is," he said, "and I know you've got a lot of shit on your plate. You need a break. A real one."

"I don't need a break. I need to get through this weekend alive."

"Then you'll take a break? Maybe even a whole-ass vacation…like a normal person?"

The sentiment made me laugh. "I don't think I've been on an actual vacation since I was a teenager."

The last time I'd gone on one was probably when my dad had taken me and a few friends to Rosemary Beach for my sixteenth birthday. The only other time after that was what should have been a week in Aspen, but I'd gotten called home early for a business emergency less than twenty-four hours into my trip. That business emergency ended up with my dad being murdered.

A sigh escaped me at the thought. I missed living a life with a sense of normalcy that my dad once provided. Things like family vacations and having friends. Just going out into the general public without a care in the world or at the risk of life and limb.

"That sounds terrible. Why don't we plan something together when all of this is over? Just the two of us?"

"Chris," I sighed. "You know we can't do that."

"Why not?" he asked, tightening his grip around me. He rubbed his hands up and down my back. His embrace felt invasive; every muscle in my spine tensed in response.

"Because. There is no two of us. You and I, we're not a thing anymore. We never were. I set boundaries, and we need to stick to them."

"Hmm." He dropped his mouth close to my ear, lowering his tone as he spoke. "You weren't saying that a few weeks ago when you called me up to your apartment."

I pressed my hands into his chest and tried backing away from him, but he didn't let go. "I know, and we shouldn't have done that. We just can't." *Alcohol is a sneaky, betraying bitch.*

"Does this have something to do with the new security guard Ivan hired?" he asked in a condescending tone.

"Security guard?" I jerked my head back and looked up at him. "You mean Roman?"

Instantly, he dropped his arms from around me and took a step back. "Roman? The guy that used to work for Elliott? That Roman?"

"Well, yeah. That would be the one." The world couldn't handle two of him.

He rested his hands on his hips and narrowed his eyes. "I thought someone got rid of him."

I held out hope that the two of them working this close in proximity wouldn't become a problem. They both had a male ego the size of Texas that was fueled by an endless dose of testosterone. Regardless, I didn't like the tone he'd suddenly taken with me, nor his reference to my team *getting rid of him*.

"Someone *did* get rid of him, but apparently not the way I or any of us had suspected."

Chris walked away, tucking himself behind his desk—a defensive tactic I used when I felt threatened or backed into a corner. "You could get rid of him again yourself. You have that power now."

"Chris!"

"What?" He shrugged dismissively. "I'm just saying. We've been operating things just fine without him up until this point. What do we need him for now?"

My shoulders slumped. This was not how I envisioned this meeting going. I originally came to hear about his finalized game plan for the event this weekend. Instead, I stood here defending Roman when I was still very much pissed off at him myself.

"Ivan brought him back as my—" I didn't want to call him my bodyguard. That just sounded...weird, but it was better than babysitter. "He's been hired to watch over me through the weekend. I don't know what else you want me to tell you."

"That's ridiculous. You already have plenty of security."

"Not enough," I retorted. "If you don't like it, take it up with Ivan."

"Ivan? Why? You're over him. You do something about it."

"I don't know what your problem is, but fix it. There's only so much Ivan or Leon or Hector or even you can do for me right now, but if Ivan thinks we could benefit from having Roman here, then so be it. I have to give this a shot."

"So he just resurrected some guy from the dead, and we're all supposed to be okay with that?"

"First off, Roman is not just *some guy*. Second, no, I am not okay with any of this, but I'm running out of time, and third, you may not know this, but Roman is like a machine with precision marksmanship. He's equipped with a very special set of skills that, unfortunate as it is, I need and nobody within a five-hundred-mile radius has." Not to mention, he wouldn't hesitate for one second to lay his life on the line for mine, with or without being paid. I couldn't think of one single man working under me who would do the same—including Chris.

"Hmm. Do those skills follow him into the bedroom?"

I glared at him with disgust. "Excuse me? What the fuck did you just say?"

"Nothing," he said, shuffling some loose papers around his desk. "It's not important. What did you need me for? You didn't come looking for me to talk about your exes."

"He is *not* my ex." Okay, so he kinda, sorta was, but that wasn't the point here, and it was none of his business. Chris and I were finished; we were no longer a thing.

He scoffed. "Whatever you gotta tell yourself."

"See! This is exactly why I needed to call things off between us. Shit just gets too complicated mixing work with pleasure." And sex with him wasn't even that good; it was convenient.

He rubbed his temples. "I just...I really fucking care about you. It bothers me that you won't let me protect you."

"Because you can't," I yelled. "That's already been proven, and I am not your problem. I never was."

"Fine. What business can I help you with? Because I have a lot of shit to do."

"Forget it. I'll take care of it myself."

Seething from head to toe, I stormed out of Chris's office, slamming the door shut as I left.

There was nothing more frustrating than being surrounded by the only two men that had ever been worth fucking...both of which had quickly turned into two big dicks.

Lyndsay Marie

I felt like shit for leaving Jameson alone. I didn't do it
because I wanted to, but she practically had steam billowing
out of her ears and looked like she was ready to launch her
dad's ten-pound antique glass ashtray at my forehead. Either
that or cry, and I was not equipped to handle the softer side
of her right now…or deal with a concussion.

      As I left her office, I cleared the entire upper level,
peeking into a few partially open doors along the way. It'd
barely been a year since I was last here, but it seemed like a
lot had changed since then. This used to be the
administration floor; now, all of the offices were vacant
except for Jameson's. Desks had been cleaned out and were
covered in a thin layer of dust. Filing cabinets were emptied,
some of their drawers left half-open. Rogue papers were
scattered across the floor. It looked like a postapocalyptic
movie scene.

Next up on my to-do list was to find Ivan. I knew his office hadn't moved. That man was going to live and die in his ten-by-ten smoke-filled room.

The door was closed when I reached his office just one floor down, and the light was off. I hit the back stairwell and came out on the river side of the casino, just beside the loading dock.

The loading dock was a massive concrete pad that jutted out of the back side of the casino—a place no patron had ever seen. The area hung out over the swampy waters in an alcove carved out of the banks of the Mississippi River. It was shielded behind a crescent-shaped island of kudzu-draped trees and unruly underbrush. It had a waterway just large enough for a boat to steer off course from the main riverway to make a drop-off or pickup, then continue on the way down the river.

Nothing had changed out here either. Hell, it looked worse. The concrete pad was dirtier and even more stained with god only knew what, and the metal roof covering the dock was peppered with rusted holes—from bullets and nature.

As expected, I found Ivan leaning against the weathered railing, staring out into the trees.

"I see some things never change," I said as I strolled up beside him.

He flicked his cigarette butt out into the water, blowing a puff of smoke out into the atmosphere. The cigarette fizzled out when it hit the water. "Around here, that's not always a bad thing."

"You're probably right." I glanced around. "Not a lot happening today?"

"Nah. We were pretty busy last week. Got some stuff coming through in a few days, after James's fundraiser. We're trying to lay low until then." He glanced around. "Speak of the devil, where is she?"

"In her office. Jordan's standing post for now."

"She ain't fired you yet?" He started to laugh, then choked as he broke out into a coughing fit.

I shook my head. "Not yet, though I'm sure she wants to."

"Hmm. You never know with her. She's been a little off her rocker lately. I think she's struggling with some things. Who fuckin' knows anymore. You know how women are."

"Yeah. I'm sure I'll be the last person she's gonna tell her problems to."

Once upon a time, not very long ago, I knew everything about her. Though the relationship we had technically didn't exist if anyone had asked; that was just the nature of the business. But between the two of us, we were all the other one had ever wanted…even if we were the only two who knew about it. Unfortunately, it didn't take long for us to become total strangers.

Ivan just shrugged.

There were two men I didn't recognize sitting with their backs against the wall near the kitchen exit. The one guy that I had known for years and was sure would never leave this place, I hadn't seen yet.

"Tater still around?"

"Of course. He ain't going nowhere. He's like a rescued animal. If I let him out into the wild now, nature will tear him to shreds."

I half laughed, but he wasn't wrong. "I've no doubt about that. He still stringing people up by the ankles?"

Ivan shook his head. "Not as often as he'd like, far as I know. I don't really ask anymore."

"Jesus. He's a real piece of work."

"Aren't we all?"

"Can't argue with that." I was no saint; the things I'd done would have me sitting on death row. But Tater? Any three-letter agency would make him disappear if they ever caught him for what he'd done. "So, I asked James for a few necessities, things I need while I'm here."

"And how'd that go?" He lit up another cigarette. "She tell you to go fuck yourself?"

"I'm sure she wanted to, but she was surprisingly agreeable. I don't feel like I asked for much, but either way, she said you'd help me with most of it."

He straightened himself upright and stretched his arms over his head. Ivan had never been the epitome of health, but he'd definitely filled out in the middle since the last time I'd seen him. What made it obvious was the fact that he still wore the same clothes that he did when he was probably twenty pounds lighter, judging by the way his shirt expanded to maximum capacity around his midline.

"Whatchu need? A gun?"

"That and a phone. I left mine behind." That was how I operated. Whenever I moved, everything was left where it sat. I had people who'd come by to clean it up, no questions asked.

"Let's do it." He stomped out his partially smoked cigarette, kicking it off the edge of the dock. "We'll finish this up in my office."

"So, who's been keeping an eye on Jameson?" I asked as we made our way across the casino floor, heading to his office. "I'm assuming she hasn't been unguarded until I got here."

"Me and the security crew. She hasn't really needed protecting, per se, until recently."

We eventually arrived at our final destination: the same dingy, smoke-stained room barely bigger than a jail cell.

Ironic.

He rounded his desk and sat down in the same old mustard-yellow leather chair that squeaked even louder under his weight. I had no doubt that chair was being held together with duct tape and a prayer.

I took a well-acquainted seat across from his desk. Unwanted memories flashed through my mind from the last time I was here as I sat down. "You ever going to upgrade this awful furniture?" I asked, picking a piece of loose vinyl from the armrest.

"Sure. It's on my list," he said with a sarcastic tone. He poured himself a drink and lit up another cigarette. "Here." He pulled a phone and a Glock out from the bottom drawer of his desk and slid them across to me. "Careful. It's loaded."

———— •◆• ————

With my new encrypted cell phone and Glock, I was beginning to feel human again. I set off to go find James. It'd been long enough since I'd had eyes on her. *The absolute longest break she'll have from me as long as I'm here.*

I'd been up since before the sun, and the muffin and coffee from earlier this morning had long worn off. I decided to take a quick detour through the main kitchen on my way back to James. Figured I'd hit Josephine up for a quick bite to eat—one that she didn't throw at me.

"Roman!" I heard my name from across the room just as I was about to push through the double swinging kitchen doors. I turned and saw Chris leaning against a wall at the entrance to the hallway that led to the new administration department. "You got a minute?"

I glanced at my watch. Not that I was really in a time crunch, but I didn't want to leave James unattended for any longer than I already had. I didn't trust her not to leave her office until I came back for her.

"Uh, yeah, but not long. What's up?"

He extended his arm, and I shook his hand. "Chris." He half-assed attempted to act like we didn't already know each other as he reintroduced himself.

Lyndsay Marie

Chris had started at Emerald Haze a few years back. He was brought on to the team as the assistant general manager. Given his family ties to the industry, he was one of the few qualified candidates to take over. After Elliott was killed, everyone moved up a rung, and he became the general manager, just after Ivan.

He'd also had his prying eyes on Jameson since day one.

"Roman," I said as I shook his soft hand. "But you already knew that."

He grinned like a used car salesman. "Yeah, I did. Mind joining me in my office? I won't keep you long. I'm sure you're busy."

"Very."

A guy like myself didn't mix and mingle with anyone from management. My job was to do exactly as I was paid to do, keep my head down and mouth shut. That never stopped me from pushing the envelope just a little. When it came to Jameson, she'd always been the proverbial princess living in an ivory tower; I was the town peasant who admired her from below. Those lines were not to be crossed, but that didn't mean they weren't…or on a regular and, eventually, daily basis.

Unfortunate as it was, while she'd always had eyes— and lips and tongue and everything else—for me, he was watching her. Always waiting to make his move. But because of how vastly different his and my roles were, it was all I could do to watch him from a distance with my mouth shut, hoping he'd stay away from her.

"Come on in. Have a seat."

"I'll stand. So what'd you need me for?"

Chris walked over to the makeshift bar behind his desk and poured himself a drink. "I just wanted to say hi. Reintroduce myself. We didn't speak much when we worked together. Figured we could get better acquainted." He spoke with his back to me—a real bitch move.

I sucked in a deep, calming breath, and the scent of Jameson's perfume invaded my nostrils, which meant she'd been here very recently. This sent a wave of rage through my veins. She wasn't supposed to leave her office. The thought of her having been in here for any reason set off something primal inside of me.

"Because we didn't work *together*." I folded my arms across my chest. "I wasn't exactly in a position to get to know people back then. I'm not about to start now."

He turned around and casually leaned back against the bar. "True. So how long are you here for?"

"I don't know. Look, as much as I'd love to sit around and bullshit, I gotta—"

"Then I'll just get to it. Keep your hands off of her," he said in a half-assed attempt at a threatening tone. "Understand?"

The fuck? "No. I don't."

"I said keep your han—"

"I heard what you said. What I don't know is what or who the fuck you're talking about. But I don't think either of us has time for this shit."

"You know exactly who I'm talking about, *Roman*. I'm talking about Jameson. She was doing just fine until you showed up. You so much as touch a hair on her head, I'll fucking kill you."

I stalked toward his desk, leaning in as close to him as I possibly could without removing the physical object between us that kept me from beating his ass. He sunk backward in retreat, completely cornered.

"I assure you, the last thing I would ever do is hurt that woman. The only reason I'm here is to keep her alive because if you or anyone in this state even had a fraction of the balls or skills it took to protect her, I wouldn't be here." His face flushed with red, and the grip on his glass tightened. "And mark my words, *Chris*, if *you* so much as lay a finger on her, *I* will fucking kill *you*. That is a promise."

Before he could respond, I shoved his desk forward into him in a fit of rage. He flinched. "That's what I thought."

I stormed out of his office, slamming the door shut behind me. I had no right to feel anything, not one single fucking emotion for Jameson. She wasn't mine anymore. Turns out time and space did nothing but make me want her even more than I ever did.

At the moment, I wanted to knock Chris's fucking teeth out and hand them back to him. But I had to keep my shit in check at the risk of her firing me. The last thing I wanted was to relinquish what little control I had over to one of these ass clowns.

This would not be an easy feat.

"Josephine," I called out when I finally entered the kitchen. I wasn't sure if it was coincidence or instinct that she had a knack for disappearing when the kitchen doors swung open. "It's Roman."

She popped out of the walk-in freezer, bringing a cloud of cold air with her. "You don't need to announce yourself. I know who you are."

"Hey, I just wanna make sure I don't need to dodge any rogue tomatoes or bullets."

She half shrugged. "Eh, it's a 50/50 risk. What can I do for you? You hungry?" She pinched my side as she breezed by with a box of frozen something tucked underneath her arm. "You look like you could eat a few meals."

I swatted her hand away. "I'll have you know, I've worked hard to maintain this waistline. Unlike *some* men around here," I said, referring to Ivan and his ever-growing belly.

She smirked. "Well, if nothing else, you'll definitely need the energy if you're gonna keep up with that one out there." She tipped her head toward the casino floor.

"Who?"

"Miss James. That one's a firecracker, you know." She shook her head with the faintest grin tugging at her lips. "She ain't the same, Romie. Hasn't been since…" Her words trailed off.

My insides twisted. I knew exactly what or *who* she was referring to. I didn't even want to imagine how much losing Elliott had changed Jameson; we'd barely scratched the surface.

"Yeah. I've noticed. Can't say I blame her."

Lyndsay Marie

"Anyways, here." She reached into an industrial-sized, stainless-steel refrigerator, pulled out a cold plate, peeled off the plastic wrap, and handed it to me. "Chicken salad on a bed of lettuce with sliced tomato and cucumber. Something tells me you're not a fried chicken, okra, and mac 'n' cheese kinda man anymore."

I smiled at her gesture. "You'd be correct. Though, I'm not sure if I'd turn that down from you."

"Maybe for dinner. Now, get. Miss Jameson's sitting out there in the main dining area eating alone. I just served her lunch. She could probably use some company," she said with a wink.

"Yes, ma'am."

That was all I needed for now—homemade food and a little reassurance. If anyone in this place knew James better than anyone anymore, it would be Josephine. Josephine had been a staple at Emerald Haze since probably before Jameson existed. It wouldn't surprise me if she knew more about ops than anyone else since probably ninety percent of business was conducted ten feet outside the kitchen walls.

I took lunch and headed out into the dining area. It didn't take long to find the woman of the week. She was one of three people sitting at one of the four-top dining tables. The other two people were an older couple well into their seventies, sitting on the opposite side of the dining area, enjoying what I had no doubt was a comped meal.

I walked up behind her, rounded the table, and took the seat across from her. "You know you shouldn't be sitting

86

out here alone, exposing yourself. You're a sitting duck out here like this."

"You left me alone. What was I supposed to do? Sit around and wait for your return?"

"That's *exactly* what you should have done. Something tells me you've been doing this long before I came back."

"Doing what?"

"Being stubborn, hardheaded, disobedient."

She glanced up from her plate and smirked. "You'd be correct. As many people as I have watching this place, you'd think I'd least be able to sit where I want and eat in peace…well, I *was*."

"No wonder Ivan pops Tums like candy."

She rolled her eyes. "Give me a break. He's been doing that for years. Don't let me stop you from living an ulcer-free life. I can take care of myself."

"I have no doubt you have, and you can, but if you could get through this event on your own, I wouldn't be sitting here."

I dug into my food just as a waitress approached, setting a glass of water down on the table in front of me.

"From Josephine," she said with a half a smile. She scurried away before I could thank her.

"Maybe," James said as she stabbed a piece of steak. She pointed it at my plate with her fork. "No barbeque or fried chicken?"

"Not if I want to stay in shape…and not a round one."

"Hmm." She smirked and took a bite of food into her mouth.

I watched as she slowly pulled the fork between her pink-tinted lips. That simple act stirred up memories that sent an old familiar sensation straight to my cock. Was she being intentional? *Highly doubtful.* Was she unintentionally sexy? *Every fucking bit of it.*

Get it together, fucker.

Picturing James on her knees with her mouth wrapped around my cock was the last thing I needed to be thinking about right now…or *ever*.

I topped off my glass with water and took a sip. "So, I ran into *Chris*."

There. That should keep my mind from wandering somewhere it didn't need to go. Figured it was a better topic than baseball.

Her head shot up, and she squared her shoulders. "Chris?" she asked with the slightest crack in her voice. "My GM?"

"That would be the one, assuming you only have one Chris on payroll. Are you fucking him?"

The steak knife slipped from her grip, causing a loud clanking sound as it landed against the edge of her ceramic plate. "Excuse me? That's awfully accusatory."

"I didn't accuse you of anything. It was just a question. You're the one taking it that way. So, are you or aren't you?"

"I'm *not* fucking him."

"Anymore." Now, *that* was accusatory. Whether she'd fucked him two months or two days ago, it'd be the last time.

"*If* I were, that's none of your business."

I leaned forward over the table, closing the space between us, and spoke at a volume that only she could hear. "That's where you're wrong. Seeing as I have to watch your every move from here on out, *everything* you do is my business. So, whatever went on between the two of you ends now...unless you plan on banging him in the bathroom."

"I might," she quipped.

Rage flashed in my eyes; there was no way she didn't see it. "Then you're no longer allowed to go to the bathroom alone."

"Is that going to be a problem for you?"

"*He* is my problem, and he won't be yours anymore if he comes near you again."

"He is my GM. We have a working relationship. Christ, what is it with you two? You're acting like man-children."

"Oh, so he's already said something to you about me, then?" Good to know. All I knew was she'd been with him in his office not too long before I'd gotten there, and the thought of her bent over his desk filled me with an insurmountable rage.

"Not really...kind of. Why does it matter? Are you jealous?"

I leaned in even closer. I wanted to make my point *very* clear. "You're goddamn right I am. That's not new

89

information to you. So don't sit there and act like you don't know what I'm capable of. As far as you're concerned, Chris no longer exists to you on anything more than a business level."

She narrowed her gaze, leaning forward. "Fuck. You. Roman. I have spent my entire life under the thumb of men telling me what to do and how to do it. I'll be damned if I'm going to sit here and let you start now."

"Don't test me, Jameson."

"What are you going to do?"

"Hmm." I sat back, relaxed, and reminded myself she wasn't the enemy here. "What am I going to do? For starters, I've got half a mind to haul you upstairs and remind you of how a real man fucks. I might not be able to have you, but the last thing I'm going to do is sit back and watch you with someone else."

If that didn't shut her up, nothing would. Seemed like it worked since she didn't argue back for a change. She just sat there with her mouth agape.

"You don't mean that."

"Don't test me."

"You're absolutely impossible."

"And I intend to stay that way. So what's on the agenda today?"

"I—for me or you?"

"Us," I clarified. "I'm officially an extension of you, and now that I have a phone, you don't have any reason to go unprotected." *Unless it's with me.*

"You mean anywhere without you," she stated matter-of-factly.

"That's exactly what I mean. Look." I softened my tone. "I'm well aware this is a lot to take in. Hell, I'm still trying to wrap my head around all of it, but something tells me if you didn't really need me, I wouldn't be here. Whether you want to admit that or not is a different story."

She let out a long, defeated sigh. "It's just...everything is so overwhelming. That's all."

"I agree. Let's start over. We got off on the wrong foot yesterday, and I apologize." My apology was sincere, and I wanted nothing more than for her to believe me. "We all have battles to fight, James. Let me help you fight yours. Please."

Demons aside—hers and mine—Jameson's life was my priority now. Nothing else mattered. I didn't expect to pick up where we'd left off and be her best friend, though there was nothing I wanted more than to be her friend *and some*. It just wasn't the right thing to do.

I just needed her to open up to me a little bit and stop shutting down every time I asked for any kind of information. I'd already ruined her life once; she needed to trust me that it wouldn't happen again.

She took a drink of water and cleared her throat. "Apology accepted...for now. You're on thin ice. But I'm sorry for being such a raging bitch to you."

"Let me guess? Comes with the territory?"

She smirked. "You already know."

Lyndsay Marie

I reached across the table and set my hand on top of hers. It was meant to be a friendly gesture, nothing more. She glanced down at our hands for a brief moment before jerking hers away.

"Relax. I didn't mean—never mind. Can we just talk? Give me something to work with here."

Her eyes surveyed the room, then flickered toward the ceiling and back down to me. *Cameras.* "Now's not the best time."

"Then when is? Give me something to work with...truthfully. It would make my job and your life a hell of a lot easier if you did."

She tossed a cloth napkin onto her plate. "Let's head back up to my office. We can finish this conversation there. People might not talk a whole lot, but they sure as hell listen."

Roman felt like he was genuinely trying to make peace with me. It was nice, but that didn't negate the fact he was hiding something important from me—like where he'd been or why he'd left. Because of that alone, I didn't know if I could even trust him. Did I want to? Yes…and no. Unfortunately, I sort of didn't have much of a choice at the moment since my life currently depended on him.

A part of me wanted to make amends with him, go back to where we were before all of…this, whatever this was. Shit, he was once my best friend, my safe place. He'd been the glue that held me together when it felt like everything around me was falling apart. Roman had always known the right words to say to make any bad situation seem less relevant to the even bigger issues going on around us.

And damn, he gave the best hugs. The kind that when his arms were around you, you just knew that without a doubt everything was going to be okay no matter what. When Roman's hand had touched mine during lunch, I'd lost all senses. Even the slightest skin-to-skin contact with him made me weak. Truth be told, it pained me to be such a bitch to him, but it was all I knew to do because his touch was kryptonite to my defenses.

The problem with him was he was just as easy to hate as he was to love, Because now he was on my ass about Chris, and I did not have the energy for their pissing contest. As it was, there was entirely too much on my plate to sit and entertain Roman's jealousy or Chris's pushy advances.

"The place looks nice," Roman observed as he looked around the casino.

I'd been so lost in thought I didn't realize I'd aimlessly wandered through the casino floor. "Thank you. It was a real labor of love."

"I like it. It's…different. Classy."

I smiled, inside and out. I was proud of how things had turned out. Revamping the place hadn't been high on my priority list, but once I'd confirmed we'd be hosting the gala this year, I knew the place needed an overhaul ASAP.

Initially, all I wanted to do was lock myself in my room, shove myself under the covers, and hide away from even the slightest inconvenience.

"We actually just finished renovations a few weeks ago. I wanted it all to be done in time for the fundraiser, for obvious reasons."

This year's theme was *Alice in Wonderland* black-tie masquerade. The gala had always taken place the weekend before Halloween, and I wanted to incorporate a sprinkling of my dad's favorite movie into the theme. So Kelly and I tossed around a few ideas, and the concept was born. She and her personal assistant, Haley, ran with it.

The fundraiser itself had grown exponentially over the years. My mom had convinced him to start the whole thing in an effort to raise awareness of child and human trafficking in the area. According to him, he was never on board with the whole thing and thought it was a terrible idea, given my own history and how I came to exist.

See, I was once a victim myself. The first time my dad had ever caught Kane trafficking people, I'd been one of them. I was just a baby, and nobody involved that night knew who I belonged to. My dad handled things on his own, and called in a few favors. The victims were released, and I stayed with Elliott and Lena, aka Dad and Mom.

Unfortunately, Mom was only able to be a part of the annual event a few times because around the time I was three, she'd contracted pneumonia that took her life. My dad continued hosting the fundraiser in memory of my mom, and now, I was going to keep it going for him.

We were already expecting the largest turnout ever for the simple fact that it had been almost two years since our last fundraiser, given that last year's had been canceled due to my dad's death right before the event was set to take place.

The recent changes I'd made to Emerald Haze were one-eighty of its original Mardi Gras theme. The original design wasn't bad, but it was long overdue and time to go.

Lyndsay Marie

I hired one of the best designers from Las Vegas, who came highly recommended from the area. They brought in a team of people who worked around the clock to bring my vision to life. When all was said and done, the décor had gone from purple, green, and gold, confetti and jesters with gemstones, to full-blown moody, gothic glam with black crystals that dripped from oversized chandeliers with shimmery diamonds and every other light fixture, mirrors for days, and gold and silver mixed-metal accents on every surface.

It was still over-the-top, as one would expect from a casino, except now it had been brought into this decade.

"I think Elliott would approve," Roman said reassuringly as he walked alongside me with his hands stuffed in his front pockets.

"I appreciate that. He was my inspiration, you know. Halloween was his favorite. It was a challenge, though, because I didn't want to ward people off by having a strict Halloween theme, so I had the designer tweak it to what you see now. The team did it all in less than six months."

"I'd say whoever came up with the final design nailed it."

"So far, no one's complained about it, at least not to my face. So I consider that a win."

"I don't see any green though," he observed.

"Oh, it's there. You know I wouldn't leave out my dad's favorite color."

I pulled out my phone, and with the tap of a few buttons, the background and uplighting faded from a soft, warm glow to a bright emerald green.

"Fully automated."

"Very clever."

We'd finally reached the back-of-house service elevator. I tapped my keypad with my e-reader. I'd never been more thankful that the ride up eleven floors would be quick because being confined in a four-by-six, walk-in-closet-sized room with Roman Stone, who not only looked every bit of mafia boss in his head-to-toe black suit but now wore cologne that smelled like sex and candy, made the already tight space feel even more suffocating.

We rode in silence, standing side by side, and when the doors finally opened, I exited first, leaving him behind. I let myself into my office, kicking the door open so it at least wouldn't slam back shut on him. Then I circled around to the back side of my desk, desperate to put as much space and furniture between us as possible. *Not that it stopped us before.*

"Lunch was nice. Thanks for not stabbing me with your fork," he quipped as he took the seat across from mine.

"Too many witnesses." I winked. "I was waiting to get you alone up here." Which, thinking about it now, probably hadn't been my brightest idea.

We both knew I wasn't immune to his advances. But I had nowhere else to go where I knew we could talk more openly without the risk of being heard or a place that didn't have a bed.

"Ha. Ha." He glanced around my office. I hadn't changed much since I'd moved in. I'd added a few basic décor pieces, removed some outdated artwork, stuck a live plant in the corner near the window. "You seem to have fallen nicely into this role."

"Pssh. I'm glad you think so. I think I've spent more days than not debating on blowing my own brains out."

"Sounds like a cop-out. You're better than that."

"Well, I must think so, too, since I'm still here."

"I can only imagine what you've been through, James, and I'm not even going to pretend like I know. But if you ever need anyone, I'm here for you."

But you weren't, was what I wanted to say. "I appreciate it. It was a hell of a transition, that's for sure."

I stared over at Roman. He looked calm, comfortable, in control…like he belonged in my chair and not me. Maybe he did. He was absolutely better equipped to do this job than me. But I had shit to prove—to myself and my staff.

"I already accepted your apology. What do you want?"

"Hmm? Nothing. Just telling you I'm sorry again. That's all."

"You're full of shit, Roman. You want something."

"Maybe." He smiled. "Okay, you're right."

"Then spill it."

He casually leaned back to one side. "Don't jump all over my ass, okay? I'm just curious—"

"If you're going to say anything about Chris, you can forget—"

"*Not* about him, or anyone else for that matter. I was going to ask if you knew how many properties there were?"

I scrunched my eyebrows together. "Properties? Why do you ask?"

"Just wondering. That's all."

I folded my arms across my chest. "No, you're not *just curious*. Roman. What are you up to? We already had this conversation once."

"James, hear me out before you shut me down. Okay? I saw the way you looked around at the cameras downstairs. I've picked up on every single one of your subtle movements—every twitch, every flinch, stare, gaze, name it. It's what I do. You've said more to me without ever speaking a word out loud. I know that you know something is going on, but you refuse to address it, but it's because you don't know how. Am I wrong?"

Fuck. He was not wrong. Not even a little bit. I hated with a passion that one of Roman's many talents was reading body language. It was something that had always come naturally to him. My dad knew it; that was just one reason he protected him.

"No. You're not wrong," I reluctantly confessed under my breath. "Sometimes I think the only reason I've lived this long is because I've kept my head buried in the sand."

"If you fully accept my apology, then you know a little forgiveness goes a long way, James. Help me help you."

I huffed. Fuck it. What was the worst that could happen? I tell him everything I know, which probably wasn't even that much, and he does what with that info? Fix all my problems? Make them worse? Guess I'd soon find out. "Aside from Emerald Haze's main resort and outlying buildings here on the property, we have one warehouse on Mud Island and one near the airport in Memphis. I'd have to look. How many do you know about?"

"The ones you just mentioned. I don't think there are any others. Have you never been to any of these?"

I already knew he wasn't going to like my answer. "No."

He raised an eyebrow. "No? As in never?"

"Nope. Not a one. I took over my dad's decades-old family business and put all of my faith into the men who were already in place running things. I never once thought to question their loyalty or motives, and I'd never had a reason to visit them."

"I'm not saying all of these people don't have your best interest at heart, but James, it might be about time you start asking some really tough questions or, at the very least, doing your own research."

I let out a huff. "This shit is so exhausting."

"Let me help you…let me in, James. You've got to if you want my help."

I wanted to—I wanted so badly to break down just a fraction of the wall I'd spent the last year putting up to protect myself from him—from anyone. I wanted to believe he had my best interest at heart, but at the moment, it was hard to trust anyone. Even him.

He held my gaze for entirely too long for long for my own comfort. I only wished I could have read him anymore the way he still could do to me.

To break whatever trance he had me in, I stood up and walked over to the massive magnolia oil painting hanging on the far side of my office. I released the latch behind the ornate gold frame and swung the heavy picture back to reveal a built-in safe in the wall. A few spins of the lock and the mechanism released with a *click*.

"All these years, I had no idea that was there."

"That's the idea." Only a few people knew this safe was here.

I reached inside and pulled out a thick manila envelope stuffed with papers and walked it over to Roman. I propped myself against my desk and held it out to him. When he went to grab it, I quickly withdrew it. "Uh, uh, uh. Not so fast. I need something from you first."

He folded his hands together, covering his mouth with steepled fingers. His eyes slowly raked over my body from head to toe and back up. "I'm listening."

I narrowed my eyes. "*Not* that."

"That's too bad."

As much as I wanted to entertain whatever idea it was he had, because, chances were, I was thinking it, too, my common sense overrode my hormones for the time being.

"There is a lot of information inside this envelope. A *lot*. Like everything my dad thought I might need to run the family business one day…god willing, and just in case. There's info in here that you won't find on any encrypted computer. I have to trust you, Roman. Like really trust you won't use any of what you find in here against me or go rogue."

"You have my word, James. You've always had my word."

"I mean it." I didn't know why I was so nervous all of a sudden. I just knew Roman had information that I didn't, and if he wanted to get anything out of me, I needed some answers from him first. "Tell me where you've been."

He closed his eyes.

Finally.

He was going to tell me *something*, and I didn't even know if it would have made a difference now. I just wanted to know; I *needed* to know.

"James," he practically groaned. "You know I can't tell you that. Not yet."

"Then when?" I yelled at him. "When do I get to know what the fuck went on around here?"

"Soon," he replied in an even tone. "I promise. I just—I need a little more time, okay?"

"Time? Time for what? You know what, fuck it, and fuck you. It's always something with you." I stalked across the room, and shoved the envelope back into the safe, slamming the door closed. Then I put the picture back into place.

I spun on my heels and started to leave my office. I didn't give a shit about him or his promises.

"Jameson, stop."

"Fuck off," I spit out as I tried passing him to get to the door.

"Stop running from me," he ordered with stern *I'm not fucking around with you anymore* force to his voice.

"Don't tell me what to do," I hissed. "You are *not* my dad."

"No, I'm not," he said with a tone that had softened, "but you didn't listen to him either. So please, at least listen to me."

ELEVEN
Roman

If there was one thing Jameson was good at, it was running. Running from emotions she didn't want to confront, running away when she was uncomfortable, running when she was sad, or hurt, or angry.

Not anymore.

Because if there was one thing I was even better at, it was catching up with someone on the run.

I quickly stood up and went after her before she reached the door. I didn't have the chance to grab her before she stopped on a dime, spun around, and caused me to run full force into her. In an effort to keep us both from falling over, I wrapped my arm around her waist, steadying her on her feet. Every muscle in her body stiffened in my hold. Then, as if she were putty in my hands, her entire body relaxed.

"Sorry, I—"

"Don't be," I whispered. "You have nothing to be sorry for. You never have."

Her respirations steadied, and every deep breath she pulled in caused her pert breasts to press into my chest. As if right on cue, and at the most inopportune moment, my cock went full-on traitor mode, growing rock solid in the span of 0.5 seconds.

Fucker.

I locked in on her gaze. "Jameson, please stop doing this. Stop running from me. I'm not the bad guy here. Not to you, anyways. But you have to quit running."

If there was one thing that I did love about myself, it was how I could read anyone like a book—Jameson was no different. Whether it was because I'd known her for nearly a decade, or she was just an easy read, her body language never let me down.

Except in this one small moment, her eyes were ablaze with fiery passion, not *leave me alone*. Everything about her screamed *touch me, make a move*, do *something*. She'd fought hard to hold back.

It was in this moment that I no longer gave a shit about her stupid fucking rules or the new NDA. She could have me sign every NDA from here to Europe, and it wouldn't stop me from doing what I was about to do.

I leaned down and placed my mouth close to her. "Try as you might," I whispered, my lips barely brushing against the shell of her ear, "to deny that there's anything between us, and you can tell yourself and everyone you know that you don't give a shit about me or us, but we both know that's a damned lie because I know, and *you* know, you feel it, too."

My cock was so fucking hard there was no way she didn't at least feel *that* pressed against her stomach.

I pulled back and studied her face—every line and crease, every emotion she'd kept bottled up, trying hard not to let her feelings show.

Her eyes fluttered closed. "I do—I feel it. I want it."

I tightened my hold around her waist and pressed my lips to hers. *Restraint was never my strong suit.*

She sucked in as if she were caught off guard by my advance. Then, within a matter of seconds, we'd gone from quarreling coworkers to one of the hottest make-out sessions I'd ever had…even with her.

Eventually, our kiss slowed until we pulled apart. I threaded my fingers into her hair, pulling a handful into my grip and forcing her to look up at me.

"Holy shit," she breathed out as my tongue slowly invaded her mouth. *Yup. She felt it.*

Cautiously, I slid my hand down her backside and cupped her ass through her tight pencil skirt. She moaned into my mouth, and I almost came on the spot. My heart pounded at a rate that probably shouldn't have been sustainable with life. Kissing Jameson like this again launched me into another galaxy.

Then, as if the universe knew we were doing something we'd both regret, her fucking office phone rang, causing us both to jump.

She quickly pulled back and shoved me away.

"I—I have to get that," she mumbled. She wiped off her mouth and answered the unsuspecting caller, trying to maintain composure.

A few minutes later, she ended the call with a very punctual "We'll meet you there."

And just like that, our fun was over…for now.

———— ◆ ————

"We need to go meet with head of security."

"Leon?"

"The one and only."

Leon was one of the longest-running security guards on Elliott's employee list. He was tall and built like a brick wall. Despite having a few years on him now, I'd still never take my chances with him in a fight. Back in his younger days, he ran with one of Memphis's well-known street gangs. Elliott found him and took him under his wing. Leon never looked back.

"Is everything okay?" I hated not knowing what the hell was going on at any given moment. Don't get me wrong, there wasn't a position within these operations I'd rather have than the one at the front lines of keeping Jameson alive, but damn, not having any inside connections anymore was going to be the death of me—hopefully, only figuratively.

"Yeah, everything's fine. He said Hector's got your security clearance."

"That's it? Just my security clearance?"

107

"Um-hmm. What were you expecting?"

"Not that with the way you answered the phone."

"It's just business, Roman. Remember that."

I had a strong feeling that statement had dual meaning, one I might address later. For now, I wanted to stay in James's good graces if it meant getting something more than a gun and a phone in my possession.

We made our way to the security dungeon—a closed-off section on the back side of the newly relocated business office area. We breezed by Chris's office without so much as a pause or a glance. Well, not by James. I gave his office door a mental middle finger.

At the end of the hallway, we made a right, down to another dead end. Hanging on the outside of the door was a black door with a gold plate on it that said SECURITY in black lettering.

James badged us inside.

The room looked the exact same—obnoxiously dim lighting, wall-to-wall high-definition CCTVs, and at least a row of men sitting in chairs, all staring at the screens in front of them, each assigned to a different area of the property. I didn't know any of them, never did.

Hector appeared from a closed office door. "James! How you doing?"

She plopped down on an empty chair across from the wall of TVs. "I'd be better if we quit letting Kane's idiots get on our property." She waved her hand dismissively toward me with an invisible eye roll. "You remember Roman, I'm assuming?"

He stretched his arm out in a friendly gesture, *unlike some people*. I shook his hand. "Of course I do. What the hell are you doing back? I thought they killed you?" he laughed, but we all knew he was serious.

"It's all one and the same anymore."

"Ain't that the truth. So where you been, then? We missed having you comin' around here."

"I've been…" I glanced down at James, who was staring a hole in my head, waiting for me to give him an answer. "Unavailable."

Hector grinned. "I get that. Well, it's great to see you. Let me get you some things Miss James has requested. I'll be right back." He stepped back into his office, the door swinging shut behind him.

"Unavailable," James mumbled as if to mock me.

I didn't acknowledge her. I just stared ahead, hands on my hips, gazing over as many of the screens as I could. *Where in the hell is her office?* Maybe I overlooked it, but I didn't see the entire floor where James's office was located—not the hallway, not the elevator lobby. None of it.

Hector emerged before I could ask. "Okay," he said. "I've got you all set up on here." He handed me a laptop with a power cord. "James will know the password. You should have access to certain requested files and even the camera feed. The archives are there, too. They're all clearly labeled on the home screen."

"A laptop?"

"Yup," he breathed heavily, as if he were hesitant to hand any of it over, "per her request."

I smirked at James. "Perfect. Thank you."

"I'm also giving you a key card that'll get you into any door on the property that requires badge entry. Even here."

I took the card and pocketed it. "Thanks, man. I appreciate this. A *lot*."

"You're welcome," James said with a snide tone.

Hector just shook his head.

"I already know," I said to him. "Thanks again."

I reached down to help James up. "Ready?"

She pushed herself up with the armrests of the chair. "Thank you, Hector. I'm sure we'll be seeing you again soon."

"Welcome. Let me know if I can get either of y'all anything else."

———————◆———————

"There. That should tide you over for a while. Why don't you head back up to your suite. I'll text you the password so you can start looking over things. I'll come check in with you shortly."

"Wait. What? Who's staying with you?' Roman asked. "Nobody. I'll be fine."

"You know I can't leave you alone."

"I said I'll be fine."

"Not happening. Where are you going?"

"Give me a break. I need to go check in on my folks, make my rounds through a few departments. It won't take long." She looked at her watch. "Maybe less than an hour."

No fucking way I was letting her go anywhere without me. "I don't care if you want to be gone for one minute or one hour, I'm not letting you out of my sight. We clear?"

"This is ridiculous."

"Call it what you want, but we've already had this discussion. Besides, you won't even know I'm there."

"Come on, Roman. You can't be serious?"

"Dead. I'm not here to hang out in a penthouse while you carry on like your life isn't in danger. Either I go with you, or you just don't check in on your people. I'm sure they'll be just fine without you."

She huffed. "Fine. Follow me, but not too close. I've gotta make my daily rounds. When I'm done, we'll head upstairs *together* and call it a day. How's that sound?"

"Like we finally agree on something. I just need to drop this laptop off first."

Less than ten minutes later, my laptop was secure in the safe in my suite, and as promised, I followed a few steps behind Jameson, staying out of her way as much as possible. Don't get me wrong, as much as I loathed being dragged around like a dog on a leash while she performed the most mundane tasks, I had zero complaints about the view of her from behind.

I'd followed Jameson around for damned near two more hours as she made her rounds. Elliott would never

111

have done all of this bullshit administrative work; he had someone else do it for him. But I guess James felt some kind of moral obligation to do everything herself...that and an innate trait to do every-fucking-thing herself.

We were just about to head up when a woman's voice called out for her.

"Oh, hey, James. There you are."

She stopped and turned toward the voice. "Kelly. Everything okay?"

"Yeah, good." Kelly Sterling approached us, eyeing me up and down. Kelly had always been a looker, but she never did anything for me. Not in the way Jameson had. From what I'd always heard about Kelly, she did a *lot* for everyone else.

"You remember Roman?" Jameson asked as she reached over and gripped onto my upper arm. *Getting a little territorial, are we?*

Kelly smiled. "How could I forget? Long time, no see."

I nodded. "Kelly. Good to see you again."

I didn't see much of Kelly when I did work around here. Mostly because she was mid-level management, always with her head in her clipboard. I'd always been just outside hired help.

"Did you need me for something? We were just wrapping things up down here. We're about to head up and call the day done."

Kelly took her focus off me and put it back on James. "Uh, yeah. No biggie. Just wanted to give you a few quick updates on this weekend, but it can wait."

"You sure?"

"Positive. Just go. It sounds like y'all are busy."

We're not, was what I wanted to tell her. I didn't define any of this as busy. It was downright boring.

"Uh, sorta. But it sounds like you have everything under control, then."

"I sure as hell try." She shifted her attention toward me. "So what brings you back to town? I thought I'd never see you again."

I caught a glimpse of James, who eyed Kelly suspiciously. "Just work. I'm only here for a couple of days."

"Awe. That's too bad," she pouted. "We miss seeing you around here."

I highly doubted Kelly, or anyone else for that matter, had missed me. I'd barely been around when I was here, and even then, I could probably count the number of times I'd ever laid eyes on Kelly on one hand. She and I weren't exactly best buds.

Jameson dug her fingers into my arm, giving Kelly a *shut the fuck up* look. "We really should get going," she said to Kelly. "Got lots to do."

"Yeah, sure. Looking forward to seeing you two around. I'll be in touch if anything changes," Kelly said. "Oh, James. One more thing. Chris was looking for you."

Lyndsay Marie

She cleared her throat. "He said text him when you aren't busy and get a free minute."

"She's always busy," I affirmed. "It was good seeing you, Kelly." I bent down and whispered in James's ear, pulling her along with me as I started walking away. "You will *not* be texting *Chris*. Whatever he needs from you can wait."

Forever.

I'd never been more relieved to be back in my own space. Roman made triple sure that I'd made it safely inside my apartment and that the door was locked before he went across the hall to his place—far away from me. He said he'd be back to check on me, though I didn't know when, which was fine by me.

All I could think about anymore was kissing him. He always knew the right things to say, how to say them. He knew exactly where to put his hands and when—all the things. But that kiss? It was soft and slow and full of passion. It was the kind of kiss that would melt any woman's panties off, and if my phone hadn't rung, I would have been bent over my desk 0.5 seconds later.

As hot as kissing him was, as much as I missed it, I regretted every second of it. We had no business crossing that line. *I* had no business crossing that line. I knew better—*we both did*. All that kiss did was remind me even more of what I wanted and needed but could not have.

I didn't know what had gotten into me when we ran into Kelly. It was like this wave of envy washed over me, and all I wanted to do was mark my territory like a possessive lunatic. I had never felt that way before—not in regards to Roman, and never toward Kelly—ever.

Eventually, I ended my day with a much-needed soak in my jetted tub, an overflowing glass of wine, and the voice of Michael Bublé serenading me through the surround sound system. It was exactly what I needed to get my mind off everything, even if it was only long enough for my hot bath water to turn cold.

———◆———

I awoke to someone banging on my front door. I thought I was dreaming at first, but the second my eyelids cracked open, a beam of blazing sunlight burned my retinas. *Shit.* I'd forgotten to close my curtains. It was nice though. I'd practically slept like the dead after half a bottle of wine and a steaming hot bath, topped off with crawling into bed with a fresh set of linen sheets that housekeeping replaced daily and the comfort of knowing Roman was just a few feet away if I needed him.

The banging started again, this time a lot louder.

I hopped out of bed and stumbled toward the door.

"I'm coming, hold on," I shouted.

"It's me," I heard Roman call out.

I unlocked and flung the door open. "Christ, what time is it?"

He held up a cafeteria tray stacked with food. "Five. Let me in, this shit's heavy."

I stood to the side and let him in. He walked over to my dining table and set the tray down.

"A.M.?"

"Isn't that the time you normally scream at the top of your lungs from the rooftop, waking up the townspeople below?"

"Ha. Ha. Not always."

"Well, I brought breakfast." He set everything up and poured two cups of coffee. "It was the best I could come up with since Josephine doesn't get here until six."

I flipped on the light above the dining room table and joined him. "It looks delicious." From what I could tell, he'd brought coffee, toast, scrambled eggs, and cut-up fruit. "Josephine's gonna have your ass if she finds out you took her precut fruit."

He pulled out a chair, waving his hand over it. I sat down, and he tucked me in, then joined me. "She'll live. Everything else I made myself."

"I'm impressed, but why the hell are you here so early?" Not that I didn't usually get an early start on my day, but every now and then, my lack of sleep caught up with me. This was just one of those days.

"Payback and because we've got shit to do, things to talk about, but first, how was your night."

I loaded up a plate with food and took a sip of coffee. "Amazing, actually. I slept like the dead. How about yours?"

"I wish I could say the same."

"What's wrong? Is it the bed?"

"Oh, no. It's definitely not the bed. The bed is a dream. I was up half the night combing through anything and everything I could access."

"Find anything good and worth investigating?" I half smirked. I knew there wasn't anything there. Not because there was anything to hide, but really, there was nothing there.

"Actually, there is…maybe." Okay, he had my attention. Even though I was still hungover and ready to crawl back into bed until noon. "It doesn't appear that Elliott had any properties other than the ones we've already talked about—here, Mud Island, and the airport—with the exception of maybe one. What's Magnolia?"

I could feel the blood drain from my face, along with my appetite. It'd been a long time since I heard that name mentioned. It wasn't a place that was talked about around here. "It—it's—"

Roman reached out and placed his hand on my shoulder. "Jesus, James. You look like shit all of a sudden. Are you feeling okay?"

"Yeah, sorry. I'm fine. It's just been a while since I've heard that name, that's all. It was my dad's estate in Collierville." Roman leaned back in his chair. Now, he looked like he was going to be sick. "Do you know about it?"

"I knew Elliott had a house away from here. I just never knew where or that it had its own name."

The thought of my childhood home and the memories we made there brought a sad smile to my face. "It's a beautiful house. Have you ever been?"

He sat in silence for a moment, staring at his untouched plate of food. "No," he finally answered. "When was the last time you were there?"

It was too damned early for shit to be this heavy. If I had known this was how my morning was going to go, I never would have answered the door.

"A little over a year ago. When I was escorted out the front door the night my dad was killed. I never looked back."

He scrunched his eyebrows together. "You've literally been here? Inside of Emerald Haze ever since? I thought you were exaggerating."

I stabbed some eggs with my fork, hoping to get a little food on my empty stomach. "I wish I were, but no. I've been here. Not because I didn't want to leave. You have no idea how many times I've dreamed about running away."

"James."

I could hear the sadness in his voice. This was not what he'd ever wanted for me; he'd always wanted better. Quite frankly, so did I, but shit happened.

"I know what you're gonna say, Roman, but it's too late. This is my life. This is what I was signed up for."

Subtly, he shook his head. "I'm so sorry."

"Don't be. This has nothing to do with you." I poured myself a glass of orange juice. The thought of coffee no longer sat well with me. "So, tell me why you're here so early that it couldn't wait until at least nine."

"You have no idea how hard it is for me to wake up this early, but I thought you'd already be ready to take on the world. Figured I'd beat you to the punch," he smirked. "Clearly, I was wrong."

"Not entirely. I think the bath, bottle of wine, and long day yesterday really did me in. I was just playing catch up."

"Well, maybe you can take a nap later. I do have *some* motive for catching you so early." I waved my hand as if to say *go on*. "First, I need to apologize to you for breaking your 'look but don't touch' rule—"

"Roman, don—"

"No. I was out of line. It won't happen again, and I'm truly sorry if I've ever hurt you—now or in the past."

I was a little taken aback by his reference to hurting me in the past. I didn't want to ask which time he was referring to, but I could only assume it was either him taking my virginity and then kicking me to the friend zone or the text he'd sent right before ghosting me after we'd spent years in the not-so-friend zone.

"I can assure you, the guy I was back then is not who I am now. That guy was a hormone-driven, horny asshole. Now, I'm just an asshole."

I couldn't help but laugh. "So you're never horny?"

He smiled. "I didn't say that, and we both know that's not true, but I'm not going to try to sleep with you because you're right. Sex makes men stupid, and stupid men get innocent people killed. I just want to—I don't even fucking know anymore. I want to keep you safe, and I want to see you happy. The thought of watching you maybe one day leave this place to go on to bigger and better things is about the only thing that makes me happy. I want more for you than anything this place could ever offer."

"It won't happen again," I assured him and partially myself. "You have no idea how hard any of this has been on me, Roman. How many nights I stayed up plotting revenge against the man who started all this, how many times I've wanted to just escape and never look back. I lost my only dad, and then…I lost you."

He reached his hand across the table, palm up, waiting for me to take it instead of just grabbing mine. I looked down at his empty hand, then up at him. After what felt like an eternity, I laid my hand in his, and he gave it a reassuring squeeze.

"You're here now, and so am I. I'm not going anywhere. Right now, let's get through this weekend, then you can run away."

He brushed his thumb back and forth over my finger. That simple touch, that one little act of tenderness from him, had me wanting to take back everything I'd said about never wanting to kiss him again and drag him straight into my bedroom.

"Thank you. And thank you for breakfast. It was nice. You did a good job."

"You're welcome."

"I need to go get ready for the day. You're already ahead of me." I forced a smile and pulled out of his grip as I stood up. "I'll try to be quick. Feel free to make yourself at home."

THIRTEEN

Roman

I felt like such an idiot as I watched Jameson disappear behind her bedroom door. So much was said in such a short amount of time, yet I didn't even cover half of what I had initially come here this early to talk to her about. Our conversation had taken a turn that I was not expecting. Regardless, it was evident that there was a lot more between us that we needed to talk about…eventually…maybe. But business came first and foremost.

Always had, always would.

It was apparent that we'd both seemingly lost our appetites, so I cleaned up what was left of breakfast, stacked our dishes back on the tray, and headed out on the balcony.

The sky was still mostly dark as night, with a sliver of sunlight creating a soft red-orange glow on the horizon. There was a slight chill in the air that would soon be replaced with the same warmth and humidity as

123

midsummer. It wouldn't be long before the peace of early morning would be replaced with a thousand cars and the hustle of patrons half willing to blow their life savings hoping to hit the jackpot.

I let out a sigh, watching my breath turn into fog every time I exhaled. The cloudy air stirred up a lot of dark memories. Shit that I wished I could forget.

The patio door slid open behind me. "The weather's perfect, isn't it?"

"It is." I turned around, and for a brief moment, it felt like the world had stopped. Jameson stood in the doorway, dressed to the nines in her typical work attire: a too-tight-for-my-liking black pencil skirt and a silk blouse—today's color choice a deep royal purple—finished off with a pair of black spiked-heel FMPs. I practically—no, I *did*—eye-fuck her from head to toe and back up again. I didn't even try to hide it this time.

"What?" she mused.

"Nothing. Absolutely nothing." All I could think was how much better that outfit would look spread out in a pile on the floor from here to her bedroom.

"You just gave me a look."

I shrugged. "Don't know what you're talking about," I lied as I quickly made my way past her, heading back inside.

She closed and locked the door. "Uh-huh. Whatever you gotta tell yourself."

"You just…you look amazing. You always do. That's all."

She grinned, playing with a dainty gold chain bracelet on her wrist. "Thank you. Feels like this"—she waved her hands over her outfit—"is about all I've got left anymore to feel good about myself. I tend to go overboard sometimes."

I walked over to her, stopping just a few inches in front of her. I reached out, tucked a loose strand of hair behind her ear, then kissed her gently on the forehead. "Don't ever change."

As I took a deep breath to keep my mind from wandering, I was hit with instant regret. Jameson smelled mildly sweet, like vanilla mixed with heaven and sex and all the dirty things I wanted to do to her but couldn't.

I backed off, putting as much space between us as possible. "Before we get going for the day, I wanted to talk about one more thing."

"Sure. It's not like we don't have time."

"I've been wondering, does Ivan ever go home at night, or does he stay here on the property around the clock?"

Once upon a time ago, Ivan had an off-site condo somewhere on Riverside Drive in Memphis. I'd never been, but I heard him talk about it in passing. He also had a wife, and I couldn't imagine she'd be okay with him being gone 24/7...or hell, maybe she enjoyed his absence.

"Sometimes he stays, sometimes he goes. I don't force him to live here. I think it depends on what he's got going on here or at home. If he does leave, he gets someone from night watch to keep an eye out. Why?" She eyed me suspiciously.

125

"I just—I don't know, James. Something feels off about, well, everything. I can't put my finger on it."

"You're not here to start an investigation. All I can tell you is we've got a decent operation going on, and you're not about to fuck it up with your wild and crazy ideas and accusations."

"I'm not accusing anyone of anything." *Yet.* She folded her arms across her chest, pushing her cleavage tighter together. *Fuck.* "Just hear me out."

"I'm listening."

"You said you haven't been to your dad's house at all? Correct?"

She reached up and grabbed the emerald pendant dangling from her necklace. A present from Elliott on her sixteenth birthday. Also another defense tactic for when she didn't have a desk to hide behind. "No."

"Do you think Ivan has anything to do with why Kane is after you?"

"What? No!" She rested her hands on her hips. "Christ. Do you know how ridiculous you sound? Ivan has done nothing but protect me in any and every way he knows how. He even brought you back from the dead to help him, for fuck's sake. Do you think he would have called you here if he had something to do with this?"

Oops. I'd struck a chord but had led her right into the conversation I needed. It was now or never. "Maybe not, but I want to go there."

Her eyebrows scrunched together. "Go where?"

I swallowed down the lump that had formed deep in the back of my throat and braced myself for the backlash. "Your dad's estate."

"No." She pushed past me, heading toward the door in an effort to leave.

I turned to follow her. "Yes. That place needs to be checked on, at the very least, and I want to be the one who does it...*without* Ivan."

She kept walking. "I said no."

I ran ahead of her and put my body between her and the only exit. "God damn it, Jameson. Stop. Fucking. Running."

"I am *not* running. I have an incredibly busy weekend with a lot to do and only a few days to get it done. That won't happen if I'm arguing with you."

"Then let me go. One time."

"It's not necessary. There's nothing there. Now, get out of my way." She reached for the door, pulling it ajar.

I slapped my hand against it, slamming it shut. "Maybe not, but you yourself don't even know for sure. I'll get Ivan or one of the guys to take over my post for a while, tell them I'm sick. I'll report anything I find back to you."

"You can't be fucking serious. Are you really standing here telling me that you think I'm just going to trust you enough to let you go poke and prod around my dad's estate? Alone?" She laughed out loud. "Are you out of your mind? Scratch that. You *are* out of your mind. Now, move. I have shit to do."

"Maybe I have completely lost it, but someone needs to at least lay eyes on that place because you clearly haven't."

"Absolutely not. I had that house locked up and sealed shut. *No one* has been there since. There's not one single reason for anyone to go back—not you, not me, not anyone."

"You sure about that?"

"On my life."

"Only one way to find out."

◆

After a stare-down from the Wild West, I eventually conceded and stepped aside, letting Jameson storm out of the penthouse. I was already at risk of getting my balls kicked into my throat. If there was one thing I knew about her that would never change, it was that all she needed was a little time alone to get lost in her own thoughts and think everything over. Once she had sorted everything out in her head and could make sense of things, she'd come around. Eventually.

I followed her around, staying far enough behind to not feel invasive, as she made her administrative rounds—yawn.

As she went from department to department, I checked my watch at least twice a minute. We were knee-deep in what could only be described as the ultimate snooze fest. That was until Chris appeared. It was as if he came out of nowhere from between some slot machines, approaching Jameson, and right on cue to liven things up a little.

Let's see where this goes.

She stopped and glanced around. *Looking for me?* She focused her attention back on him when she didn't see me, as if she were alone. I hated that I couldn't hear what they were talking about, but she pulled out her phone and showed him the screen. They talked for another minute, and then he leaned in closer to her, saying something he wanted only her to hear. She leaned away from him ever so slightly, said something back, then started to walk away. I watched them for a second or two before I followed at a distance. I knew in my gut he'd been waiting for this moment. He'd really thought in his shit-for-brains that I'd actually left her alone.

They walked casually side by side, innocently enough, until he reached behind her and copped a feel of her ass. She swatted his hand away and kept walking. He seemed to laugh at the gesture. I, on the other hand, saw red as heat seared through my veins.

I quickly made my way up behind the unsuspecting couple in only a handful of long, easy strides. When I was within arm's reach, I tapped Chris on the shoulder. He turned around, and I decked him square in the jaw. He immediately lost his balance and fell to the floor on his knees.

"Roman!" Jameson screamed. "What the hell?" She reached for me, but I shoved her with one hand to her chest, pushing her out of the way.

I squatted down and leaned in his face. "Motherfucker. Get up."

"Fuck you." His words slurred, and blood pooled in the crease of his lips.

"No, thanks. Word on the street is you're a lousy lay."

He cut his eyes to James, then back to me, and smiled. "Yeah. You hit like a bitch."

He clambered to his feet and lunged at me, knocking us both to the ground. He took a swing at me from above, grazing the side of my face just as I turned my head, causing him to punch the floor. I easily overpowered him, rolling him over onto his back. As soon as I did, I unleashed a series of closed-fist hits straight to his face.

"Don't ever put your hands on her again," I heaved between thrown licks. Chris's blood splattered from his face off to the side in tiny flecks all over me and the carpet beneath him.

Jameson's scream in the background for me to stop was barely audible over the ringing in my ears.

It didn't take long before I felt hands pulling at my shirt and arms, dragging me off him.

"Roman," Leon's deep voice calmly ordered as he lifted me up. "That's enough."

Jordan ran over and helped Chris to his feet.

He was a bloody mess, his face and shirt destroyed. He tried shrugging Jordan away. "Get off of me. I can take him."

Ivan stood off to the side, casually leaning up against a slot machine, shaking his head in disbelief, a smug grin on his face at the circus I'd created. Jameson stood shakily beside him with tears streaming down her cheeks.

It was barely eleven in the morning, and thankfully, the patrons were still far and few between this time of day.

Chris was still being held upright by Jordan's hands.

I licked my lips; a metallic taste coated my tongue. I didn't know if it was his blood or mine.

"*You* hit like a bitch," I casually said to him.

"Don't worry. Next time, I'll just fucking shoot you."

"Hmm. Something tells me there won't be a next time."

Lyndsay Marie

FOURTEEN
Jameson

I stood frozen in complete and utter shock as I watched the nightmare unfold in slow motion. It was as though everything going on around me were a lucid dream. Except it wasn't. Roman fucked Chris up—straight up whooped his ass—and I was pretty sure Chris had no idea what had hit him initially.

Security showed up in the nick of time, pulling the two apart. Thank fuck for my guys because there was a handful of patrons watching in horror from the table games, and there was no way in hell I could have intervened successfully. Ivan was as useful as a fork in tomato soup.

I wiped my face dry as Roman approached. "I'm— fuck." He ran his bloodied hand through his hair. "I'm sorry about that. He just—"

"Go get yourself cleaned up. Ivan can take over from here." My vision had returned, and my body finally calmed from shaking to toe with adrenaline. I needed some space and time to cool off. So did he. "I'll find you in a bit."

"Yes, ma'am." He didn't argue this time. His voice was soft and low, barely audible over the dings and rings and music blaring around us.

"You okay?" Ivan asked me as Roman walked away.

"A little shaky, but I'm fine."

"Chris shoulda seen that one comin' a mile away."

"Really? Roman's fucking unhinged. That was completely unnecessary."

"Eh, maybe a little much, but that's why we need him around." He grinned. "Plus, *we* saw it comin'. I was checking on things in the surveillance room. I told Hector to keep an eye out. Soon as he saw Chris, we came running."

"Well, the pissing contests around here are getting old. It's a damned good thing you came when you did, or he might've killed him."

"Doubt it. He mighta beat him within an inch of his life, but I bet Chris won't touch you again."

I had no doubt Ivan was dead serious. Truth be told, as scary as that was to watch, I was slightly grateful for Roman. Something deep and dark inside of me felt a rush of excitement at the insane actions of one man—that Roman would come to my defense so quickly and to such an extreme over something as simple as another man putting his hand on me.

At this point, I wanted nothing else to do with Chris unless it was work related. Even then, that was debatable. He'd already been out of line telling me how much he missed having me bent over his desk, then had the audacity to cop a cheap feel. The thought of his hands anywhere on me anymore made me want to vomit.

I shivered at the thought.

Ivan lit up a cigarette. We were in one of the few places I allowed smoking inside, and I didn't even want it here. "You want me to tell Roman to take the rest of the day off? Let him cool down?"

I thought about his offer for a second. "No, thank you. I'll be fine." Roman and I had other business to handle, and I didn't need Ivan or anyone else around. "He'll get over it."

"You sure? I don't mind. It's not like Cindy's gonna bitch and whine about me not being home another night."

Cindy had been Ivan's wife for longer than I'd been alive. I didn't know how the hell she'd stayed with him so long in this line of work, but she did. She just stayed as far away from here as possible. Mostly, I think it was having access to his credit cards and her proximity to the Main Street Mall.

"I'm sure. Just text me later and let me know how Chris is. He's the one who needs to take the next day or two off."

I still needed him here, but the way he'd been beaten, I wasn't entirely sure he'd even make it to the fundraiser this weekend.

Ivan laughed. "You're probably right about that. I think they hauled him to the clinic to get checked out. I'll pop in and see."

"Thanks. While you're at it, get someone to give buffet comps or hotel vouchers to anyone and everyone on the floor. Not that it'll stop them from talking on social media, but it'll make them feel better about what just happened."

"You got it, boss. I'm taking off. I got eyes on you. Let me know if you need anything."

I felt like a fish out of water in my own casino. I barely knew my own crew anymore; I had no one to turn to for answers now that I was the one at the top of the chain of command. Something had started to feel very off about every rung below me.

Just as fast as the fight had broken out, things had already seemingly gone back to normal...whatever that was anymore. No one had run out of here screaming for their lives; people were still playing the slots and table games, unbothered.

My phone dinged with a text as I contemplated heading to my own bar and getting drunk before noon.

Roman: Are you okay?
Me: No! I'm not fucking OKAY!

I typed it out but immediately deleted my response.

Me: Yes. I'm fine.
Roman: Do you need me?
Me: More than you know.

Lyndsay Marie

Delete, delete, delete.

What the hell was wrong with me? My intrusive thoughts were not about to win this battle. How I felt about Roman at the moment, good or bad, didn't matter. What mattered was getting through the weekend alive. What I cared about even less was him knowing how I felt about him right now.

Me: I'm planning out the rest of the day. Taking as much of it off as possible.

Because I needed a fucking break. My body felt like it'd just run the St. Jude Marathon. I couldn't remember the last time I didn't have to watch over my shoulder. Last night was the first decent night's sleep I'd had since I could remember.

Roman: Just let me know what you need from me. You know where I'll be.

I didn't respond. I tucked my phone into a pocket that I'd had sewn inside the waistband of all of my work skirts and pants. It was the only way I could keep my hands free and still carry around a phone.

My stomach growled. What little breakfast I'd eaten earlier that morning had long gone. That was my cue to vacate the area and head to the kitchen.

"Josephine?" I called out as a courtesy when I entered the space. The woman had a knack for popping up out of nowhere and scaring the shit out of people.

"You looking for me?" I knew she was here, yet her voice still startled me from behind.

"Jesus Christ, Josephine, you've got to quit doing that." I put my hand over my heart. "I've had enough scares for one day."

"So I heard." She breezed past me with a stainless-steel dish in one hand and big-ass butcher knife in the other. "You came to my kitchen. I'm just working; you're the one who's jumpy."

"It's been a hell of a morning. What do you have to drink around here?"

She gave me the side-eye. "Ma'am, this ain't that kinda kitchen. You want food? I got you. Sweet tea? No problem. What you're looking for is at the bar." She waved her knife toward the door, causing me to duck out of the way.

I propped up against the island countertop and folded my arms. "Ma'am. I know what goes on here. Where is it?"

"Eh." She shrugged.

Typical. Everyone always wanted to be vague; nobody ever wanted to be forthright about anything.

Lyndsay Marie

I glanced around the empty kitchen. "Where's everyone else? It's like you're always the only one ever in here."

"Because my people are *working*. I give them what they need to do their job and send them out of my way. Where's my Romie? Ain't he supposed to be following you around or something?" She pulled a handful of carrots out of the bin and started chopping.

I rolled my head from shoulder to shoulder and massaged the back of my neck. "Your *Romie* is taking the rest of the day off."

Maybe.

"Hmm. Sounds serious." She set her knife down and disappeared into a storage room. A second later, she came out with a muffin in one hand and a syrup bottle in the other. "Take a few squirts of this, but don't let anyone see you. Then tell me what's really going on."

I grabbed the bottle. "Really? Aunt Jemima? I don't need syrup." She gave the bottle a shake in my grip, and the liquid sloshed around. "Oooh." I flipped the top and tipped it back. My throat burned like a mother, but I swallowed down a few swigs of the drink. "Jesus Christ. What in the backwoods redneck shit is this?"

She took the bottle from me with a smile. "You'll appreciate that backwoods redneck shit in a few minutes."

I released my breath and thought I was going to blow out actual flames. "Thanks for that, anyway."

"Now," she said, going back to cutting. "Talk. My crew's gonna be back soon to get refills."

138

I gave her a recap of my morning, telling her everything I'd witnessed from the time I hit the casino floor until the time Chris physically hit the floor. She didn't talk; she just listened to me rant.

"So what's the problem?" she finally asked.

I jerked my head back. "What's the problem? Did you hear anything I just told you?"

"Of course. Y'all brought Roman back to do a job. He did it. I don't see the issue."

"Josephine! You can't be serious."

"You're lucky Roman gave him a second chance. I've known that man just as many years as you, but I know him a lot better. I've watched him grow up from a boy to a man. You don't know the shit these guys had him doing out there." She flicked her eyes toward the back door. I glanced at it and got a sick feeling. Maybe it was the shot I'd just taken that caused my stomach to churn. "They made a man out of him real early on, you know what I mean?"

Every hair on my body stood on end because I knew exactly what she'd meant. Ivan had hired Roman to do their dirty work, unfathomable deeds that I didn't even want to try to pretend I knew anything about. I could only imagine what he'd been put through.

"You're right. Maybe all this isn't for—"

"Plus, he loves you," she said without looking up from the vegetables.

"What?"

"You heard me. I didn't stutter. Now, get out of my kitchen. I got work to do."

"Josephine! You can't just—"

She physically spun me around and shooed me away. "Go. Bye. See you later."

Shit! This day just kept getting better and better. I reluctantly left Nellie's kitchen with a very strong buzz. She never did tell me what was in the bottle, and I'd probably never know. All I knew was that it wasn't syrup, and it was probably as old as me, if not older.

With hazy vision, I tapped out a text to Kelly.

Me: Got a minute?

I'd already started making my way toward her office before waiting for her to reply. Her office was located between the main casino and event center on the ground floor of the hotel tower and clear on the other side of the building from where I was. It was already a hell of a walk as it was. Doing it with a buzz would be a whole different story.

My phone dinged.

Kelly: Always. I'll be in my office. My happy place. My zen. Ohhhm.
Me: Nerd. OMW.

A few minutes later, I stumbled into Kelly's office and plopped down on her sofa. She was sitting behind her desk, typing away.

"Is it hot in here to you, or is it just me?" I fanned my shirt out, trying to create a breeze. "Can you open a window or something?"

She glanced at me over the top of her computer screen with a confused look on her face. "There is no window…and from the looks of it, it's just you. You good? 'Cause you look like shit. Your face is all red."

"Nellie. She gave me some—"

"Shit. Did you sip her syrup?"

"Sip? More like chugged a few shots. You know about it?"

"Yeah, most of us do. I took that shit one time. Never again. I felt sick for two days."

"Christ. I think she tried to kill me. How come I didn't know about it?"

"I think that's obvious. She didn't warn you first? Jesus. One of her family members down the river makes it. That bottle is probably older than both of us combined."

"Tastes like it."

"You shoulda known better than to drink some unknown brown liquid out of a syrup bottle."

"I've made worse decisions."

"Hmm. You might not feel that way in the morning. Why're you drinking this early? It's barely noon."

"You'd drink, too, if you watched what I just witnessed."

"What's going on?" she asked, closing her laptop.

I let out a heavy sigh, followed by a hiccup. "Let's see, where should I start? Oh, I know. How about Roman whooped Chris's ass out on the gaming floor just a little while ago."

Her eyes widened. "Get the fuck out. No he did not!"

I lay back, practically melting into her overstuffed couch. "I wish I were lying. Chris copped a feel of my ass. Roman saw it and lost his shit. Right there in front of everyone."

Kelly practically busted out laughing. "Does Chris *not* know who he's fucking with here? Goddamned idiot. He must have a death wish."

"It's not funny! You should have seen Chris!"

"I'm sure Roman rocked his fuckin' world. How is he? Is he still alive?"

I just shook my head in disbelief. "Yeah, for now. I have no idea how he is at the moment. Ivan's supposed to keep me updated. Jordan dragged him off the floor, I think to the clinic."

"He'll learn real quick Roman is a fuck around and find out kinda guy. Or maybe he won't, and you'll be less one team member. Where is Roman, anyway?"

"I know, I know. He's waiting for my signal. I sent him to his suite until I figured out what I wanted to do for the rest of the day."

"That's probably for the best. Let him cool off."

"Anyway, moving on. How's things going with our event this weekend?"

"So far, so good. Things are falling into place. I got the food and beverage menus delivered this morning."

"Ooh. How they look?"

She held one up for me to see. "Amazing."

Even from across the room, I could tell they were just as immaculate as I had envisioned. Everything from the black velvet paper down to the shimmery silver and gold foil writing. Even the back had been embossed with our logo.

"What did we end up going with for food?"

We had a limited menu because, one, the less people had to worry about food, the more attention they could focus on writing checks, and two, Josephine was up my ass about what she was and wasn't willing to do.

"Let's see…crab cake aioli, pulled pork barbeque sliders with smoked bourbon sauce, prosciutto-wrapped melon, and beef Wellington bites with creamy Dijon mustard dipping sauce. Those are just the main course apps."

"Shit, that sounds so good right now. What about dessert?"

"I was getting there." She cleared her throat. "Then for dessert, we have peach cobbler with French vanilla ice cream, pecan pie balls with caramel dipping sauce, and banana pudding cheesecake."

"You're killing me. That literally sounds the best."

"Oh, it will be. So don't even think about counting your calories. Best just plan on eating your weight in finger-food."

"Deal. Did you decide on a signature drink? All of the ones you'd sent me sounded amazing, too."

"Yup. Me, Haley, and a few others sat here one night at the bar and had Pablo make us all of them."

"And?" I asked anxiously.

She smirked. "Black widow martini."

"Love it."

"We'll still have local craft beer, a flaming cocktail, a smoking cocktail, and a few classics."

"What about the live band?"

"All lined up. Flowers and lighting have both been confirmed. We're rocking right along."

"You're amazing."

"I know. What else you need from me?"

"Everything. That's what else."

She swiveled her chair back and forth. "You're gonna have to elaborate."

I let out a whiny moan. My alcohol brain fog had me feeling some kind of way…that's if that were even considered alcohol that Josephine had given me.

"Can I ask you a question?"

"Of course. Isn't that your job?"

"Well, yeah, I guess. But this isn't about work."

"Oh! Even better. Fire away, then."

My stomach knotted in anticipation, but I knew I had to ask her about Roman. So many other people seemed to know an entirely different side to him than me. I wanted to *know* him the way everyone else did. "What's he like? When I'm not around?"

"What's who like? What do you mean?"

"Roman. It's just—I don't know. Everyone seems to know a different version of him than me."

She shrugged. "He seems the same as he's always been to me."

"I guess."

"Look, don't take this the wrong way, but the Roman you got and the Roman the rest of us know are two totally different people. He didn't want to be the guy everyone expected him to be when he was with you. He could let his guard down with you, right? Isn't that all any of us ever want?"

"Yeah, you're probably right." The problem was almost no one knew about us. They didn't know we'd ever been together or that we were even friends. He'd always just been part of a business transaction to my dad. I was never allowed to interact with him for anything more than that.

"He's grown up a *lot* since the last time he was here. He's always been a looker, but holy shit. Have you seen him?"

I sighed. "Yeah, I see him." And I'd felt the front of his body pressed against mine, savored the sweet taste of his tongue as it invaded my mouth. The thought of our superhot and unfortunately super-short make-out session sent a sensation through my entire body straight between my legs. *Damned alcohol.*

Lyndsay Marie

She propped her elbows on her desk and rested her chin in her hands. "Y'all have lived two completely different lives since day one. You were always the untouchable princess; he was the village villain. You gotta consider what he's been through. Who knows where he's been or what they've had him doing. You know how this line of work can be—how it *is*. But you've only ever seen it from the outside looking in, you know, 'cause Elliott shielded you from a lot."

"I guess you're right." Just in the last day or so, I'd actually considered pursuing Roman again, testing the waters to see where he stood. I didn't know if that was a good idea or quite possibly the dumbest thing I'd ever considered. We had a history…operative word *had*. I needed to remind myself that just because he looked at me like a dessert waiting to be devoured didn't mean he wanted *me* again. He'd only be here for a few more days, and then he'd be gone just as fast as he'd shown up. "And given my track record with men, it's probably best I just sit this one out."

"Ma'am, I don't wanna hear shit about your track record. I've got worse luck than Taylor Swift—spent my entire life picking the wrong men. I just wish I could have found a way to capitalize on it. Hell, I've cooked meals for men I should've poisoned." Kelly stood up and made her way over, causing my head to bob when she sat down. I almost threw up. "You still love him, don't you?"

I didn't respond. Anything I said at this point would be held and used against me forever, so I just kept my mouth shut and let the room spin.

"You know it's okay to still be in love. Shit. You deserve love, too. Even with him."

I gripped the arm of the couch and shot straight up. Bad idea. If there were any remnants of breakfast in my system, surely they were on their way back up. "Jesus Christ. I am *not* in love. And definitely *not* with him."

I have a love for Roman, there was no denying that. But I was not in love with him. The kind of trust I needed to be *in* love with him had yet to be earned. It was one thing for me to want to jump his dick; it was another thing entirely to give him my heart...again. I'd made that mistake once already, and I'd decided going back down that road would probably get us both killed.

"Whatever you gotta tell yourself. I saw it years ago—hell, we all did. Well, the ones with half a brain around here."

"It's just not like that."

She tilted her head to the side. "Okay." She patted me on the leg, then started to stand up.

I huffed. "Where are you going?"

"Some of us got work to do."

"Fine," I conceded. "Is it that obvious?" I had too much on my plate to be catching feelings for someone...much less worry about other people noticing it, too, right now.

She sat back down. "I mean, it's not like you walk around here wearing 'I Love Roman' on the front of a T-shirt, but anyone who's ever paid attention probably picked up on it. You think no one used to see the two of y'all sneaking off and hiding from time to time? Why do you think Alina from housekeeping gave you her key card? She got sick of you asking to borrow hers."

"Ugggh." I buried my face in my hands. "You don't understand. My dad would have killed us if he knew—then and now."

"Would have. You're a grown-ass adult now, and your dad isn't around anymore, God love him." She put her arm around my back. "So, what's your excuse?"

I threw her a look. "For starters, everything. It's him."

"So? What's that got anything to do with it? We all know what he does for work, or he wouldn't be here. Plus, he's fucking hot. How can you not want that?"

"Nobody said I didn't want him, but I don't know if you've noticed I don't exactly have time for love. Hell, I barely have time to shower. I have a casino to run, idiot minions to ward off, a massive fundraiser to coordinate, barges coming and going. The list never ends."

"Well, let's see. You've got a team of guys running your casino. Roman and security are keeping the idiot minions away. Me and Haley got the event covered. Ivan and his binkle nuts crew take care of the boats."

"Kelly, you're amazing."

"I know! Now, let's at least get you laid. You can do that on your own, can't you?"

"No! Absolutely not." I tried sitting up but was quickly pulled back down by an unseen force. *Damn it, Josephine!* "I'm too busy right now to even think about having sex." Okay, so that wasn't entirely true. I'd thought about sleeping with Roman at least once an hour since he came back.

"Sounds like an excuse to me. You need a good fucking. 'Cause from what you've told me about—"

"Don't say a word. I already know where you're going." She was about to call out Chris.

I shuddered at the flashback of the few times we were together. He wasn't the worst I'd ever had, just the worst I could remember in a very long time. For the record, convenient sex is dumb sex, and it's never as good as you think it is in the moment. At least not for me.

"I'm just saying. A little dick would do you some good."

"It's not little," I mumbled under my breath.

"Ohmigod, Jameson Magnolia Hazentree! You already slept with him again, didn't you?"

I bit my bottom lip to keep from spilling my guts. The alcohol didn't help. I made a mental note to find out what Josephine kept in that bottle.

"You did, didn't you? Was he good? Please tell me it was as amazing as you remember."

"No! Well, not exactly." *Not yet.*

"What do you mean, not exactly? You either did or you didn't? Spill the tea, bitch. I've got to get back to work."

I was so embarrassed and for no good reason. Kelly was my best and only female friend—the only one I trusted to confide in when it came to non-work-related stuff. "We didn't sleep together, but I've...felt it?"

"Is that a question? Or are you telling me?"

"Ugh. It's not a question. I did. Okay? Better?"

"You're a damn mess." She stood up. "Go fuck that man 'cause there's no way in hell he's gonna turn you down. And don't come talk to me again until you do."

FIFTEEN
Jameson

I left Kelly and headed up to see Roman. I figured by now, we'd both had enough time to cool off. Only now, I had a million more things to think about, and inappropriate ideas floating around my mind that didn't need to be there, and just enough of a confidence boost to try to do them. Thankfully, my buzz had started wearing off on the long walk over, so by the time I reached him, logic would kick in, and all of this would be a nonissue.

I knocked on Roman's door. I could have just walked in using my master key, but God only knew what I'd be barging in on—naked would've been fine by me.

Within a few seconds, the door opened. Roman was still wearing the same clothes, but his face and hands were clean.

Damn.

He looked around the hallway. "You alone?"

"Of course I'm alone. My bodyguard left me." I pushed past him and walked into his suite.

"Come on in," he mumbled sarcastically as he closed the door. "What do you mean I left you? You sent me away. Where's Ivan?"

"I told him to take the rest of the day off. We have things to do." I eyed him up and down him. "Why haven't you showered yet?"

"I was waiting for you."

"Me? I'm not showering with you." I'd already seen him wet and wrapped in nothing but a towel once. That paled in comparison to the thought of him in the actual shower, dripping wet…with water…naked…shit.

"I meant I was waiting to hear back from you. I didn't want to be in the shower, and you need me for something."

"I guess that's fair." I looked around his suite. It was still pristine, like he hadn't been staying here for the last couple of days. The only evidence of him being here was a huge duffle bag on the floor beside the couch and the laptop security had given him open on the kitchen bar with a half-empty beer bottle beside it.

"Find anything useful?" I asked, pointing toward his setup.

"Depends how you look at it. I've just been going over employees. I went as far back as six months before I left. Doesn't seem like anyone new has been added since."

"Well, I haven't needed anyone. We've been managing everything with the team we currently have. The one my dad put together."

He walked over to the bar, sat down, and closed the computer.

"I've been thinking about your proposition?" I actually hadn't given it a second thought since he'd suggested it. I've been too damned busy, but now was just as good a time as any to bring it up.

"Which one?" he smirked because we both knew there was only one. "I didn't know there was more on the table."

"Never mind." I shook my head. "I've been thinking about going back to my dad's estate."

"And what did you decide?"

I propped against the countertop. "I'll let you go on one condition."

He took a swig of his beer. "What would that be?"

"You can go, but you have to take me with you."

"James," he sighed. "I don't think that's a good idea."

I shrugged. "It's that or not at all. You're here to watch over me; this won't be an exception. Either I go with you, or neither of us goes."

He sat in silence, contemplating the idea, knowing there was no way for him to ever get away from me now without suspicion. "Okay."

"Okay?"

"Of course. What other choice do I have?"

"Hmm. I guess none, really. But—" I paused. "—if we don't see anything out of the ordinary, and I mean one single thing, you drop it. All of it."

"And if we do?"

"I'll deal with it if the time comes." I pushed off the bar and made my way toward the door. "I'm going back to my room to do some work on my computer. If you need me, you can reach me on my cell. If you get hungry, ring the kitchen. You can text room service from the app on your phone."

"Good to know." His voice spoke from a very close distance. I had no idea he'd even gotten up.

I turned around, and he was standing right behind me. "Be ready by eight tonight. I'll come get you."

"Sounds good. You don't think Ivan is going to pop up out of nowhere, come looking for us?"

"Doubt it. He's supposed to update me on Chris before he leaves for the day. Speaking of"—I didn't really want to bring this up, but—"what the fuck that was about, anyway?"

"What? He earned it."

"Seriously? Not to that extent." Maybe he had earned it a little, but seeing it play out live was like something out of a movie. Everything moved in real time and slow motion all at once. "You could have killed him. You didn't have to go that hard."

"He touched you," he answered casually. "I already warned him once."

I jerked my head back. "You warned him? When?"

He stared down at me but didn't say anything. "What difference does it make?"

"I'm an adult. I'm allowed to be touched."

He turned and walked away, swiping his beer bottle off the counter and tossing it into the trash. "Not by him. Not anymore."

I stormed after him. "You can't be fucking serious right now."

"Oh, I am dead serious, and if he touches you again, neither of us is going to have to worry about him doing it a third time."

"Roman. You can't just kill people for putting their hand on me or my ass."

He walked back toward me, stopping just inches away from my face. "See, that's where you're wrong. I can and I will. Don't fucking test me either."

"Let me remind you, I am *not* your property."

He stared me down, his chest expanding and contracting with every breath. His eyes flicked back and forth, searching mine. There was something there, something else he wanted to say but didn't. Instead, he turned and walked away, heading into his bedroom. "Go to your suite. I'll deal with you later."

"I thought you didn't want me to be alone?" I challenged, causing him to stop dead in his tracks. "You'll deal with me now."

"Don't challenge me, Jameson."

"What the fuck is your problem?"

He spun around to face me. "You. I'm not going to stand by for one more second and watch another man put his hands on you for any reason. Not now, not ever."

"Ever? You don't get that kind of say in my life. You're only here for a few more days, then I'll be the last thing you'll have to worry about."

"Maybe so, but in the meantime, I do. You are *my* problem—not Ivan's or Chris's or anyone else's around here. Got it?"

"I'm damned sure not yours either."

"Yeah." He lowered his voice, and his entire demeanor changed. "Guaranteed, no one else will ever care about you the way I do."

He reached up, probably to touch me in some sort of intimate way. I had to stay strong. I swatted him away. He was irritating the shit out of me. In some sick and twisted way, I wanted to slap him and fuck him at the same time.

"Keep your hands off of me. You already crossed a line this morning when you practically shoved your tongue down my throat."

"Hmm. You didn't seem to have a problem with my tongue down your throat *or* my hands on you then."

"Things have changed." I was weak and already walking a very thin line with Roman. I was one look, one touch, one breath away from reaching my breaking point with him. If I didn't stand strong now, I never would, and we'd end up tangled together where we stood. I hated him— I hated that I wanted him even more. "And if you touch me like that again, I'll have you on your knees faster than you can snort a line of coke off a stripper's ass."

He cocked an eyebrow with a casual smirk. "You have a serious attitude problem."

"So I've been told."

"You'd probably lose half of it if you spent more time on your knees."

SIXTEEN
Roman

Jameson had no idea the restraint it took for me to push her away, but I needed her as far away from me as possible at the moment. I'd already sent Leon a text asking him to send someone to keep an eye on her front door and to call me if anyone came or went. Between shadowing James on her admin rounds, her attitude, and dealing with Chris—and I wasn't even close to being done with that motherfucker yet—I felt like I'd lost the entire day doing abso-fucking-lutely nothing.

The thought alone of Chris's hand on her ass—or anywhere else on her body—made my blood boil. Clearly, he hadn't gotten the memo that she was through with him. Not that it mattered in the grand scheme of things—she was right. She was a grown-ass woman allowed to do whatever the fuck she wanted to do. She was allowed to do things that made her feel good…even if they were with someone else.

Just not while I was still around. Once I was gone, she could do whatever she wanted to do.

Though I still should have killed him right there when I had the chance. The only reason I backed off was out of respect for Leon. It had nothing to do with my physical abilities and everything to do with keeping my current *job*. Because if I fucked up and Jameson got rid of me, there wouldn't be a soul around who would protect her like I could.

I didn't know where the hell the day had gone, but by the time I'd made it back to my suite, it was already late afternoon, and I'd missed lunch. After a quick shower to wash away the remnants of that asshole's blood, I ordered myself some dinner from the guest kitchen—medium-rare cheeseburger loaded with lettuce, tomato, red onion, all the sauces they could offer, and a side of sweet potato fries. Not the healthiest choice, but given my current circumstances, I needed a nice, heavy meal to make myself feel somewhat better about my situation.

For starters, I'd never been so frustrated with myself and my incredibly high sex drive as I had been as of late. Normally, my need to breed wasn't this uncontrollable. It was even worse now having to be around James—the only female I'd found myself remotely attracted to, yet she was the last person I should want to touch.

Three. More. Days, I reminded myself. That was all I needed to do—make it through the next three days alongside *her*. Then, all of this would be a moot point. I could go back to pretending like she didn't exist.

Lyndsay Marie

In the meantime, I tried watching TV as a distraction. That didn't work. I could have gone the porn and jack-off route, but I didn't need Jameson getting a bill for some smut movie—like she needed anything else to hold over my head. I thought about hitting the gym, but I needed to stay as close to James as possible, just in case. I'd looked through enough spreadsheets with employee names it made my eyes cross.

As I lay in bed, the harder I tried to distract myself, the dirtier the thoughts of Jameson grew. All I could see was the sparkle in her eyes and how the edges of her eyes creased when she laughed, how her perfectly plump lips framed them. Which led me to wonder what her mouth would feel like wrapped around my cock—it'd been way too long. The image of her down on her knees in front of me took over. All I could visualize was her knelt in front of me, gripping my cock, guiding it into her mouth and sucking me off.

"Fuck," I cursed out loud as my erection grew painfully and exponentially rock hard. "Cold shower it is," I conceded.

I undressed and headed to the suite's massive bathroom. I turned on the shower, and water shot out of almost every surface from the ceiling to the walls—jets everywhere. It was just what I needed to wash off the remnants from earlier and get her off my mind. Plus, I had the bathroom all to myself, so hi-ho, hi-ho, it's off to bust a nut I go.

Steam swirled around me as I stepped inside. I quickly washed my hair and scrubbed away the grime of the day. As I reached for the conditioner, the lights in the bathroom dimmed, causing me to take pause.

My heart pounded inside my chest at a beat barely sustainable for life. I was supposed to be the only one in my suite. *Or so I thought.*

I wiped away steam that had fogged up the glass, blocking my view.

"It's just me," a *very* familiar called out, barely audible over the running water.

James? The hell was she doing in my bathroom? "I'm kinda busy here." I snatched the towel that I'd flung over the top of the shower wall and quickly wrapped it around my waist without even turning the water off. As I reached for the door, it swung open. "Jameson, the fuck?"

She stepped inside the shower, completely. fucking. naked, and pulled the door shut behind her. "I came over here to talk before we head out. I heard the water running. Figured I'd join you."

I took a step back, my entire body practically trembling from head to toe at her invasion. I'd dealt with some *very* scary men in my lifetime; nothing compared to Jameson butt-ass naked within arm's reach. "We can talk *anywhere* else but here and *with* your clothes on."

My cock sprang back to life. The only thing that held it back was the towel that I had in a death grip.

"We could, but that doesn't sound like as much fun." She closed the space between us until my back was to the wall. The cold marble wall gave me a temporary jolt but quickly warmed up as hot water poured down on both of us from every angle.

Lyndsay Marie

Seeing Jameson's smooth, naked body covered with water, watching it bead and drip down her shoulders and chest until it rolled off her pebbled nipples, had my cock as hard as it had ever been. I sucked in a deep breath and tightened my grip on the towel as I waited for her next move. There was no way in hell I was going to do anything but stand here like a fucking idiot.

"Maybe not as much fun," I assured, "but definitely smarter."

"Hmm." That was all the noise she made. A fucking *hmm*.

She reached out and splayed her hands over my chest, then slid them down and gently pinched my nipples.

"Ah." I flinched. "What are you doing? Have you been drinking?"

She smirked. "Nope. Just having...a little fun. Figured I'd take your advice and give myself an attitude adjustment."

Fuck. I closed my eyes for a split second, trying to process what was going on. "This—we cannot—" My words cut off when I felt a hand on my cock through the towel. My eyes flew open. "James. Don—"

She reached up, placing her finger over my mouth to shoosh me. Then, without warning, she peeled open the front of my towel, and my cock popped out from between the layers of the soaked cotton material. I dropped my head back against the wall with a *thunk* as she wrapped her hands around me and slid her grip up and down my shaft.

"Fuck," I hissed through my clenched jaw.

"Feels good, don't it?" she purred.

"You know goddamned well it does. But why the fuck are you doing this to me?"

"Because I want to…?"

So much for my towel. It was useless, so I let it drop to my feet in a sopping, wet pile. She slowly pumped her hand from base to tip, occasionally rubbing her thumb over my head, which was now slick with precum.

"You need to stop while you're ahead," I warned her. "You're playing with fire." I wanted nothing more than to spin her around, bend her over the shower bench, and bury my cock inside of her pussy balls-deep, fucking her into oblivion. She had no idea the restraint it took me to not do any of that.

"Maybe I like the burn," she countered back as she lowered herself to her knees on the shower floor.

Instinctively, I reached out and grabbed a fistful of her dripping wet hair. "What about your rules?"

"You forget, I make the rules; I can break them."

I looked down and watched James's next move. Her tongue slinked out of her mouth, and she licked the precum that dripped from the tip of my cock. I almost came on the spot. Then, she cut her eyes upward, looking at me through her jet-black eyelashes as she wrapped her lips around the head of my cock and sucked me into her mouth.

"God damn," I declared as I watched on. She had one hand wrapped around my shaft, pumping as she took me into her mouth as far as she could. She moaned, sending vibrations from my dick to my shoulders. *Fuck it.* If this was what she wanted, then who was I to not give it to her? With a fistful of her hair, I tightened my grip and held her head in place as I started fucking her mouth. I moved slowly at first, testing the waters. When she didn't bite my cock off, I went for it, pumping faster. "Ah, yeah, that's it. Take my cock like the good girl you are."

Her eyes closed tight, and I knew the power had shifted. She thought she'd come in here with all the control. *Little did she know*.

Her other hand joined the first one, and she jacked me off while I fucked her mouth. She enjoyed this just as much, if not more, than I did.

"Look at me," I commanded. Slowly, she opened her eyes and looked up at me. "This what you wanted?" She barely nodded. "You want me to come in your mouth?" She moaned in response, half closing her eyes. "Fuck. Look at me." I was close, and I was torn. As amazing as this felt, I wanted to come in her cunt. The thought alone sent me into a tailspin. "Suck harder."

She did exactly as told, sealing a vacuum grip around my cock. My balls tightened as my pending orgasm threatened. I held her head in place and gave a few quick thrusts until the first release of cum came barreling through my cock and down her throat. I slowed my pace but didn't stop pumping. Not until I was sure I'd dumped every pent-up drop of cum I had in me into her mouth. Then, as my release slowed, I eased out of her mouth and released her hair from my grip.

I helped her to her feet. "You okay?" I asked her. Her face was flushed and eyes teary. "That was a lot. I'm sorry if I was too rough."

She tipped her head back under the water and let it run into her mouth. Then she spit it out down the drain. "Don't apologize," she said in a soft tone. "I asked for it."

She wasn't wrong, but I still felt bad for some reason. Jameson was not some whore to use at my will, and I'd basically just treated her like one. Before I could say anything else, she turned and got out of the shower without saying another word.

I stood underneath the water for a few minutes, letting my guilt wash down the drain. "Fuck." Every ounce of pleasure I'd felt left just as fast as I'd come. I never should have done that. I should have shoved her out when I had the chance.

Not wanting to waste any more time wallowing around in my own self-pity, I shut the water off, grabbed a dry towel out of the linen closet, and rushed out of the bathroom after her.

"James?" I called out for her as I made my way through the suite. "Shit." It was too late. She'd already left.

Haphazardly, I tossed my clothes on and made a beeline after her, banking on her having gone back to her place across the hall.

"James?" My voice rang out as I knocked on her door. She didn't respond, so I knocked again. "It's me. Open up."

Lyndsay Marie

I reached into my wallet to pull out my master key and realized it was gone. *That little shit.* She must have taken it with her. Just as I raised my hand to knock again, the door opened.

"Relax. I was changing." Jameson casually strolled out of her apartment like she hadn't sucked me off less than five minutes ago. "Here." She shoved my missing key at me as she breezed by, heading down the hall toward the elevator.

"Don't you think we need to talk?" I asked, stunned by her sudden change in demeanor.

"Nope. I got nothing to say. Now, let's go before I change my mind."

I pocketed my key and caught up with her. I threw my arm in front of her to block her. "James." I searched her face for some kind of answer, but she refused to make eye contact. "Look at me. Please."

"Can we just go? You want to do this; I do not."

"Yeah, we can, but what the hell was that back there? You did not have to—"

She pushed me out of the way. "Didn't have to what? Do *that*? I'm well aware of my obligations. Maybe that was just something I needed to get out of my system. You ever think of that?"

"Well, no. I don't guess I have. But—"

"Then there really isn't anything to talk about, is there." She completely ignored my attempts to figure out what the hell had gotten into her. "You coming or not?" she asked, blocking the door that kept trying to close.

I didn't say another word, and why should I have even tried? She clearly didn't want to talk. I just shook my head and joined her. It wasn't worth the argument...yet.

SEVENTEEN
Roman

"We'll have to take your car." We strolled past security, making our way out of the casino. He nodded as we walked by. I did the same in return. "All I have is my bike."

"Ooh. That could be fun. I haven't been on the back of a bike in forever."

I smirked at the thought of flying down the highway with Jameson clutched to me like a backpack. "I have no doubt it would be, but not tonight. Maybe some other time." Though I was pretty sure it would never happen.

As we walked out, I couldn't help but wonder if anyone in surveillance had spotted us and watched us leave, wondering where in the hell we'd be going. Jameson didn't seem bothered, and I didn't ask. If anyone did question us, I'd come up with some excuse on the fly.

We exited through a lesser-used side entrance that led out to a long, covered walkway that connected the casino to the parking garage. The night was cool, with little to no humidity for a change, to the point I could see my breath in the air. That was the thing about the weather in the south, specifically this time of year. You might freeze your balls off one night and sweat them off the next...more often on the same day. Tonight was one of those in-between nights where you didn't do either.

We took the stairs down to the gated underground area reserved for two things: upper management and invite-only guests. Jameson's cars were parked near the front under a sign that read RESERVED.

"Well, we have two choices. My Camry or my dad's car?"

"You're joking. Is this even a choice?" Elliott's car was an Audi RS e-tron with over 600 horsepower and could top out at sixty miles per hour in three seconds. Jameson's Camry four-door family sedan was gifted to her on her sixteenth birthday.

"Good thing I didn't bring my keys, then." She tossed me the keys and winked.

Little minx.

I felt like a fucking king sliding behind the wheel into the driver's seat. The car was in pristine condition, not a speck of dust to be found on any surface. Not surprising since it probably hadn't been used in months. "You'll have to tell me where to go."

"I'll make it even easier on you." She started typing her dad's address into the navigation system. It popped up as HOME. "Just follow the green line."

169

Lyndsay Marie

As I backed the car out of its spot, I noticed James already had her shoes off and her legs crossed with her feet tucked under her. She probably hadn't been able to sit in peace and quiet while someone else drove her around and worried about the world in who knew how long.

"You ready, passenger princess?"

"As I'll ever be. Let's get this over with."

We left the property and exited the highway, taking the off-ramp onto the interstate. I'd always wanted to drive this car since the day Elliott had it dropped off the back of the hauler. I didn't know how much use he'd ever gotten out of it, seeing as he'd only had it for a few months.

One thing was sure: no one had ever taken it wide open. *Not like I was about to do*. A car like this needed that every now and then. The Audi accelerated with ease, hugging the curve of the road as we merged onto I-69. We *very* quickly topped out at 110 by the time the lines on the road had straightened out.

I glanced over at James. Her lips were pursed, and she had a death grip on the seat at her sides. I let off the gas and set the cruise to 80.

"Something tells me you don't take this car out much."

"I don't take this car out at all. I don't need to."

"You should try it sometime. It's fun."

"You're crazy," she said, keeping most of her thoughts to herself. She probably wanted to tell me I was out of my fucking mind. *She wouldn't be wrong*. We rode in silence for as long as I could stand. Eventually, I figured now would be the perfect opportunity to talk about what she'd done to me in the shower since she had nowhere to run.

"So, you gonna tell me what that was about back there?"

"What was what?"

"You know what I'm talking about. Don't do shit like that because you think it's what I want or I'm going to like it. I mean, I enjoyed the hell out of it, but this isn't about me."

"Who said I did it for you? Not everything is about you."

"You're the one with this *look but don't touch* rule…or does that apply to everyone but you? Because we've already broken that rule. Twice."

"What's it matter to you if you enjoyed it so much?"

"Okay then." *Two can play this game.* "When do I get to return the favor?"

"Excuse me?"

"You heard me." I could practically hear her swallow down her emotions. She knew my head game was strong. Jameson hadn't ever *not* come with me. She knew damned well what she'd be getting into…or missing out on.

She folded her arms across her chest. "I—you don't. Not ever. Like I said, that wasn't about you. It was a onetime thing. It won't happen again."

"Suit yourself." We'd already made it through Hernando and were over halfway to Byhalia. According to the map, we were less than thirty minutes out from our final destination. "You'll regret that decision later."

"Hmm. We'll see."

We rode out the last half hour of our trip without another word to each other. I double-checked the location as I turned into the neighborhood with four minutes to spare, then ended the trip on the navigation and turned the display screen off.

Houses were decked out with fall décor, some Halloween. One house had put out two gigantic skeletons at least twelve feet tall. A few of the trees had started losing their leaves, peppering their pristine yards with decaying debris, which would no doubt be gone by midmorning by the time the landscapers had left.

Magnolia Estate was an antebellum-style home standing three stories tall in the front, with massive white columns flanking the top of a curved brick staircase that led up to the front door. Above the columns was a balcony overlooking the front yard and golf course across the street. The house was reminiscent of what you'd expect to see in a movie like *Gone with the Wind*.

When we arrived, I drove past the house and turned around in a cove around the corner. Then, I parked across the street on the golf course side just out of view of the house, killing the lights on the car. I had a clear enough view of the driveway and front of the house, except for the big-ass magnolia tree that blocked a lot of the side and back corner.

"Can you see anything?" Jameson asked as we parked. "'Cause I can't see shit with that big-ass tree blocking my view."

My initial thought was to be parked far enough away so that I could still see what I needed to and for Jameson to see as little as possible. My plan seemed to have worked. "I can see enough. You ever thought about having that tree cut down? Or at the very least trimmed back?" Not that it really mattered. According to her, no one was ever here or supposed to be.

I was just making conversation at this point.

"Yeah, I'll get right on that. It's right at the top of my to-do list, just behind not dying this weekend."

"I'm sorry. I didn't mean it like that."

"No, it's fine. The tree probably hasn't been trimmed in years. My dad always liked the privacy."

"I wonder what the neighbors think about the house being empty for so long. Anyone ever ask you about it?"

"Pssh. The neighbors don't give a shit about me or this house as long as the yard is kept up and the shingles aren't flying off the roof." She adjusted in her seat and stared at the house, a pensive look on her face. I wanted to ask what was on her mind, but I already knew.

"Are there cameras around?" It'd never crossed my mind until now that the house might be just as heavily monitored as the damned casino. *Probably should have thought of that last year.* Though after a few lines of white powder encouragement, nothing mattered.

"Yeah, but just on the front and back door. Nothing on the inside or side door."

"They monitored?"

"No. At least not at the casino. Maybe on my dad's old laptop. It's funny. This neighborhood was supposed to be one of the safest in Shelby County. It's why he said he'd chosen to build here. Golf course on one side, privacy and security all around. It was the only place where he ever felt normal. Nobody ever asked what he did for a living, and we were never worried about anything happening to us here. It was like we were normal here. Hmph. Ironic."

I didn't know what to say to that. "Ironic it is, but I don't think any of these people would be considered normal if you got to know them."

"Maybe not."

"I noticed you added quite a few cameras outside your office. What's up with that?"

"I had them installed during renovations a few months ago. I thought one of the contractors was poking around my office when I had the place renovated. Nothing ever came of it, but it still left me with an uneasy feeling, ya know?"

"I didn't see any of those new cameras on the feed."

"Probably because only two of the cameras work. The rest are just for show."

"You're joking. So only two of those cameras work? Out of all of them?" I hadn't sat and counted, but there were a lot more than just two cameras in that hallway.

"Yup."

I wanted to bang my head against the steering wheel. What the hell was she doing? "What about in the surveillance room? I didn't see the outside of your office on there."

"Those are monitored remotely off the main feed. Hector has one of his men watching those separately."

"Interesting. And are there any more dummy cameras on the property?"

"A few. Mostly at the exits. All the ones on the casino floor are original and functional. I didn't need to add a hundred more camera feeds for surveillance to have to watch."

"That explains a lot. Who all knows those are dummy cameras?"

She grinned. "Just me."

"Jesus Christ."

"At least my plan worked. I had a bunch of blank cameras installed, and nothing's disappeared from my office since."

"Wait. You've had stuff come up missing from your office? Like what?" That was news to me. Shit, everything was news to me at this point.

"Mainly a few former employee files. Sometimes my chair would be out of place, or my pen would be out on my desk when I know I put it back in the holder. Could've just been my own doing and not even realizing it. Maybe I'm going crazy. Who knows."

"Who else has access to your office besides you?"

"Just Ivan."

"Hmm."

"Don't go there, Roman."

I held my hands up. "I'm not saying a word." But it did rocket him to the top of my suspicious person's list, as if he hadn't already been there. "Does he ever come here and check in on things?"

She half shrugged. "Who knows. I wouldn't think so since there's no need."

"So you've just been letting this place sit around and collect dust?"

"It would seem so."

"That's a shame."

She shifted in her seat toward me. "That coming back to where my dad took his last breath hasn't been at the top of my priority list? I mean, god forbid I have to subject myself to a constant reminder of someone shooting my dad in our home, ruining my entire childhood."

"Shit, I'm sorry. I didn't mean it like that. I just meant that—" My train of thought derailed when a tree between Magnolia Estate and the neighbor's backyard was illuminated by the soft glow of a warm, yellow light. It wasn't much, maybe a bathroom light or even a night-light? I couldn't tell because I didn't know the lay of the house on the second floor. I just knew it wasn't very bright, and it came from the back.

"You just meant what?"

"Sorry." I tried to backtrack, but I couldn't remember what the fuck we were just talking about. "You're sure no one has been here? Not even a weekly or monthly cleaning crew?"

"When I took over, I gave my security crew direct orders to have the house deep-cleaned one last time and then seal it off. My dad didn't usually do business at home. There was no reason for *any* of us to come back here, then or now."

"I think you put way too much trust in your staff."

"What makes you say that?"

"Just a thought."

"Well, I don't like the way you think. You're acting suspicious as hell right now."

"I'm not, James. Seems like you're not doing enough thinking when it comes to shit around here. Not asking enough questions."

"I don't have time, and unless you know something that I don't, this conversation is over."

I felt bad for pressing the issue. Especially since this was her first time back to the only place she'd ever known as home, and I'd just stirred up some really shitty memories for her. But fuck. She'd either been living in total denial all this time, or she really didn't have a fucking clue what could be going on right underneath her nose.

I didn't press the issue, and now, the car was quiet...too quiet. So I turned on the radio with the volume down low for background noise. She needed the distraction, and I didn't need her trying to read me like a book right now. "This okay?"

"It's fine."

"Anything in particular you wanna listen to?"

"Not really. Anything beats the hell out of slot machines ringing all day. You know, I couldn't even tell you the last time I listened to the radio?"

"Really? You don't listen to Spotify or anything in your office while you work?"

"Nope. I have no idea what music is new anymore. Don't really care."

"You should. The least you can do is have some semblance of a life outside of work."

"Yeah, right. I don't have the time or the energy. Getting four hours of sleep in a row feels like Christmas."

I reclined the seat back with my hands behind my head, trying to appear relaxed. Internally, I was buzzing with adrenaline, knowing there was someone in this fucking house that no one was supposed to be in, and Jameson was none the wiser. "You're gonna dig yourself an early grave doing this shit."

"Oh fucking well. It'll be worth it in the end if I can put a bullet in Kane's skull. He's the asshole who landed me in this position to begin with."

"Don't be so sure of that."

"Excuse me? Who else would have done it? Because nobody wanted my dad dead or to see everything he's worked his entire life for come to an end more than Kane. Do you know who did it? 'Cause I can't think of one fucking person."

"I can," I mumbled under my breath.

"Really? You can? Then who?"

"Nothing. Forget it." I'd already said entirely too much.

"This is such bullshit. You seem to know a hell of a lot for someone who doesn't know anything."

"I—I just—fuck. I don't trust anyone I know or anything I hear anymore, not that I ever have."

"And I should? You still won't even tell me where you've been or why you went away, for fuck's sake. You seem to have forgotten where we started, just how far we go back."

Every fiber in my being practically boiled with anger at the thought of her thinking she was disposable to me, that I'd just walk out of her life without explanation because I'd wanted to. She and I both knew the line of work I did, and it didn't leave much room for a personal life, but for her? I'd made that sacrifice. I took the risk of seeing and being with her any and every chance I had, even though it put us both at risk of losing everything.

I rose up in my seat. "Really? You think I forgot? Then how's this for forgetting?" Her eyebrows scrunched together when I reached over, catching her off guard, and grabbed her by the front of her T-shirt, practically pulling her over the middle console. Our faces were barely an inch apart. "Don't you ever think for one more second I forgot how far we go back. I remember every stolen glance, every touch, every graze of your fingertips across my skin. I remember every text you've ever sent me telling me when and where to meet you so we could sneak off, even for just a few stolen minutes. I remember the way the flavor of your strawberry lip gloss lingered on my lips hours after you'd

179

been there." I held her in place as I leaned forward and pressed my lips to hers. She tensed up for a split second, then relaxed and opened her mouth to mine. Then, she let out a soft moan that caused my dick to harden to its fullest potential as our tongues made contact.

Fuck.

What the hell were we doing? We could not be doing this…not again.

Our kiss deepened. Jameson got up on her knees and hovered over me, pushing me back. If we didn't stop, I was going to yank her into my lap and fuck her right here.

She held my shirt in a death grip, pulling me into her kiss.

It was as if she'd been reading my mind.

My cock strained against the inside of my pants. *Down, boy.* This was not the time nor the place, no matter how hard she made me.

Reluctantly, I pulled away from her, both of us completely out of breath, and guided her back into her seat on her side of the car.

I wiped my mouth with my hand. "Fuck. We gotta stop."

"God, I hate you," she huffed.

"I'm sorry. We—I shouldn't have done that. We can't do this."

I glanced up at the house. It was now just as dark as it had been when we arrived.

"You know, you used to tell me everything. *We* told each other everything. There were no secrets between us.

Now, you won't tell me anything. You just shut me up with your mouth. It's not fair."

I knew exactly where this was going. She was right. It wasn't a fair tactic to use against her, even though she'd done it with me.

"Babe. I already told you I didn't have a choice."

"Oh, you did." She checked herself out in the visor mirror, wiping her mouth and fixing a few strands of hair that had fallen loose.

"I guess you're right. My only other option if I didn't leave was to get my ass dragged down the river behind a barge from here to Louisiana. That hardly beat the alternative, which was to take the assignment I was given, then disappear."

I shoved my hands in my hair. There was so much I wanted to tell her that I needed her to know. But telling her any of it now would only hurt her more than it would help. "You weren't supposed to be here when they got rid of me. You were supposed to be in Colorado." My voice trailed off at the thought of it all.

"Trust me. I wish I never would have come back."

I took a deep breath, trying to untie the knot in my stomach. It was time for me to give her something, even just a shred of information. I was her only hope of knowing where I'd been because she and I both knew she wouldn't get that information from anyone else. "Nashville," I forced out at a volume just barely louder than the radio.

She slammed the visor closed. "What?"

"Before you even ask me again. Nashville."

"Nashville?" Her voice was soft and low. *Shit.* "That's where you were?"

"Yeah." I didn't even want her knowing that much, but she deserved better than what she'd been given.

"This whole time, you've been four hours away from me?" Her voice cracked, and I knew she was on the verge of tears. "Who sent you away? Who did this?"

Tread lightly. "You aren't going to like my answer."

"Jus—just tell me who."

"Elliott."

EIGHTEEN
Jameson

Roman had just dropped the biggest bomb on me. I could feel every drop of blood drain from my face as my world spun around me.

It was…my *dad*? He was the one who'd sent Roman away? No fucking way. I didn't believe him.

And Roman had been only four hours away from me this entire time? Somewhere between his admission and my tears, I went from horny as hell and ready to bang his brains out right here and now—*sorry, Dad*—to wanting to puke in his lap.

"My dad sent you away? Why?" That didn't make any sense. In what world would my dad send Roman away from here, and why?

This was the most defeated I think I had ever felt since this circus had started and I took over things. Now this?

Lyndsay Marie

"I quit trying to figure shit out a long time ago."

"What were you doing there?" We didn't have property out there or family business in Nashville."

He closed his eyes and gripped the steering wheel. *Come on, Roman. Talk to me.* He was starting to piss me off with his secrecy.

He opened his eyes and gazed up at the house. "Scouting," he answered flatly without adding any unnecessary details.

"Scouting for what? I'm gonna need you to elaborate. Maybe be a little more specific than that."

He blew out a frustrated breath, but at least he was finally talking. This was all I'd wanted since laying eyes on him again. He was the only person who could offer up any explanation because no one else was going to tell me anything, even if they did know. Roman was my last hope in figuring out my next move, and he'd just practically pulled a checkmate on me.

"Prospective clients, buyers, artwork, intellectual property. Anything that could be easily confiscated or rerouted and turned for a quick profit. Stuff that didn't take up a lot of storage space or leave a trail that couldn't easily be erased."

My mind reeled with a million more questions that I knew wouldn't be answered. Not tonight, at least.

"I don't know what pisses me off more, the fact that you vanished without so much as a goodbye text or the fact that you've only been four hours away from me. All the while, I sat here thinking you were dead the entire fucking time."

My life was a fucking joke at this point, and I was the ass end of it. Everyone was laughing except for me.

He shook his head. "I'm glad you think it was that easy for me. Just like you, I did what I was told to do. Except things end a little different for people like me if we refuse to do as we're told." As much as I'd hated to admit, he was right. We only ever did what we had to do to stay alive. "Can we talk about something else already?"

"Sure," I conceded, I'm sure much to his approval. Though this conversation was far from over. "What would *you* like to talk about?"

Roman stared intently at the house. I still didn't know what he thought he was going to find. Quite frankly, I thought this whole excursion was a big waste of time. I had no reason to believe that there had been anything going on behind my back.

Roman reached across the console and grabbed my hand, threading his fingers with mine. His tender gesture caught me off guard. My first instinct was to pull away, but his touch felt sincere, not invasive or manipulative. "Okay, let's see." He thought for a second, and for a singular moment, it'd felt like the old Roman was coming back around. The one who used to ask me random and silly questions, something to get my mind off everything. "If you could've done anything differently with your life, rules aside, what would you have done?"

Oof. I did not think we were going there. I could think of a million things I'd have done completely differently. "Honestly? I'd go to college."

"Really? Yeah?"

"Yeah, I would."

He nodded. "And what would you study?"

I already knew exactly what I'd have done. It was something I'd always been drawn to. "Psychology," I stated. "Specifically, criminal psychology with a focus on forensics."

He smirked. "I bet Elliott would have loved that."

"Hah. Yeah, right. We both know he would have locked me in solitary confinement and tossed the key."

Okay, maybe not really, but my dad had only ever wanted me to take over the family business one day. There was no room for higher education in my future.

Roman rubbed his thumb back and forth over mine. God, I missed human touch. I missed *his* touch. It'd been so long, though I never forgot what he felt like. "Your dad loved you. I think if you'd fought hard enough, he would have covered you if you wanted it bad enough. All he ever wanted was to see you happy."

I sighed. "Maybe. Sometimes I wish I could go back in time, maybe Colorado, start over."

"Then what?"

"Not come back here."

NINETEEN
Roman

I could tell James was getting sick of sitting here, and quite frankly, so was I. I hadn't seen much, but I'd seen more than enough. We'd been here for almost two hours, and nothing had changed since the light incident, and I still didn't know what to make of that.

"We should've gotten snacks," she stated matter-of-factly.

"Snacks?"

"Yeah. You know? Chips, M&M's, or at the very least, a Coke. I'm getting thirsty."

"You can't be serious." I grinned. I should've known Jameson was going to want food. She'd already had a hard time sitting still as it was. Eating gave her something to do during times that required her to sit for more than five minutes. "I'll remember that for next time."

"Good thing there won't be a next time." She stretched her legs out in front of her. "I'm bored and hungry. I didn't eat dinner. Now, I have to pee."

"So, I take it you're ready to go."

"Very."

I gave the house one last glance. It was still just as dark as it'd been when we'd arrived; the mystery light would no doubt not be turning back on anytime soon. "I agree. Let's go."

"You want to check in on the other two properties while we're out?"

She curled up and laid her head on the middle console. "No. I want to eat and go to bed."

"Don't get too comfy." I put the car into drive and coasted a few houses away before turning on the lights. "There's one more stop I wanna make."

It was sometime after midnight when we finally rolled into the underground garage. Our bellies were full of barbeque from her favorite BBQ joint, the Pit, and she was sound asleep in the passenger seat. I hated to even wake her up, but we'd surely catch the attention of any and every prying eye if I carried her inside.

I nudged her awake and walked her back up to her penthouse. Once I knew she was safely inside, I turned myself in for the night in my own suite across the hall.

Tomorrow was a new day, and I needed to have a chat with Ivan ASAP.

As soon as I locked myself inside, I fired up my borrowed laptop and started digging. I didn't know what I was looking for, but I went through file after file that I had access to. Everything was a red flag, and everyone was an enemy at this point.

I checked the camera feeds. A few of them glitched out here and there, but things appeared to be status quo. The hallways were empty, doors were secured. There wasn't a whole lot of activity at this hour during the week. My camera feed didn't have access to the hallway outside of Jameson's office. *No surprise there.*

A small stray cat casually sauntered across the back dock, stopping to lick its paw before carrying on whatever journey it had been on.

It was almost two in the morning, and there was no way in hell I was gonna sleep now. Not after tonight. I no longer trusted leaving Jameson unattended, even as close as she was being right across the hall from me. I wanted to check on her one last time for my own reassurance.

When I opened the door of my suite, music spilled out into the hallway from behind Jameson's door.

The hell? I thought she'd been asleep the whole time.

I walked over and put my ear up to her door. Eighties rock music played from inside her penthouse.

I checked the door handle—it was still locked.

I turned to go back to my place when something crashed from inside.

I knocked my knuckles against the door. "James?" No answer. I knocked and called for her again. Nothing. "Jameson. Open up, or I'm coming in."

Still no response.

189

I stuck my ear up to the door again and listened harder. All I could hear was music that had now been turned down. "God damn it." The last thing I wanted to do was invade her private space uninvited.

"Last chance," I called out into the door.

When she didn't respond, I pulled out my key card. The light turned green as I badged myself inside. Music played from her bedroom. I scanned the penthouse as I made my way through. Everything seemed normal, from what I could tell.

I placed my hand on my gun and called for her again, slowly making my way across the living room. Her bedroom door was slightly ajar. I nudged it open with my toe just as Jameson stumbled out from behind it, laughing to herself with a bottle of wine tight in her grip.

She jumped back and let out a screech when she finally noticed me. "What the hell! You scared the shit out of me, Roman!"

"Sorry. I heard something crash."

"Did you think to knock?"

"You've gotta be fucking kidding me," I mouthed under my breath. "I *did* knock—twice—and I called your name—more than twice."

As much as I would have loved to have stood around, bitching back and forth, my mind had all but shut down at the sight of her. She'd taken her tight ponytail down, letting her hair hang in loose, unruly waves. She'd changed out of her head-to-toe all-black ensemble in exchange for nothing but a gray, faded vintage Guns N' Roses T-shirt that stopped just beneath the waistband of a pair of black lace panties.

She curled her toes, digging her neon pink-painted toenails into the carpet. "Well, I was in the bathroom. I didn't hear you."

To keep my eyes from continuously raking over every inch of her body, I stared at the tiny freckle on her forehead, just above her left eye.

I cleared my throat. "Fair enough. So what crashed?"

"A shelf." She nodded behind me. "I stumbled on the edge of the carpet and caught myself on it. It fell off the wall."

I looked back and saw the shelf, resting face down on top of her coffee table. Then, I eyed the bottle dangling from her grasp. "Are you drunk?"

"Not really."

"I don't care if you are. You're allowed to drink." I knew Jameson. She was drunk as shit right now. I could see it in her eyes. "It's just really late. We have a busy day ahead of us."

"After tonight, I think I've earned it."

"I didn't say you didn't. You want me to fix that shelf for you?"

"No, it's fine. I'll get someone from maintenance to rehang it."

She stepped forward, closing the short distance between us.

Lyndsay Marie

I took a step back, glancing down at her standing inches in front of me. "Now that I know you're safe, I'll resume my post. Try not to hurt yourself in here."

As I turned to walk away, I heard a *thud*. I looked down behind me to find the bottle of wine she'd been holding lying on the floor. When I turned back around to face her, she grabbed the front of my shirt and pulled me into her.

"Um, what the hell are you doing?" I asked, thoroughly confused.

"I'm not ready for you to leave yet."

Two hours ago, I would have been all over this opportunity. Now? No fucking way. "You are *very* drunk right now. I don't think this is a good idea. Actually, I know it's not. This is a terrible idea."

"I've made worse decisions. I think you owe me."

"I wha—"

She loosened her grip on my shirt and pushed me back. "Now, go, sit. You're already here. You might as well let me get you a drink."

"Not necessary." My words fell on deaf ears. She'd already worked her way around me and disappeared into the kitchen...and I watched her the entire time she walked away. My dick perked to life at the sight of her ass cheeks peeking out of the bottom of her high-cut panties.

Down, boy.

Now more than ever, I needed to be on my A game. We were both in a vulnerable state of mind—hers from drinking. Me? I had no excuse other than my primal instincts were kicking into high gear, and when it came to Jameson, she was my kryptonite.

Still, against my better judgment, I took a seat on the end of her couch closest to my only escape route—the one I should have been running out of.

She reappeared a moment later with two shots—one in each hand. "Here," she said, handing me a glass. "Let's toast…to us?"

I grabbed the offering and set it down on the end table beside the couch. "Let's not."

"That's rude." Shot glass in hand, she climbed onto my lap and straddled me. "I invited you to stay for a drink, you drink."

"James," I warned. "Don't do this. Not now."

"Now's the perfect time. I've had just enough to drink to let my guard down and not change my mind. Unlike some people."

"That sounds like the absolute worst time."

She ground down on my lap, rocking her hips. "Hmm…is that your gun, or are you just happy to see me."

"Both, actually."

"Do you know how long it's been since I've been thoroughly *fucked*?"

"Nope. Not a clue. And I don't need to know." I didn't want to know. That was not something I wanted to think about when it came to Jameson, much less a conversation I cared about having with her. Because the only person that came to mind was Chris. I closed my eyes and prayed to someone, *anyone*, for some kind of guidance here because if left to my own devices, I was probably going to fuck her raw. "You've managed to go this long. I'm not going to be the one to change it now. Not tonight."

She tossed back her shot and slammed the empty glass down on the table beside my full one causing it to slosh and spill over. "You're probably right. If I'm going to break my streak, I'll need a real man to do it."

"Hmm. Chris wasn't?"

"You going to drink this or what?" she asked, ignoring my question.

"No. It's all yours." She picked up my glass and tossed it back. "If you're done here, I'll go. We'll just act like none of this ever happened."

"Hmm. It's a damn shame you don't want me. I just got waxed at the spa a few days ago." She hooked her finger into the crotch of her panties and pulled them to the side, exposing a *lot* of bare skin, showing off her fresh wax job. This time, I looked without even trying to hide it, and *fuck*.

I sucked in a deep breath, holding it deep in my lungs until it physically burned. Then, I slowly blew it out.

"You asked when it was going to be your turn to return the favor. How about now?"

My hands were planted firmly at my sides as I gripped the couch cushion, damn near ripping the fabric with my fingertips. "James. Don't do this."

Did I want to? Judging by the way my cock strained against the inside of my jeans, that was affirmative. Right now though? Hard pass. I wasn't about to put her in a position to accuse me of taking advantage of her or her waking up with regret. Not that she would, but it wasn't worth the risk.

"Touch me."

"Absolutely not."

"Please?" Her voice had gone from hard and demanding to soft and pleading.

Now she was begging me. Never in a million years did I ever think I'd have the control to tell Jameson no, much less her beg for me.

"No fucking way," I swallowed, my words ragged.

"Why the hell not?"

"I—I just can't." Despite my granite-hard and painful erection, I was *not* caving in. I'd already fucked up and let my hormones get the best of me when I practically attacked her in her office. Then, I let her suck me off earlier tonight. Plus, our hot make-out session. That was more than enough crossing a line for me.

She slipped her delicate fingers between her legs, and they disappeared into her panties, her eyes closed. "Roman," she moaned quietly, "I need you." Her hips started to rock ever so slightly as she finger-fucked herself on my lap.

"James. God damn it." My restraint was dissipating by the second. "Please stop."

She reached down between us and grabbed my dick. Then, she leaned forward and ran her tongue from the dip at the bottom of my neck up the side to my earlobe. My entire body tensed. "I don't think you really want me to," she whispered.

Lyndsay Marie

I reached up and gripped onto her hips, digging my fingers into her soft flesh. "No, I don't. What I really want to do is flip you over, face down on this couch, fuck you senseless from behind, and come inside that pretty little pussy of yours. But you've had way too much to drink."

This was pure hell for me, and she knew it. A year ago, I never would have turned down this opportunity. She and I used to sneak off every other chance we had and fuck like rabbits. While it was fun and exciting at first, the more time we'd spent together getting to know each other, the more I did it because I cared about her. I still did.

I had one head telling me to give in, just give her what she wanted—what I wanted. My other head told me to back off; she'd sober up, and by morning, she'd be beating herself up over this. Because the last thing I wanted to do was take advantage of her.

Sensibility finally won.

In one smooth move, I picked her up, spun around, and sat her down on the couch next to where I'd been sitting.

"What the hell, Roman? You can't just—"

"Listen to me. I fucking told you no," I practically barked out at her. "I just—" I shoved my fingers into my hair with both hands. I wanted to rip out every strand by the root. "I just—we can't. Not right now."

"You can't? You didn't try and stop me when I was sucking your dick!"

"Oh, for the love of god. I didn't ask for that. *You* did that on your own."

"And you didn't try to stop me. Rest assured, I won't let it happen again."

"I—I'm sorr—"

"Just get the fuck out," she yelled. "Now. Get out!"

I wasn't about to sit here and argue with her. I turned around, heading toward the door to make my exit. "I'll be outside if you need me."

"I will *never* need you!"

As I closed the door behind me, something shattered against the wall—a shot glass and my ego.

TWENTY
Jameson

I used to lie awake in bed at night, fantasizing about having that small-town, warm and fuzzy feeling kind of romance in my life—the one where Prince Charming trots gracefully into my wretched kingdom on a white horse to sweep me off my feet, and then we would ride off into the sunset together to live out our happily ever after. A real Hallmark movie—what a joke!

Not anymore.

Not even close.

My nights were spent falling asleep with murder mysteries or true crime documentaries playing in the background on my bedroom TV. Second to that, my time was spent plotting revenge against my dad's killer. I hardly classified either of those as romantic. *I guess maybe to the right person, it could be.*

When I wasn't dreaming about 101 ways to seek revenge on my enemy, I was in charge of running morally gray operations out of a small-time casino on the banks of the outskirts of Memphis. *Some inheritance.*

I scoffed at the thought.

Life hadn't always been like this. At one point, in my mind, I would've been well on my way to a crime-free lifestyle. One where I was saving people, not taking them away—a life filled with peace of mind, knowing I'd made a difference in this world. I never wanted to be the one coordinating the movement of drugs and guns or stolen artwork or always having to watch my back, wondering who was on my team, who needed to be taken out, and knowing the difference between the two.

That had always been my dad's life until he'd so graciously handed it down to me.

Instead, I'd been put in a position to give up on my dreams, albeit unrealistic as they were, in exchange for getting my hands on the piece of shit who took everything from me with a promise to fuck his world up when I did. Would it bring my dad back? No. But would it make me feel a hell of a lot better? Absolutely. After all my dad had ever done for me, I at least owed him that much.

I thought I'd had it all figured out…and then *he* came back.

I shouldn't want him. Not even a little bit, not even at all.

But I did, more than ever.

That truth was a tough pill to swallow. An even harder concept to grasp was Roman didn't want me. There were times when I'd thought he did, but when I gave him every opportunity to have me, he pushed me aside. I'd already told myself a thousand times *this is the last time*, yet I still caved.

Every. Fucking. Time.

He did not.

Rolling over with a pounding head, I grabbed my phone off my nightstand. Panic set in at the date on my lock screen. Less than twenty-four hours now until the gala. That was it, and I couldn't feel less ready in my life. I could potentially be counting down the hours until my demise, all of the way down to the very last minute.

After a few calming breaths, it was back to business.

I checked my email, glanced over my calendar and to-do list, then caught up on a few overnight texts—making sure I didn't send any drunk texts to *anyone* that I might regret.

Nope.

I breathed a sigh of relief. Crisis averted…sort of. Not sending any illicit texts to Roman didn't negate the fact that I'd tried to seduce him, *again*, and had failed miserably.

I checked in with Ivan to see how Chris was doing, see if he'd taken the day off or if he'd decided to brave the elements and come into work today.

Before physically dragging myself out of bed, I reviewed the camera footage outside my door. "You have got to be kidding me," I huffed out loud.

This was getting ridiculous. I kicked the covers off, threw on the wine-stained Def Leppard T-shirt I'd had on the night before, and trudged to the kitchen. If I was going to face this day and Roman, I needed a cup of coffee ASAP.

My phone buzzed with a new text.

Ivan: Haven't seen him since yesterday. Office door is closed.

Me: He okay? Anything broken?

Please say no, please say no.

Ivan: Not far as I know. His face and eyes are swollen, black and blue. He'll live.

That was reassuring, though I was sure he did look like shit.

Me: Thanks. See you soon.

Once I felt like I had enough caffeine in my bloodstream to tackle the next few hours, I cleaned up the shattered shot glass that I'd thrown across the room at Roman as he left me high and dry last night—again—and headed to the shower.

Getting ready for the day, I slipped on a royal blue low-cut silk blouse with my favorite black lacy push-up bra. Something a tad bit on the sexy side, still a little bit business.

Lyndsay Marie

After pulling on a pair of high-waisted black trousers and tucking my phone into place in the inside pocket, I slid my feet into my favorite shiny black heels with the red bottoms. I dried and styled my hair, gave it a final fluff with my fingers, pinning it back, and swiped on some red lipstick to match the bottom of my shoes. Then, I gave myself a few strategic spritzes of Baccarat Rouge 540 to seal the deal.

On my way out, I made a quick pit stop for a second cup of coffee. *One of us is going to need it.*

As I exited my penthouse, fresh coffee in tow, I stepped over Roman. He'd slept on the floor, curled up in front of my doorway. It was a good thing the only people who had access to this floor were us and staff members. I'd hate to explain to a paying guest why it looked like a homeless man was sleeping in the hallway.

I nudged him on the shoulder with my toe. He slowly stirred awake with a grunt. "You have an entire suite, Roman, and a very comfortable bed. Get off the floor."

"Good morning to you, too," he groaned as he sat up, scrubbing his hands down his face.

I scoffed. "There's nothing good about this morning. I have a hangover from hell, I'm out of Tylenol, and I walk out to find you sleeping on the floor outside of my door."

He stretched his arms over his head as he stood up. The hem of the bottom of his untucked T-shirt rose just slightly, showing off a sliver of his smooth, tanned skin and a hint of a happy trail. *It's too early for this, James. Did you already forget what happened last night...and every other fucking time before because he won't cave in to you? Hmm?*

"Not the worst place I've ever had to sleep. I could have been in the bed next to you."

I rolled my eyes. "Good thing you didn't *have* to sleep in either of those places. You're the one who chose the hallway. Here." I handed him the cup of coffee I'd just made. "Coffee with a splash of milk, no sugar."

"Thank you." He took a sip. The slightest hint of a grin pulled at the corner of his lips. "Aw, you remember how I like my coffee?"

"Lucky guess." I wasn't about to tell him I'd never forgotten. "Consider it an apology for last night. I was out of line."

"Apology accepted. You sure you don't need it?"

"Do I look like I do?"

"Eh."

"I've been worse. I'll just grab another cup downstairs."

"Sounds good. What's on the agenda today?"

I eyed him up and down. "For starters, you look like you need a shower more than I did this morning. Why don't you go do that, then meet me in my office. We'll figure it out from there."

"Sometimes I think you're just trying to get rid of me."

"If I wanted to get rid of you, I could." Which was true. If he'd said that three days ago, my answer would have been different. Because three days ago, I *wanted* to get rid of him. "I'm just used to working solo."

"You know I don't like you being alone."

"I'll manage."

"Okay, I'm not supposed to leave you alone. Better?"

"Fine." I rolled my eyes. "Would it make you feel any better if I get someone from security to meet me there and stay with me?"

"Very much so."

I pulled out my cell and dialed up the surveillance office. Jordan answered. "Hey, Jordan. Can you meet me at my office in five? Roman's got some things he needs to handle this morning. Thank you." I ended the call. "Better?" I mocked him.

"Much." He brushed by me, the hair on his arm tickling against mine as he passed, his gaze locked on me the entire time. "See you soon. Stay out of trouble." He disappeared into his own suite and closed the door.

As soon as the door shut, I closed my eyes for a brief moment, thinking back to just a few hours ago. I was so embarrassed about my behavior. It would take more than one moment of weakness or lapse in judgment on his part to succumb to me.

He was right about one thing: he didn't ask me to go down on him. I did that on my own...and I didn't regret it. Not one bit. Hell, despite my own frustrations, I might just be dumb enough to consider doing it again if the opportunity presented itself.

TWENTY-ONE
Roman

Reluctantly, I left James under the care of Jordan and not even with him initially. I'd trusted her to get to her office unattended, where he'd meet her there and watch over her until I made it down. Not ideal, but I needed to get away from her for a little bit without making it obvious that was what I was doing, which was exactly why I didn't put up too much of a fight when she'd suggested leaving me to get ready for the day. It was time for me and Ivan to have a little chat. Someone somewhere knew something, and if anyone had insider information, it would be him.

I took the quickest shower I'd ever taken in my life, opting not to shave 'cause fuck it at this point. I dressed in my typical black attire, threw on my watch, tucked my Glock safely into place, and headed out. My first stop: Ivan's office.

The lights were out, so I went out to the docks, his home away from home. Ivan was the most predictable fuck I'd ever known.

Unlike last night, when the temps had actually cooled down to a tolerable number, today was a new day and felt like Satan's asshole outside.

Tater was sitting on the rickety metal railing, swinging his twiggy legs over the edge.

"Thinking about jumping?" I asked as I walked up beside him.

Makes one of us.

"Not a chance." He tipped his head to face me. "I heard you was back. Guess the rumors were true. Welcome."

"Thanks. I wouldn't say it's been welcoming, but I'm here."

"I heard that."

He wasn't a big guy by any stretch, probably a third less my weight and an inch or so taller. He probably showered once a week and combed his hair even less. But he was reliable when it came to questionable favors. No questions asked.

"You see Ivan lately?"

"Not in about ten, maybe fifteen minutes. I been coming and going, but last I saw, he walked around over there." He nodded toward the part of the dock that was wrapped around the side of the building going toward the front.

The area was semi-secluded, still covered by the metal overhang and shielded by overgrown brush from the riverbank. There was a grated metal stairway that led to a second-floor mechanical room just above the kitchen. It was a good place to go when you wanted to be out of sight.

"Well," he said, jumping down off the railing, "things to do." He patted me on the shoulder as he walked by. "Good seeing you, man."

"Yeah, you too."

A wispy billow of smoke floated from the side of the building on what little breeze Mississippi had to offer at the moment. "Bingo."

I took one last glance around. Unless someone was over there with him, he and I were alone. I grabbed a steel rod leaning against the side of the building by the back door, one that had either been used to prop the door open or bash in someone's skull. Sometimes both. I wedged one end of the pole under the back door handle, kicking the bottom against the concrete ground, making sure it was secure enough that if anyone tried to get out here, they'd at least struggle, and I'd buy myself a few more seconds.

I'd studied the camera feeds. There were only two cameras out here—both facing the back door. Neither of them pointed toward the side where I needed to go.

I quietly walked to where Ivan was hiding. Before I rounded the corner to confront him, I stopped when I realized he was talking to someone.

"Tell me about it. I know." Silent pause. "I don't know what the fuck else to do. I got him here." Silent pause.

Lyndsay Marie

He was on the phone.

I pressed my back to the building and listened, being cautious to stay out of sight.

"He wasn't supposed to go poking and prodding around. Now, his feelings are getting in the way." Another silent pause. "How was I supposed to stop him?" Pause. "Well, far as I know, everything is still going as planned. We'll just roll with it for now. Yeah, she's fine. Falling right into place."

"The fuck," I cursed quietly under my breath. I didn't know what was going on, but I'd heard enough.

I pulled my gun out from my waistband, jerked the slide back, cocking it into place, and closed the space between us. I tapped Ivan on the shoulder as I approached him from behind.

"Listen, I gotta g—" As he turned around, I snatched the phone out of his grip and tossed it into the murky water below.

He watched in horror as it started to sink, then looked back at me. "The fuck is wrong with you?"

"You're about to find out." With a death grip on my Glock and a finger on the trigger, I shoved the barrel into his fat neck underneath his chin.

His hands went into the air in surrender as he stumbled back into the guardrail. "Woah. Wha—what's going on."

"I ask the questions. Not you. Who the fuck was that? Who were you talking to just now?"

Sweat beaded on his forehead, and his face turned beet red. "That was, uh, just an old friend."

I turned the safety off with the flick of my thumb. *Green means go.* "Try again."

He squeezed his eyes shut tight for a brief moment, either praying to his god for this to be quick and painless or debating on what to tell me based on how much he thought I'd heard. "Fuck," he huffed.

"Three. Start talking, or I'll blow your fucking brains out right here, right now. Zero regrets." Something I'd thought about doing many times before.

"Rom—it's not like that."

"Two. If I get to one, you're fish bait."

His eyes darted toward the dock, probably hoping someone would round the corner right about now, find us, and save his ass. "Don't worry. Nobody's getting out that door easily." I gave the gun a strong shove further up into his neck fat. "On—"

"Fine. Fine." He heaved. "I'll talk. Just not—not here. Not now. Okay?"

"Now seems like an alright time to me."

He swallowed. My gun jumped as his throat bobbed against the tip. "W—where's James?"

"With Jordan. Is she safe with him?"

He nodded. "Yeah."

"You sure?"

"Ye—yeah, I'm sure." The sweat that had collected on his forehead now trickled down his temples. "Fuck, it's hot. We need to go somewhere else."

Lyndsay Marie

I heard the back door rattle. Someone was trying to get out. "If anything happens to her, you're as good as dead," I assured.

"I swear it won't. How much time you got?"

"As long as I need for you to tell me the truth."

———————◆———————

Ivan and I spent the next hour driving around the property on a maintenance golf cart that we'd jacked from their garage. I'd learned more about Emerald Haze in the last fifty-two minutes than I had in the sixteen years I'd done work there. Now I knew everything. Well, Ivan had at least reassured me he'd told me everything. I didn't get the feeling he was in a position to lie to me now.

I drove back to the maintenance garage and parked the golf cart. "That's it? Nothing else?" I asked him.

"Listen, I've told you more than you were ever supposed to know. If anyone finds out, and I mean anyone, I'm shit outta luck. I mean, we coulda killed each other at any point, had us a real western shootout, and nobody woulda been none the wiser, but I got nothing left to hide." He lit probably his tenth cigarette and took a long, relieving drag. "I told you because I trust you to not tell anyone else. I'm risking a lotta lives and our entire operation unraveling."

"I need to go." I hung the keys back up in their place on the wall. "Keep me updated," I told him as I started making my way back inside.

But not before making a quick phone call.

He picked up on the fourth ring without greeting.

"River," I said into the receiver. "It's me."

"The empire must be falling if you're calling me," he replied.

I palmed the back of my neck and squeezed in a lame attempt to rub out some of the tension. My brother was only one of two people I trusted more than myself. "It will if I don't get some help.

TWENTY-TWO
Jameson

Roman was taking longer than I would have thought, and for some reason, his lingering absence made me very uncomfortable. Considering he didn't want to be away from me at all, I'd expected him here within ten minutes or less of my departure from his proverbial grip.

Regardless, there was still work to be done, with or without him.

I'd managed to get updates from Kelly about the upcoming gala, make sure everything was still running on track. *It is.* Then, I texted Chris to see how he was doing. His only reply? *I'm fine.* Chris was mad-mad. I didn't blame him.

I tossed my phone down on my desk and got lost in my own work. By the time I looked up, almost an hour had passed, and I still hadn't heard from Roman. A part of me wanted to call or text and ask him if he was okay, but I also didn't want him to think I cared too much about him.

There was a knock on the door. "Hey, boss?"

"What?" I called out to Jordan, who was still standing guard outside my office.

"You got company," he notified me.

"I'm not in the mood right now." I couldn't even imagine who wanted to see me. I didn't have anything blocked out or scheduled on my calendar, and no one had let me know they were on their way.

"Um, I think you're gonna want to hear what they have to say."

"Unless they've got Girl Scout cookies, I'm not interested."

"He said it's about Magnolia?" Jordan's voice was low, barely audible through the wooden door. "Said you'd understand."

My heart sank into the pit of my stomach. *Magnolia?* Until last night, not so much as a word had been breathed about my dad's estate. Not to my face, anyway. Now, someone was standing outside of my office door with a message for me regarding it?

Against my better judgment, I buzzed the door open with a security button installed underneath my desk. The locking mechanism released, and Jordan swung the door open.

I stood up to greet my mystery guest. A man I didn't recognize appeared in the doorway. He wasn't very tall, maybe my height, and barely had twenty pounds on me. Odds seemed in my favor if I needed to defend myself.

Hell of a time for Roman to not be here.

213

Jordan stood behind him, just off to the side.

The man grinned. "You're even prettier in person."

"You didn't come here to compliment me. Say what you need to say, then leave."

He stepped through the threshold, crossing into my office. "In private."

He nodded toward Jordan as if to say *he goes*.

Jordan gave me a *what would you like me to do* look over the man's shoulder. *Shoot him in the back of the head* came to mind, but I hated the idea. I'd just had this office repainted.

"You can shut the door, but he stays there," I told the guy. This way, at the very least, if he did shoot me, he wouldn't make it past security upon his departure.

The guy shrugged. "Fine." Then, he used his foot to shove the door closed without taking his eyes off me. As soon as the door shut, he reached under his shirt down the front of his pants, pulled out a gun, and aimed it at me.

I rolled my eyes. "Jesus Christ," I mumbled under my breath.

"You're gonna need him if you get squirrely. Now, hands up where I can see them."

"Could you be any more predictable?"

"Now," he ordered.

I slowly raised my hands in the air at shoulder level. Shit. Now I couldn't unlock the door from my desk if I needed to. They'd just have to find another way inside.

The idiot had a gun pointed at my face. One twitch and I was toast…guess I'd grossly underestimated this guy, and he definitely didn't have cookies for sale.

"You think you're gonna shoot me?" I asked, keeping my voice steady despite having a probably loaded gun pointed at me.

"I might if I have to." He half shrugged.

"Honestly, I don't give a fuck at this point," I lied. I did give a fuck, kind of. "I'm sick of dealing with shit around here, anyway. Feel free to take me out," I challenged him.

"You're making this way too easy." He smiled. I almost flinched. This guy was missing half of his teeth, and the ones left were hanging by a thread.

"Maybe. But you won't get away with it. As soon as you open that door, we'll both be dead."

If this was one of Kane's idiots, I knew he wouldn't dare kill me and think he was going to get away with it one way or the other. Kane wanted to make my death a spectacle, and this wasn't it. Whoever this guy was had to have known that much. He could be new. Kane was known to blow through cronies faster than a hooker giving blowjobs to make rent. Maybe he just didn't give a shit.

"My, uh, boss. He said you need to stay away. Quit getting nosey."

"I don't know what the fuck you're talking about."

"He said you'd say that, but you know exactly what he's talking about."

"Tell your boss he can fuck right off. Better yet, tell him if he wants me to do something, then he can come see me himself. I don't take third-party orders."

"He isn't gonna do that. You've been creeping around places you shouldn't be." He waved his gun carelessly in the air as he spoke. *Amateur.*

"I go wherever the fuck I want to go. If that's a problem, tough shit."

"You're a real smart-ass." He cocked the hammer back.

Oops. Maybe he was dumb enough to shoot me. That's if he could fucking aim straight.

Where the hell is Roman? The one damned time I actually needed him for what he was here to do, and he was MIA.

"So I've been told. If we're done here, feel free to leave."

"Stay away from Magnolia."

"Yeah, you said that already."

I wanted to know who in the hell knew where we went last night. *How* did anyone know I went to my dad's estate? The only people who would have seen us leave were in the surveillance room.

There was another knock at my door. "Now's not the time," I called out.

"James?"

"Who's that?" the idiot wanted to know.

Roman knocked again. "James?" His voice was laced with warning. The door handle shook. "Open up."

I had flashbacks to last time I didn't answer the door. I knew if I waited long enough, Roman was getting inside of here one way or the other. Now, whether or not he'd find me alive was a whole different story.

I shrugged with my hands in the air. "Now what?"

"Tell him to come in. Let's play."

This moron. "I can't. It's locked."

He stepped to the side as he waved the gun toward the door. "Open it."

"I can do it from here, but I have to move my hands."

"Naw. I don't think so. Come open this fucking door the old-fashioned way."

Keeping my hands in the air so he could see that I was unarmed, I cautiously rounded my desk, removing the only barrier between us.

As I reached for the door handle, Roman knocked again. Hard. "James. Last warning. Open this fucking door, or I will."

"Do you always let your peasant workers talk to you like that?"

"Hold on," I called out.

I'd barely twisted the handle to release the latch before Roman came barreling through it, his own weapon drawn.

The intrusion caused me to stumble backward into my desk. The door flung wide open, bounced back against the bookshelf behind it, then closed and locked again. Now, it was the three of us—me, Roman, and this squirrely guy, who I still didn't know if he was actually harmless or not.

217

Lyndsay Marie

Roman leveled his gun with a steady grip directly at the idiot's head. The idiot pointed his gun from me to Roman, only his arms were a lot shakier.

I wanted to laugh at how comical this situation had become. Roman had at least six inches in height over him and probably six inches in dick. Not to mention, he had a body built of solid muscle. This guy's body was made of years of Southern fried fat that had solidified into a skeleton.

"Who the fuck are you?" Roman demanded, gun aimed at the intruder.

"Who the fuck are you?" he spit back at Roman.

"You don't get to ask the questions around here." Roman cocked his gun.

The idiot smiled. "Oh, you must be that new pussy bodyguard who apparently can't do his job. I heard 'bout you."

Roman flicked his gaze at me, then back at our *guest*, never moving his aim from his target. "Honestly," Roman said, "I don't need to know your name to kill you. The less I know about you, the better. I'm not even counting to three. You're just going to leave."

Roman slowly inched his way further into the room with his back to me. He made a wide circle around my desk, positioning himself between me and the idiot until he was completely blocked out of my view by Roman's body. This left the doorway—our only exit—blocked by the idiot but left him exposed to security from behind…and where the fuck were they, anyway?

With Roman's back to me, I carefully reached up and wrapped my hand around the grip of the gun that he'd wedged in the waist of the back of his pants.

I glanced down. Our lives were on the line, and what did I do? Checked out his well-defined muscles tensing through his custom-cut button-down shirt and his tight, bubble ass wrapped up in his perfectly fitting dress pants like a present that had been personally wrapped and gifted to me by Santa himself.

"I'm not scared of you," the guy said.

"I'm not trying to scare you. I'm trying to get you to leave without having to blow your fucking brains out in front of the lady and have you dragged out of here by your feet," Roman assured.

"You're not very bright, are you, bodyguard boy?"

"Smart enough to know where to shoot you without making a mess, just dumb enough to send you back to Kane with your head on a platter."

The last thing I heard were the words "fuck you, boy" and the sound of a click.

Then another.

And another.

"What the hell?" Our intruder looked down at his gun, confused.

"Safety's on, fucker." Roman pulled the trigger of his own gun. The guy screamed out as the gun he'd been holding went flying from his hand across the room.

I yanked the gun from Roman's waist just as the idiot hit the floor on his knees, clutching his hand, screaming and crying.

Someone pounded on my door. "James. Open up."

I pressed the lock release button underneath my desk, and the office door flew open. Jordan and Ivan both appeared in the doorway.

"What the—?" Ivan started first. He looked between us, then at the guy screaming on the floor. "What the hell is going on?"

"We had a visitor," I said.

"Yeah, no shit."

The idiot rolled around, clutching his hand to his chest.

"You shoot him?" Ivan wanted to know, looking at the gun in my hand.

I shook my head. "No. Roman beat me to it."

The guy continued screaming in pain. "Fuck. You shot me. Motherfucker. I'll kill you. Ahh, god damn it."

"I can't believe you only shot his finger off," I said to Roman, who was still standing in front of me. "You know he'll be back."

"I never intended to not kill him." He faced me, then wrapped his arm around my waist and pulled me into his chest. "Cover your ears."

I did what he told me to, and then, without taking his eyes off me or so much as a blink, he leveled his gun to the side and pulled the trigger. I flinched from head to toe in his arms at the crack of his gun going off.

The room fell silent as the screaming ceased.

"Hope you got your body bag ready," he said, his gaze still locked in on mine. "It's time to send Kane a real message."

TWENTY-THREE
Roman

The last thing I wanted to do was shoot this poor fucker in front of Jameson, but he wouldn't stop screaming, and it was pissing me off. That and I wasn't about to give him a chance to even think about trying to come back.

Problem solved.

As much as I wanted to know who he was, his identification was the last thing I was concerned about at the moment. I needed to get her out of here first.

"Holy shit," I heard Ivan say. "That was impressive."

"He didn't even look," Jordan said quietly to Ivan.

I wanted to tell him, *yeah, no shit. Why do you think Ivan brought me here?*

"How'd he get here?" I asked Jordan since he was the one who was supposed to be standing post.

"I—he just got off the elevator. Came down here faster than I could respond."

"And you let him in here, why?" I asked James, knowing she was the only one who could have opened the door.

"He knew," she whispered.

I scrunched my eyebrows together. "Knew what?" Because at this point, I didn't know up from down, who knew what, or whether I was coming or going anymore.

"Magnolia. He told me—us—to stay away."

Fuck. "Get him out of here," I said to Ivan and Jordan. "Take him out of the building and off the property. Just make sure he gets to Kane before the end of the day."

"Yeah, sure. Got it," Jordan acknowledged.

Ivan just shook his head and half laughed in amusement. "We'll take care of it."

I loosened my grip around James, holding her at arm's length. "You okay?"

She looked up at me. "Y—yeah." She swallowed. "I'm…okay. I think. Thank you."

I brushed a loose strand of hair away from her face and tucked it behind her ear. "That's what I'm here for."

Jordan radioed for backup. We needed to leave, but I didn't want to have to step over this guy. I also didn't want to sit here with a dead body any longer than we already had.

"He didn't hurt you, did he?" I looked her over. She seemed fine, no visible marks.

She shook her head. "No."

Lyndsay Marie

I steadied my breathing. "We need to get you out of here. Come on." I grabbed her hand and led her toward the door, shielding her from the man with a bullet hole in his forehead. I positioned her ahead of me, just outside the door, keeping her back to me as I leaned over to Ivan. "You recognize him?"

He shook his head. "Nah. Never seen him. Still probably one of Kane's guys. You know how he goes through men."

Either way, he wasn't my problem anymore. He was going back to Kane, and he could figure out what to do with the guy's body.

What I wanted to know more than his identity was how he'd gotten ahold of one of our employee uniforms. He was wearing an Emerald Haze button-down shirt and black dress pants. The pants were basic; anyone could get them, but the shirts were issued through HR and embroidered with the employee's name during orientation and returned upon dismissal. His name spot had been left blank.

I kept a tight grip on James and walked us back to her penthouse. We passed Cody from security running in the opposite direction as we trekked across the casino floor.

We eventually reached the top floor of the hotel and stopped in the middle of the hallway. There were two options—her place or mine. The doors were directly across the hall from one another, and it didn't matter which one we used; I wasn't leaving her alone again.

"Are you sure you're okay?" I asked when we reached the middle point between her place and mine.

"Yeah, I'm fine, actually. I'm just ready to get this shit over with so I can put it behind me. All I wanted was to host this fundraiser in honor of my dad. I didn't know it was going to turn into a life-or-death fiasco."

"I agree, but it is, and I'm here. But right now, where to?"

"What do you mean?"

"Whose place are we going to, mine or yours? Because I'm not leaving you alone."

"I'll be fine…at least for the rest of the day. Kane's never sent two men back-to-back."

"Are you crazy? Before you answer, let me answer that for you—you're crazy. At this point, you'll be lucky if you shower alone from now on."

"Why?" Her shoulders slumped. "What difference does it make now? Kane isn't letting this go, and my own men fucked up and almost got me killed…again. I'm just not safe anywhere anymore."

"Look at me." My gut twisted. I felt the same way, but as long as I was here, I would stop at nothing to protect her. Not even because it was my job anymore, but because it was her. My leaving her under Jordan's watch was a big fucking mistake, one that I would never make again. Though my time alone with Ivan had been more than productive and informative, to say the least. My only mission now was to become Jameson's shadow as much as possible from here on out.

I reached under her chin and tilted her face up. "Look at me. You have nothing to worry about. Okay? Your life is mine. I'm not going anywhere. Ever."

She rolled her eyes. "Don't say ever. You're only here because you're being paid. You'll be gone again in a few days."

"You can't be serious. Is that what you think?" If she only knew the shit I'd been through today alone, just in the last couple of hours, she wouldn't remotely feel that way. She didn't have a fucking clue what I was up against.

"It's just—I have so much going on and so much to do, and it really hit me that when this is over, you're leaving. Whether I make it out alive, you get to walk out of here a free man. All I want is to leave."

With any luck, it'll be with me. "Come here." I pulled her into me and wrapped my arms around her.

"Why do you care so much?" she asked with her face buried in my chest.

For starters, *because I fucking love you. I've always loved you. I never stopped loving you.* All the things I wanted to say but couldn't. Instead of telling her how I'd felt, I went with the next best thing. Maybe not the most appropriate time, but the opportunity presented itself, and I wasn't turning back this time.

"Because if anything happens to you, I can't do this."

Catching her off guard, I lifted her off the ground and backed her up against my door.

Decision made.

She let out a gasp, but I caught her mouth with mine before she could protest. As soon as our lips locked, her entire body relaxed in my arms. She moaned into my mouth as she physically melted into me. *That's my girl.* She wanted this just as much as me. That much I already knew. And as many chances that we've had, then backed out of, this was not going to be one of those times. It was time to stop playing around.

I reached behind her and cupped her ass with both hands, giving it a firm squeeze as I slid my tongue deeper into her mouth. She welcomed it in, sucking on it the slightest before gently dragging it between her teeth. This got a moan out of me.

"Isn't this breaking my rules?" she asked with a sly grin.

"Oh, it most definitely is, but you said yourself that you make the rules, Miss Hazentree. If I'm being honest, I don't give a fuck about your rules anymore."

"You're right," she whispered. "I do make the rules, which also means I can break them. So whatever it is you plan on doing to me, please don't stop. No more stopping."

While holding her up against the wall with one arm, I reached into my back pocket with the other, pulled out my key card, and unlocked the door behind her. "Not a chance in hell."

I wrapped her legs tighter around my waist as I carried her inside, shoving the door closed with my foot.

She cradled my face between her hands, bringing her mouth back to mine as her delicate tongue dipped between my lips. Kissing Jameson felt like having life breathed back into me.

I walked over to my bed and carefully sat her down on the edge.

"No going back?" she asked with the slightest hesitation in her voice.

I knelt in front of her. "No, Jameson. No going back." *I couldn't, even if I wanted to.*

"These need to go," she said, slipping her shoes off one at a time, flicking them to the side.

"No, *these* need to go." I grabbed the waistband of her dress pants, pulling them downward. She rose slightly off the bed as I dragged them down…her panties coming off with them.

This wasn't the first time we had ever been intimate, but definitely the longest we'd ever gone without each other. *It will not be our last.*

I ran my palms slowly up and down her thighs. When I reached her knees, I coaxed her legs apart, spreading her open.

"Oh, god," she moaned softly.

"Lay back," I demanded. She propped herself back on her elbows and stared down at me. "All the way."

"What if I don't trus—" I cut her off midsentence when I pressed my tongue to her pussy.

"Oh," she moaned out.

I wished I could have seen her face, how her eyes fluttered closed at the sensation of my tongue as I dragged it up her slit or the way her mouth formed the perfect O when she moaned with pleasure when I gently flicked my tongue over her clit.

She fisted her hands into my hair, pulling handfuls of it into her grip, forcing my face deeper into her. I did not object.

She arched her back, moaning louder and louder, rocking her hips against my mouth as I licked and sucked and ate her out. I slowly slid two fingers into her tight, wet pussy, curling them against her inner walls. The faster I moved my fingers inside, the harder she clenched down on me.

"Rom—Roman," she breathed. "I'm clo—"

Her hips bucked beneath me as I coaxed her first orgasm out of her. Her juices covered my face and dripped down into my hand.

As her breathing steadied, I withdrew my fingers and stood up. "You okay?"

She smiled. "I'm better than okay. Holy shit, I needed that."

"I'm not done with you yet."

She sat up on the edge of the bed and pulled me toward her. "Good. Because I don't want you to be."

I grabbed the hem of my T-shirt and pulled it over my head, tossing it to the floor beside her pants and shoes. She reached up and dragged her fingernails across my chest and down my abdomen. When she reached the hem of my pants, she gave them a tug. "These need to go."

"You don't have to tell me twice." I unhooked my belt, unbuttoned, and pulled my own pants off.

"These, too," she said, referring to my silk boxers. She hooked her finger into the elastic band and pulled, then let it snap back.

"Careful what you wish for." I slid them off and gave her what she asked for.

"Hmm. Come closer."

I stepped forward, just inches away from her. She wrapped her hand around my cock and stroked me from base to tip with a firm grip. She leaned forward and licked the bead of precum that spilled from the tip. I reached out and grabbed the back of her head, coaxing her forward.

She licked the head of my cock, then pulled me into her mouth, letting out a moan as she sucked me in.

"Fuck," I hissed. Her going down on me would never get old—the feel of her wet lips sliding against my shaft, her hand wrapped around me, jerking me off at the same time she sucked me in. All of it had me on edge.

She moaned again as the head of my cock hit the back of her throat. I almost came.

"James, fuck, slow down." I pulled back. "Christ, you're gonna make me come."

She grinned, wiping off her mouth. "And? Isn't that the idea?"

I leaned down and kissed her swollen, dark pink lips. "Yeah, it is. But I don't want to come in your mouth this time."

"Then what are you waiting for?"

"I'm not done with you yet." I planted a gentle kiss on the side of her mouth, then kissed along her jawline to her ear. I nibbled on her earlobe, then licked and kissed my way down her neck until I reached her breast.

She arched her back, urging me on. I wrapped my mouth on one nipple, then the other, sucking, flicking my tongue, focusing on one at a time. My cock nestled between her thighs as I urged her to lie back on the bed. Her legs spread slightly apart, allowing the head of my cock to rub against her wet pussy.

"Roman." She lifted her hips. "I need you."

I grabbed my cock and rubbed her pussy up and down with the tip. "I'm all yours."

She wrapped her legs around my waist, and I pushed myself inside of her in one long, slow movement, burying myself as deep into her as I could go.

"Ah, god," she called out loud. Her pussy tightened around my cock as I moved in and out of her, harder and faster.

I grabbed onto her shoulders, pulling her downward as I thrust upward. "Fuck. James. Your pussy's so goddamned tight. And mine. All. Fucking. Mine."

We panted, our bodies drenched slick with sweat as I fucked her with everything I had.

What felt like years of pent-up frustration, want, need, desire, anger, unspoken feelings—all of it—came barreling out of me in the form of rough and raw sex, topped off with single-handedly the most mind-blowing orgasm I've ever had with the woman who was unknowingly responsible for every single one of those emotions.

And fuck.

Lyndsay Marie

Every minute I'd ever spent wondering what her pussy would feel like wrapped around my dick again, every second I'd thought about being inside of her all night long, wondering if we'd ever even make it this far, was worth the wait.

Because now I know.

TWENTY-FOUR

We spent the rest of the day and entire night locked away in Roman's suite…specifically his bed. I didn't know who needed who more, but it didn't even matter. We'd all but become one person. At one point, I'd tried to get away for a while and go back to work, but there was no way he was letting me go. Roman had me in his clutch, and in more ways than one.

During one break, I did text Ivan, told him to take over things for the rest of the day and have Chris handle any administrative fires that came through since he'd decided to come into work for a little while. Then I got back to Kelly, who'd blown my phone up wanting to know what the hell went down and why I wasn't responding to her. *Because Roman is going down on me.* But she'd already figured it out by the time I'd responded to her.

Lyndsay Marie

I was lying in Roman's bed, wrapped in his arms with my head on his bare chest, leg thrown over his thighs. This was exactly what I'd been needing, what I'd missed so much. The physical act of being with a man could have come from anyone, but Roman and I always had this connection.

"Are you glad to be back?" I asked him as I traced my finger along his chest and abdomen in a figure eight.

"Hmm. Considering the circumstances, not really. But because it's you, yes. If you'd been anyone else, I don't think I'd care enough to put forth half the effort." He ran his hand up and down my arm. Taking my wrist in his grip, he guided my hand down until he wrapped my fingers around his rock-hard erection. "I know something else that doesn't take any effort."

"Hmm. I see." With his cock firm in my grip, I stroked him up and down.

The thought of having him inside of me again, over and over, had me dripping down the inside of my thighs. I couldn't believe either of us had anything left to give after the night we'd just had. Apparently, judging by his rock-hard erection, we had plenty left.

"What about this?" I asked as I rolled over on top of him. "How much effort do you think it would take to finish?"

He grabbed onto my hips and pushed me down onto him as he thrust upward, gliding his length between my legs. "You or me?"

"Yes." I held on to his chest as he slid back and forth, coating himself slick. The pressure of the length of his cock

234

gliding across my sensitive clit was enough to damn near make me come on the spot.

He lined himself up for entry, then slowly pushed inside. I lowered down onto him until I was seated on his lap and he was inside of me as deep as he could possibly go.

"Fuck," he hissed. "You're so fucking tight and wet. I don't think feeling you like this will ever get old. God, I've missed this so much."

I slowly rocked my hips, grinding and rubbing against him.

"You seem to have that effect on me." I kissed and licked up his neck, across his stubbled jaw, to his ear. "I'd kiss you on the mouth, but, you know, morning breath." Something neither one of us liked. Then again, does anyone actually *like* it, or is it just tolerable under certain circumstances?

"Is it still considered morning breath if we've hardly slept?"

I smiled. "Yes."

"I'll tell you what I don't mind," he said, grinding his hips upward, pushing in deeper.

"Hmm. What don't you mind?" I nipped his earlobe between my teeth, grinding back down.

"Morning pussy." Roman leaned up and wrapped his mouth around my nipple, taking it in and sucking hard. He sat us up, grabbed onto my shoulders, and pulled me downward. I wrapped my legs around his waist and rode him with everything I had left in me.

Lyndsay Marie

--- ◆ ---

It was midmorning by the time we'd finished our last session. Just *poof*, half the day gone already. I didn't even care anymore. Roman had fucked any give-a-damn I had left right out of me.

Despite my protesting, Roman eventually got up and headed to the shower. I wrapped myself in the bedsheet and watched him as he disappeared into the bathroom. As much as I'd wanted to join him, I declined his offer because I really did need to do *some* work today.

I'd somehow lost track of all time and neglected all of my duties for the last twenty-four hours. Okay, so I knew exactly how time had gotten away, and it showed by the sheer volume of missed calls, text messages, and unread emails I had waiting for me.

First on the list was to call Ivan back. I'd just disconnected my call with him when Roman appeared from the steam-filled bathroom, towel wrapped around his waist. If not for the conversation I'd just had, I might find this scenario more appealing.

"What's wrong?" Roman asked.

"He talked to him," I said, clutching my phone. My stomach turned and twisted into knots. Not only because I hadn't eaten since we ordered room service the night before but because Ivan had talked to Kane.

On the phone.

He stalked over to me and sat down on the edge of the bed. "Who talked to who? What are you talking about?"

"Ivan," I said, looking up at Roman. "He talked to Kane, said I need to call him."

If Ivan thought I needed to call Kane, then I most definitely needed to call him, which was the exact opposite of what I wanted to do.

"Guess he got my message. Did he leave you his number?"

I nodded. "Ivan texted it to me."

"Call him."

"Now?" What the hell? I'd just had one of the best nights of my life, and he expected me to potentially ruin everything with a phone call to the man who wanted me dead?

"Yes. Now. I think it's time to have that in-person meeting he's been wanting."

"Are you sure? 'Cause that doesn't sound like a good idea. Actually, that sounds like a horrible idea. Maybe your worst one yet."

"Nothing's a good idea at this point, but we've poked the bear. Let's at least see what he has to say."

I bit my bottom lip as I stared down at my phone. It was almost noon. I was still naked, wearing only a bed sheet. I was sure Kane was up for the day, dressed to the nines and ready to take on the world like a southern Dr. Evil.

"Hey." Roman reached out, placing his hand underneath my chin and tilting my head to look up at him. "It's going to be okay. You know I'm not letting anything happen to you, right?"

At this point, I wasn't so sure even he could stop this. "Yeah," I sighed.

"I mean it, James. All I'm asking is that you call him. You can use my house-issued phone if you want to, but you're the only one he'll talk to. Let's see what he has to say."

In my mind, the plan had always been to take Kane down. The problem was I couldn't just give my men orders to risk life and limb, storming onto Kane's property like it was the invasion of Normandy, without solid evidence that he'd single-handedly been the person responsible for my dad's death. *Just a strong suspicion* didn't work in this industry. It worked for me, but there still had to be some form of underlying mutual respect...until lines were physically crossed.

Unfortunately, Kane thought I'd crossed those lines, and once he stuck me on his radar, my ass was as good as grass as far as he was concerned.

"God, I hope you're right," I mumbled under my breath, half to Roman, half to the powers to be, because I needed all the encouragement and support I could get.

With shaky hands, I grabbed Roman's phone and dialed the number in Ivan's text.

Kane answered after only a few rings. "I got your...message," he droned, his voice laced with amusement. "Nice shot, if I do say so myself."

"Thanks." As much as I would have loved to have taken credit for it, too bad it wasn't mine.

"Did you keep his finger as a consolation prize?" he laughed. I didn't respond. But I did wonder what ever came of his finger. I didn't want to find it in the corner of my office later. "That was a bold move. I didn't think you had it in you."

"You'd be amazed what a woman will do when pushed to her limit." I put the call on speakerphone so Roman could hear.

"Still, I'm impressed."

"I wasn't trying to impress you," I deadpanned.

"Well, as much as I appreciate your gift, there's just one minor problem."

I rolled my eyes. "There's always a problem, is there not?"

"You returned that unlucky man to the wrong sender."

He's bluffing.

I swallowed down the lump in my throat, trying to steady my voice. "What are you talking about?"

I glanced up at Roman. He just stared down at our clothes haphazardly tossed on the floor, his face void of any emotion or expression.

"He wasn't one of mine."

Suddenly, everything made even less sense than it already did with him. "Then enlighten me. Who was he working for?"

"Don't know, don't care. And it's not my job to find out. He came for you, not me."

I was speechless at this point, my mind reeling. Someone else had sent that man to me with a message to stay away from my dad's estate?

"I don't believe you."

"Seems like you have a lot more enemies than you realize."

"Lucky me. Except I don't go around pissing people off on purpose. It'll be easy to figure out," I lied. I didn't have the slightest fucking clue who'd sent that man if Kane wasn't the one who did. I didn't even know where to start anymore.

"Maybe it's time we have our long-overdue in-person meeting you've been putting off," he drawled in a thick Southern accent that made me want to puke. "Have a little one-on-one chitchat. Don't you think?"

"Yeah," I reluctantly agreed. "Let's." As in, let's hurry up and get this shit over with.

"How's tomorrow work for you?"

How about never. "Next week," I pressed, hoping he would catch my hint since I already knew he had a hit out on me that he planned on having carried out this weekend.

He laughed. "Oh, you're just full of jokes, aren't you? So cute. Tomorrow," he stated again, this time with less amusement in his tone.

I looked at Roman for guidance. He mouthed the word *today*.

I covered the mouthpiece of the phone and held it away from us. "What?" I whisper-yelled. "Are you insane? We ca—"

He covered my mouth with his hand, again silently mouthing the word *today*.

I threw his hand down.

"Can't," I said to Kane. "I'm busy that day. This afternoon actually works best for me."

"Fine. I'll send one of my cars. How's that sound?"

"That sounds shitty. You come here or not at all."

I could practically hear him smiling through the phone. "Fine. I'm not scared."

Shit. I was.

As soon as the call ended, Roman set everything into action so fast it made my head spin. He was on the phone with Ivan and coordinating with surveillance before my brain even processed the fact that this was actually happening. I was about to come face-to-face with Kane for the first time since taking over my dad's business. My dad, on the other hand, was probably turning over in his grave.

---- ✦ ----

There had always been this unspoken yet understood rule that you didn't just go around all willy-nilly killing the ringleader of your competition because they did business differently than you. You killed them when they crossed a line...and only when you could prove it.

I'd stayed tried and true to that rule.

Apparently, Kane felt differently. He'd thought that I'd crossed some fucking proverbial line first and that he had all the evidence he seemed to have needed to eliminate me.

241

Lyndsay Marie

This was the first time I'd seen Kane in person in years. It wasn't like he attended family gatherings or dropped in to see how we were. The last time I'd known him to be here was when he and my dad had a meeting in my dad's office. To this day, I didn't know what that meeting was about or why it took place.

This was the first time I'd have met him as his rival.

"Relax." Roman helped me into my wire, tucking the little transmitter box into the waistband of my skirt. "Remember, he's on your turf. He knows you're gonna have a bunch of trigger-happy men with loaded guns around every corner. He's not stupid enough to try anything now. That's not how he works."

I released a long, calming breath. "I know. I'm just leery. That's all."

"Trust me, you have every right to be. But we're all here, we've got you. *I've* got you. Okay?"

"Okay." I tugged at the front of my shirt and brushed my hands down my skirt, as if my appearance mattered anymore.

Roman tucked the thin cord beneath my bra strap. The back of his hand grazed over the swell of my breast as he secured the wire behind the cup of my bra. Then, he clipped a tiny mic to the lace between my breasts.

"There. All set. Just wanted to make sure the wire isn't visible." He winked.

Of all times, coming face-to-face with the man who wanted me dead was not the time to be horny, yet, here I was, ready to risk it all for another earth-shattering orgasm.

Instead, I settled for a piping hot, panty-melting kiss…just in case it was my last.

Roman pulled back, both of us out of breath. "What was that for?"

"Everything," I said, wiping my lips, trying to fix my smeared makeup without a mirror.

"You need to get out of here before I call Kane myself and reschedule this meeting for never."

"Fine. I'll go. But only because you told me to."

He smacked my ass as I walked away. "Go get 'em, tiger. I'll see you downstairs."

I met Ivan at the door, and we made our way downstairs on what felt like a walk of shame.

The dining area where everything had been staged was located on the far side of the casino, situated between the gaming floor and corridor to the hotel. For guests, it meant they had to pass by food on their way to and from their room. For me, it meant I had a clear line of sight to the front door and hotel entrance.

I took my seat at the table that had been set up and strategically arranged in place so I wouldn't have any blind spots. With my back toward the wall, I glanced around the room. I didn't see anyone standing post, and my men were there, watching and waiting, ready to strike at a moment's notice.

After what felt like an eternity, a tall, lean figure dressed head to toe in a dark burgundy, custom-fitted suit accented with gold strode over to me.

Lyndsay Marie

He grinned as he approached. "You've grown up since the last time I saw you. How long has it been? Years?"

"I'm okay with that." He took the seat directly across from me.

He seemed to have aged a *lot*. I guess stress and time did that to a person. His hair had turned solid gray, and his face was lined with wrinkles at every corner.

"It's been what? Four, five years?" he asked, lighting up a cigar he'd pulled from his coat pocket.

"Not long enough," I quipped. "I see you've downgraded your taste." I tipped my chin toward the cigar wedged between his thin lips. It was a King of Denmark, somewhere in the $5K-a-pop range. Not that the money mattered to him; it was probably stolen anyway. But someone somewhere else was pissed off and still waiting for their missing smokes.

He smiled as he blew out a plume. "You're good." He held the King between his fingers, examining it. "This is just a backup until my next boat arrives. You know how that goes. So, how have you been?" He glanced around the casino before returning his gaze to me. "Seems like things are going very well for you here, all things considered."

"Everything is going just fine, yes." Except for that one tiny problem where he kept sending his men over here to try to kill me.

"You've made some renovations, I see."

"I did. But I'm sure you already knew that."

244

"Indeed, I did." He flicked an ash onto the floor. *Asshole*. "Word out there now is you've hired new security? Yeah?"

"I've increased my staff." I narrowed my eyes to him. "Where is this going? Did you just want to meet up to ask me about my staff? 'Cause I've got things to do. Busy weekend and all. You know how that is."

"By one," he stated. "Is it lover boy? Where has he been, anyway?"

"Cut the shit, Kane. What do you want?"

"It is him, isn't it?" he asked, completely ignoring me. "That's so cute. A modern-day Bonnie and Clyde. You really don't need him though."

"Clearly, I do. You keep sending your henchmen over here, trying to intimidate me, when all they're doing is getting in my way and on my last damned nerve."

"You seem like a smart girl, but you're a terrible host." He ignored me completely. "You haven't even offered me a drink or anything."

I snapped my arm in the air, waving over a cocktail waitress. "This man would like a drink," I told her when she approached us.

"Yes, sir. What would you like?" she asked, a hint of nervousness in her voice.

"Surprise me. Whatever's the most expensive. Jameson here doesn't mind." He glanced at me with a smirk.

"Yes, sir." She scurried away to the bar to fetch his shitty drink.

"What do you want from me?" I asked, getting back to it.

"You know, I always liked that about you, Jameson. You're a take-no-shit, get-straight-to-business kinda gal…or so I've heard." He took one last puff from his cigar, then snuffed it out. I didn't say anything, just glared at him. "You're a tough cookie to crack. So, I guess we'll get to it, then. You blocked one of my deliveries…a very specia—"

"I did no such thing."

Any hint of amusement in his demeanor disappeared. "Don't play stupid. That cutesy shit doesn't work with me. Quite frankly, I don't give a flying fuck whether you swam out into the river and pulled my boat off course yourself with your teeth or got one of your puppets to do it for you, but someone here did, and my entire boat, along with all of its contents, is still missing."

"I don't give a shit about—" The waitress approached and set his drink down on the table in front of him. When she walked away, I continued in a hushed tone. "I don't give a shit about you or your boats or your precious fucking cargo. The only thing I'm concerned about are my own problems. You should try minding your business sometime. It's fucking liberating."

"I don't generally cross lines. Not until mine is fucked with." He took a sip from his glass—Don Julio on the rocks. I knew because it was the most expensive drink staff was allowed to serve customers, and he was not a paying guest. "Don? You can do better than that."

"I reserve the best for the best. Let me get to the point because I have shit to do. Stop sending your men over here trying to toy with me. Otherwise, you can look forward to getting each one sent back to you, maybe still in one piece if you're lucky."

"You're just like your dad, you know that? Always want to play hero, save the fucking day. I've got news for you: you're not him, and you can't save them all."

"You're wasting my time and yours."

"Like I told you, that wasn't my man. Not anymore. You'd think all those years you spent alongside Elliott, you'd have learned something." He took a slow pull from his glass. "You took something of mine, and I want it back."

"I already told you I didn't take your *precious cargo.*"

"I've got a missing boat that's worth more than the one we're sitting on now, and it veered off course right here," he said, poking his finger into the tabletop. "I'll let you do the math."

"Let me get this straight. Because you can't keep track of your own shit, that's somehow my problem?"

"It very much is your problem. If it had disappeared at someone else's property upstream, then it would be *their* problem."

"Give me a fucking break." I leaned back in my chair, folding my arms across my chest. This shit was comical at best.

"Oh, something is going to break, but I'm thinking more along the lines of legs and a few necks if I don't get my boat *and* its contents back. So do whatever you have to do to make that happen, but make it quick. Your time is running out."

"The only thing I ever messed with of yours was that feeder boat that I sunk because I found one of my men with a bullet in his forehead. Unlike me, you got your boat back."

"Sounds like you need men with sharper skills."

Asshole. "Sounds like you need better tracking equipment."

He smirked. *At least one of us finds this funny.* "See, that's my problem. My missing boat *was* tracked, and it was last pinged on radar less than a hundred feet upstream from your dock."

"Sounds like a personal problem."

"This isn't a game you want to play with me. Elliott tried that, and look where it landed him."

"Hmm. I always knew it was you." Though hearing his confession out loud did not give me quite the relief I'd hoped it would. It only made the void in the pit of my stomach even deeper.

He smiled and shook his head. "Just because he got what he had coming to him doesn't mean I'm the one who did it. He built an enemy list a mile long. But that's what happens when you try to play the hero in a villain's world." He paused to sip his drink. *I should've poisoned him when I had the chance.* "Maybe you're not as smart as you've come across, so I'll educate you. You don't know a fucking thing about how any of this works. Now you've wasted the last year of your life trying to figure out how to take me down, and this entire time, the real killer is still out there, probably walking around your own goddamned casino floor." He reached his arm under his coat and pulled out a Glock. He set it on the table and slid it over to me. "If you believe so deeply in your soft heart that I'm the one who killed Elliott, now's your chance." He waved his hand over the gun like it was a prize on *The Price is Right*. "Take it. Pull the trigger."

My hands shook in my lap as my thoughts raced at a million miles per hour.

This was it. The singular moment I'd waited for and lost what had felt like years of sleep and life over. He was dropping the weapon in my hand, giving me this opportunity practically wrapped up and tied with a bow.

I wondered where Roman was hiding, what was running through his mind right now, if he thought I'd snap up this opportunity before it was too late. I had no doubt he wanted to kill him more than I did at the moment.

Knowing Ivan, he'd probably shit his pants by now.

"I'd rather slit your throat open with a dull butter knife from my own kitchen and watch the life bleed out of you all over this white tablecloth."

He leaned forward. "Then fucking do it, Jameson," he challenged. I stared down at the loaded gun, heavily contemplating if killing him right here and now was worth the risk. "Why haven't you killed me yet? You have just as many resources as me, do you not? But you can't do it, can you? Because now, you're not so sure."

I locked eyes with him, staring into pure, soulless evil. "I want you and your men to back off. Stay off of my property."

"I'm afraid I can't do that." He grabbed his gun off the table, casually spinning it around his finger, causing me to flinch. All he had to do was turn it on me and I'd be toast. "Your dad should have left you where he found you. Again, he just had to be a hero." He pushed himself away from the table as though he was about to leave.

"Excuse me? What the fuck does that mean?" I could feel my blood practically drain from my entire being.

He smirked. "You really don't know, do you? You should have stuck to your dreams and gone with academics. Stay in your lane, Jameson. This is much bigger than you're equipped to handle."

I knew exactly what he was talking about. My history wasn't something I thought had been made public information.

"How dare you come here into *my* casino and spew out meaningless bullshit and lies."

"Lies? You need to get your head out of your ass. I'd tell you to ask Elliott, but—"

"Get the fuck out of here," I shouted as I stood up, pointing toward the front door. "You fucking piece of shit. Just get the fuck out. We're done here."

Not my brightest moment, but I'd had enough of his shit. It was time for him to go.

Background chatter around us ceased. All eyes were on us now. *Fuck. Not again.*

"If you're going to be in this line of work," he drawled in a calm and even tone, "you should probably control your raging hormones." An evil grin spread across his face. "You'll figure it out one day…or maybe you won't. I don't give a shit either way." He winked as he stood. "I'll see you…Saturday, is it? I'll have to check my invite."

"Fuck you."

I glared at him as he buttoned up his sport coat without saying another word and walked away.

Lyndsay Marie

TWENTY-FIVE
Roman

I stood at my post in the shadows, watching and listening to the entire exchange between Jameson and Kane, knowing that this could single-handedly be the most pivotal move in her entire career and life.

Kane was not new to me. He wasn't new to anyone. I'd known him for as long as I'd been in the business, though he and I had never met face-to-face. This was about as close as I wanted to be to him.

The work I'd done to know the things that I did about him, his business, and his personal life all happened behind the scenes, obtaining and extracting information on a single person as much as one could. There were things I knew about him that would have justified me ending him right here and now, but the timing wasn't right...yet.

Nobody wanted him blown off the face of the Earth than me right now.

Finger on the trigger, I was itching for him to make the slightest fucking twitch so that I could put a hollow point between his eyes right there in the middle of a casino, patrons be damned.

I'd also promised James I wouldn't do anything unless I absolutely had to. Unfortunately for me, Kane didn't so much as get a single hair out of line the entire time…and then he slid his gun across the table.

"Just wait," I whispered into my mic to everyone on the channel. I wanted to wait and see where this was going.

Don't do it. I knew how badly she'd wanted this. Hell, we all did.

She held her ground. *Atta girl.*

Kane continued to egg her on, taunting her, practically begging for her to lose her cool…and then she did.

He'd pushed the right button. *Fuck.*

Kane kept his cool the entire time, even as she lost her shit and kicked him out. He casually slid back in his chair, stood up, and smiled at her like he'd just claimed victory over her.

I watched as he strode casually across the room, leaving through the main entrance, whistling some stupid ass tune as he left.

Jameson stood frozen and completely dumbfounded, right where Kane had left her.

"I need to get out of here," she mumbled as she started to walk away.

I caught Leon out of the corner of my eye coming toward us. I held up my hand to stop him.

"I got her," I said over the radio.

"Jameson," I called out to get her attention.

She kept forging ahead, ignoring my plea, as if she were on a mission.

I followed behind her, picking up my pace to catch up to her. "Jameson Magnolia Hazentree."

That worked.

She stopped short at the sound of her government name and spun around on her heels, narrowing her gaze. "What?"

"Where are you going?"

"Crazy. I'm going fucking crazy." *Relatable.* "Did you hear him back there? Did you hear what he said?"

"Yeah, I heard him." I darted my eyes around the room, then pulled my earpiece out and turned it off. "Not here, not now."

She huffed. "I just—I don't get it. All I wanted to do was host a fundraiser. Just one fucking time. Preferably without the risk of dying, and move on from all of this." She waved her hand in the air. "Better yet, I want out. I just—I don't think I can do this anymore."

I wanted her out of all this shit, too. Hopefully, she was serious because if I had my way, she would be when all was said and done. If I'd known how this was how things were going to turn out, I never would have taken the job from the beginning.

It was too late now. I was in way too deep and over my head. She had no idea just how much she was, too.

"I know, but we need to get you out of here."

She nodded in agreement. "Yeah, fine. Let's go."

I led her upstairs back to her place. Figured she'd be most comfortable there than anywhere else.

"Come. Sit down." I walked her over to her couch.

She plopped down with a sigh of relief.

I knelt in front of her. "Take a deep breath. We'll get through this. Right now, the only thing I want you to focus on is Haunted Hearts. Get as much money for charity out of these uppity pricks as you possibly can. That's what Elliott would have wanted; that's what you want. Not you sitting here worried about Kane and his bullshit. That's my job."

"It's not an easy thing to do right now when my life is on the line."

"I know it's not, but as long as I'm alive, nothing is going to happen to you. You understand that? Nothing."

"I hope you're right about all of this because I'm not sure about anything anymore."

The last thing I wanted her to know was I didn't know a damned thing either.

My phone rang. A rare occurrence, considering how few people had this number. Though, I had a feeling about who it was.

I slipped the pocket from my phone and glanced at the screen. UNKNOWN flashed across the screen.

"Ivan?" Jameson asked.

"Uh, yeah. I need to take this. I'll be right back." I stepped out onto the balcony, pulling the sliding door closed behind me.

"Yeah," I said, swiping up on the screen to answer the call.

"Roman, baby bro."

"Make it quick. James is inside, burning a hole in the back of my head right now."

He laughed. "I wouldn't expect anything less. I'm here."

"Damn, you move fast." Not wanting to be too suspicious, I stared down at my feet but kept the bottom of the door in my peripheral. If Jameson walked up, I'd see her feet.

"What can I say? You called and asked me for my help. That's what I do. Bail you out when your ass gets in over your head."

"Yeah, yeah, well, if I'd had any fucking clue about what I was getting into in the first place, I'd be in Costa Rica instead."

"Somehow, I doubt that. Anyway, I'm on-site."

I glanced up at James. She hadn't moved. She was still sitting on the couch, reclined back with her eyes closed and feet propped up on the coffee table.

"Good. Right now, what I need is a burner or two. Can you handle that much?" I asked with a smart-ass tone.

There wasn't much he couldn't handle, that I knew for a fact. My brother could wipe out entire three-letter government agency computer programs or erase the dark web with the press of a few keystrokes if he really wanted to.

"Lucky you, I came prepared," he assured. "How you wanna go about doing this?"

"I'm gonna get Ivan to cover for me, hold Jameson off, so we can chat in person. It'll be tricky since I'm supposed to be her shadow."

I didn't want to leave James alone with anyone, but I damned sure wasn't about to leave her unattended, especially since I'd already reassured her I wouldn't leave her side. But I had to get away for a few minutes without creating any suspicion on her end. I thought for a second, coming up with a game plan on the fly, then told him when and where to meet me.

"Looking forward to it. I just hope you're right with all this." I could practically hear him shaking his head, his tone void of all sarcasm.

"Yeah, me fucking too," I said, ending our call.

I stared at Jameson across the room. She hadn't moved an inch, and I secretly hoped she'd fallen asleep.

A few seconds later, she cracked open one eye. When she caught me staring, they both flew open.

"Yeah, yeah. I'm coming." Not that she'd heard me.

Jameson and I spent the rest of the afternoon going over last-minute details about the upcoming fundraiser—normally a task she'd be doing with Kelly and one that I found mundane. But the more she spoke about the gala, the more I could feel her passion for this event pouring out of her. Plus, it took her mind off everything else.

Lyndsay Marie

It didn't take long before the conversation eventually shifted back to business. She had me go over the guest list with a fine-toothed comb, which, unbeknownst to her, I had already done…four times. But just to appease her, I did it a fifth.

We talked about her role and expectations for the night. The goal was for her to be a host, enjoy the evening, and reap the reward for all of the hard work she'd put into it over the last year.

My goal was to keep her alive.

I reassured her everything on my end was squared away. I'd already been in contact with security to make sure that we had everything covered on our end. All entrances and exits on the casino side would be guarded and completely inaccessible by anyone except for security, approved staff, and, worst case, emergencies. Then, it was exit only.

Leon already had his own plan in place when it came to the main event. He'd made sure there were enough men available there would be someone standing guard inside and out and around every corner, rerouting any unknown or uninvited guests back to their car or to another casino.

Jameson had assured me that their marketing department had been announcing for months that the casino would be closed for a private event. Guests staying at the hotel could stay, but their access to the casino would be cut off for the day and night.

In a perfect world, we had a plan in place that would, in theory, run like a well-oiled machine. The reality of it all was this was probably going to end up a shitshow of epic proportions.

Either way, at least one person, if not more, was not going to make it to see Sunday morning.

We would not be one of them.

We'd been sitting on the couch for way too long. My ass had gone numb, and time was running out before I needed to meet up with River. If I didn't show up in a timely manner, he'd most definitely come looking for me himself.

"I need to meet with Leon. You okay with Ivan taking over for a few minutes?"

She arched an eyebrow. "Mr. I'm Never Leaving You Alone Again wants to leave me alone again? Seems suspicious."

"Well, it's not. And I'm not leaving you alone— you'll be with Ivan. Considering the shit we have going on, I just need to go over a few things with him before tomorrow, that's all. Didn't think you'd want the added stress." Okay, so that was partly true. The less she knew, the better for everyone. She needed to focus on hosting first and foremost. "It won't take long. We just need to iron out a few details."

"Who am I to stop you? Do what you need to do."

"So then you won't stop me from doing this?"

"Doing wha—"

Her words trailed off mid-sentence when I leaned over and pressed my lips to hers. It was the only thing I could think of doing to get her mind off my leaving.

She always liked to play dirty. *I play dirtier.*

259

She softly moaned into my mouth, a sure sign she wasn't going to object or stop me.

Her body slowly moved in time with our kiss. I could already feel myself getting hard. *Shit.* This was supposed to be about her, not me. I grabbed the back of her head and pulled her into me. Our tongues slid across each other's. All I could think about was how her pussy tasted.

Fuck.

Just as quickly as I'd come on to her, I pulled away. As much as I enjoyed her, I had shit to do that required my clothes to stay on.

"What was that for?" she asked, wiping her mouth with her hand.

"Nothing in particular. Just giving in to temptation." I stood up and helped her to her feet. "But I really need to go. I told Leon I'd be there by now."

"Fine. But we're not finished."

I pulled her into me and kissed her on the forehead. "Looking forward to picking things up again later."

Fuck. I was supposed to meet River five minutes ago, and I hadn't texted Ivan to make sure he was even available to take over for me. At this point, I was going to start heading in that direction and figure out what to do with James along the way.

I shot Ivan a text and hoped for the best.

Me: I need a few minutes. You free?
Ivan: Yeah. Say when?

Me: Now. Main floor.

Thank fuck he responded.

James and I made our way downstairs to the casino floor to meet Ivan. I spotted Ivan immediately. If it hadn't been for our *very* eye-opening conversation, I'd never have trusted to leave her with him. Given the recent shift in power between us, he was no longer in a position to question me.

"Sorry for throwing her on you last minute," I said to Ivan as we met up.

Jameson slapped the back of her hand against my chest. "You say that like he's my babysitter."

"I mean..."

She narrowed her eyes, giving me the kind of look a mother gives her misbehaving toddler.

I smirked at her and winked, knowing damn well how much it would irritate her. I'm sure I'd pay for it later.

"No worries," he said. "I just seen Kelly. She mentioned wanting to see James for some things. I don't know for what. Girly shit, I suppose."

"Sounds good. I'm about to piss myself anyway. You two have fun. I'll catch up with you soon."

Ivan went one way with Jameson, and I went the other, making a beeline for the main public bathroom.

A wet floor sign blocked the doorway. I skirted around it anyway.

"Bathroom's closed," the janitor called out with his back to me.

Lyndsay Marie

"Sorry. Can't hold it."

I walked past the man mopping the floor, heading to the last urinal. As soon as I started to piss, the back of one of my knees buckled out from under me.

"What the fuck?"

I almost broke my neck looking back over my shoulder, attempting not to piss everywhere, only to find River standing behind me. He looked ridiculous in an Emerald Haze cleaning crew uniform, mop in hand.

He grinned. "Nice suit."

"Thanks, asshole." I adjusted my pants and personal parts back into place, then quickly glanced around the bathroom, squatting down to peek underneath the stall doors, looking for anyone else who might be quietly eavesdropping while dropping a deuce.

"Do you not think I already did that?"

"This isn't where I told you to meet me," I whisper-yelled.

He treated this shit like a joke. I saw exactly zero humor in his little costume and scheme.

"Oh, I know. Your idea was dog shit. Catching you with your pants down was much better."

"How'd you know…never mind. I don't want to know. I don't have time for your humor right now. Ivan can only hold James for so long."

He reached into one of his pockets and pulled out a phone. "Per your request."

I took the phone from him. "Just one?"

"That's all you need."

Christ. River had zero idea what I needed at the moment. "Meet me in my suite in five." I gave him the room number. "Don't be late."

"10-4." He went back to mindlessly mopping the bathroom floor.

"Next time, try using water."

———— ✦ ————

"Thanks for actually meeting me here. It's not exactly an easy feat to conduct business in a public bathroom," I said sarcastically.

We met back up at my suite as agreed without a minute to spare.

"I've worked in worse conditions. This is a nice setup you got here. Doesn't look like you've been here almost a week."

"Because I haven't. That and I've been staying at James's the last couple of nights."

"Oh, yeah?" He waggled his eyebrows. "You hittin' that again already? That didn't take long."

"Fuck off." I wasn't about to tell him that I wasn't just *hitting it*. I'd let myself slip and catch feelings for her again, though I wasn't entirely sure they'd ever gone away. I'd just learned how to suppress them because...reasons. "I'm in a hurry. Ivan's got her distracted, but I need to get back before she comes looking for me."

I pulled a beer from the fridge and handed it to River.

"Thanks, man." He cracked it open and took a long pull from the bottle before setting it on the bedside nightstand. "So, as fast as you can, tell me exactly what's going on."

"It's complicated."

He threw himself on his back onto my bed and casually stretched out with arms behind his head and legs crossed at the ankles. "I don't know about you, but I've got all the time in the world."

"What? No computers to hack? Government files to steal?"

He lifted a shoulder. "Things are slow right now, what can I say?"

I sighed. This was literally my brother. The man who'd bailed me out of everything from lying about my grades on my report card to taking the blame for a murder, then making all of the case files disappear.

The only people who understood our relationship were us.

I spent the next few minutes giving him a quick rundown about everything that had been going on, from the night I'd left Memphis a year ago down to the moment I called him right after my conversation with Ivan.

He stared at me silently, completely dumbfounded.

"Exactly."

He blinked.

"River. Say something."

"I mean...Jesus Christ. I knew you were up shit's creek without a paddle when you called, but damn. This is..."

"Shut the fuck up. That's not very reassuring."

"I'm not here to reassure you. I'm just trying to save your ass."

"Obviously, I think you can help, or you wouldn't even be here right now."

"Maybe I just wanted to check out this spectacular view of the Mighty Mississip?"

"You're such a dick."

"It's what I do." He winked. "Now, I guess since I'm in on this because you just told me your dirty little secret, guess now's a good time to tell me about tomorrow. What do you need me to do for you?"

"Burn an empire to the ground."

TWENTY-SIX

Jameson

Time had flown by in a whirlwind. One minute, I was sitting at my desk with a dream in my heart and an idea floating around in my mind like dust in the wind. The next thing I knew, my team and I were balls to the wall, working to bring my wild and crazy idea to life.

I could picture it all so clearly—the glitz and glam, the lights, guests dressed in clothing that cost more than a new car, throwing money at Haunted Hearts charity, endless food and laughter.

Now, it all seemed like a fever dream.

Somewhere amongst all of the chaos, it felt like my plans had started to unravel. I questioned whether or not forging ahead was even a smart idea at this point, especially after meeting with Kane face-to-face. All it did was leave me with more questions than answers. Though things had seemingly cooled down since we'd spoken in person and he'd stopped sending me threatening messages and assassination attempts, his silence felt like the calm before the storm.

The day had finally come.

Now, here I was, a few hours away from the Haunted Hearts Gala, and to say that I was scared shitless was the understatement of the century.

As promised, Roman had hardly left my side; I'd even invited him to share my bed. He didn't try to fight me on it. It was nice having someone to cuddle up next to for a change, even if it were him. For the first time in a very long time, I felt safe. Having Roman near me again made my world feel almost normal, even though everything about him was far from normal.

We'd gotten an early start on the day. I spent the morning making one last quick round through every department, from housekeeping to security, the kitchen to the loading docks, making sure everyone had everything they needed to get through the day and night. Tomorrow, things would be back to business as usual.

Tonight was going to be a long one.

"We need to head to my apartment so I can start getting ready. I'm supposed to be meeting Lana from the day spa in—" I checked the time. "—ten minutes."

Once again, Kelly, my literal saving grace, had arranged for Lana to come in on her day off to do my hair and makeup because she knew I'd forget to set it up.

News flash: I did.

Lyndsay Marie

We made it upstairs just in time to meet Lana trudging down the hall with a huge black suitcase in tow.

Roman grabbed the case from her and hauled it into my apartment. "Christ. What's in this thing?"

"Makeup, hair tools, towels. All kinds of shit."

"It feels like a two-hundred-and-twenty-pound dead body," he stated.

She arched an eyebrow. "That's oddly specific."

"Don't ask."

As soon as we were inside, Lana got to work setting out all of her supplies. She ran power cords across the floor to plug in hair tools I'd never seen in my life. Most of them didn't even look like they were made for hair. While her smorgasbord of tools heated up, she turned my dining room table into a buffet of makeup, hair spray, and an endless sea of bottles of who knew what.

Then, she sat me down in a chair and wasted no time getting to work.

Not a day had gone by in over a decade that I didn't do my own hair or makeup, but the way Lana worked was like pure magic. I should have felt like a movie star, and to some degree, I did. But I also felt guilty. Here I was, getting all dolled up for one of my and over a thousand other people's biggest events of the year, knowing my life, and possibly theirs, were all at risk.

Except they didn't have a clue.

I glanced over at Roman while Lana blotted on my foundation. He was sitting in one of the side chairs, going back and forth between working on the laptop and seemingly texting someone on his phone…a phone I didn't recognize.

"New phone?" I asked.

"Um, no." He quickly stuffed it into his front pocket. "Ivan would never. He's too cheap."

"Hmm." He wasn't wrong about Ivan. Then again, Ivan seemed to have no problem spending my money. Maybe I was mistaken about the whole phone thing. It was hard to tell from across the room with squinty eyes.

"Close your eyes," Lana said as she loaded up a small brush with eyeshadow. "Need to do your eyes." She swiped her fluffy makeup brush across my lids. "Okay, now, open and look up."

She rubbed something under my bottom lashes.

"I just want to make it through the night." I was half speaking to myself and half to anyone who would listen.

I heard Roman's laptop close. Then, he appeared in my peripheral as he walked up beside me, bent down, and kissed me on the forehead. "And you will. We all will."

A knock on the door startled us all. Even Lana shot upright.

"Expecting someone?" he asked.

"Could be my dress." I fucking hoped it was and not someone with a dozen roses and a surprise gun.

Roman disappeared to answer the door and returned a moment later.

"You'd be correct." He hung the black garment bag on the doorframe leading into my bedroom.

"Two? What's the other one?"

He smirked. "That one's mine."

"Yours? Did you get a suit?"

"Of course. You didn't think I was going to show up for your special night in the same shit I've been wearing, did you?"

"Well, no, I don't guess. How did you get it?" This man had way too many secrets.

Sneaky bastard.

"The other day. I found Kelly's number in the contact list on my phone and sent her a text asking for her help. She had someone from the shop take my measurements the other night. Kelly handled the rest."

"Well, aren't you sneaky." I mean, really. If I missed that much, what else did I not know about him?

"Only when I have to be." He winked.

"We're almost done," Lana assured. "I just need to do your lips and finish your hair. You'll be all set."

"Sounds good. Thank you, you're a lifesaver."

She finished working her magic, and an hour or so later, she was done, cleaned up, and out the door.

I tightened my cotton robe around my waist and went to see Roman out on the balcony. He was casually leaning against the railing, decked to the nines in his custom-fitted suit, the back side of him looking like the cover of a *GQ* magazine, as he stared out at the river.

It was hard to believe a man like him had the type of history and lived the life that he did.

I cleared my throat as I stepped outside. "Excuse me, Mr. Stone."

He pushed off the railing and turned to face me. His mouth fell open.

"God damn," he finally muttered under his breath.

"Holy shit" was my own response as he turned around.

The sight of this tall, dark, and holy-shitballs-Batman's-twin-fuck-me-running, dangerous man had me thinking I might need to reschedule this entire event. He looked deliciously edible.

He walked forward, closing the distance between us. He stopped just a few inches short of me, reaching his hands through the opening of my robe, splaying his warm hands across my hips as he pulled me into him.

"You look absolutely beautiful, Miss Hazentree. Just…stunning."

I wrapped my arms behind his neck and pushed up on my tiptoes. His hands slid around to my ass, and my robe fell open between us. "I'm not even ready yet."

He squeezed my bare ass as I nuzzled my face into his neck, breathing in whatever cologne he had on.

Fucked-up as Roman and I were, I could get used to this. I missed this…I missed him.

It was hard to believe almost a week had gone by, and already, he'd be gone by tomorrow, if not tonight when the party was over.

"And you're not going to be coming to me like this half-naked, tempting me on every level, you little minx. Don't you have somewhere important to be tonight?"

Lyndsay Marie

"Ha. Ha." Reluctantly, I pulled slightly away, secured my robe back into place, and tied it. Tight. Because he was right. Despite my wanting him, we did have somewhere we needed to be. "I actually just came out here to tell you I'm going to go finish getting ready."

He took my hand in his and held me at arm's length.

I eye-fucked him from head to toe, not even trying to hide it anymore. "You, sir, look absolutely, deliciously fuckable. Whoever made your suit did a fantastic job."

"Some old guy named Armani. Now, take your fine ass inside and finish getting ready before I bend you over this balcony and ruin your makeup and your night."

I pressed up on my toes, placing a kiss first on the corner of his mouth, then along his freshly shaven jawline, and down his neck to the collar of his starched white dress shirt. He let out a low growl when I reached between us and rubbed him through his tuxedo pants. He was already rock solid.

"Hmm. You're worried about ruining my makeup? Who said you were gonna fuck my mouth?"

He pulled me flush against him. "You asked for it."

His fingers curled and dug into my hip through the thick cotton robe that I wished I wasn't wearing as his other hand untied my belt and made its way through the opening in the front.

I shifted my legs slightly apart, giving him the access he silently asked for as his warm fingers slipped between my legs. Slowly, he slid one, then another finger inside of me. I dropped my forehead to his chest and held on to his arms for support as his fingers moved in and out of me.

"You're already so fucking wet." He worked his hand, slowly pushing deeper, working his long fingers until I was on the verge of coming. He knew it, too. "Not yet," he whispered in my ear.

"Please. I'm so close."

"I know." He pulled out of me and spun me around.

"Roman. What are you doing?" He guided me forward with his hands on my shoulders. I was now looking down over the parking lot and the entire casino property.

I'd never been more grateful for the sun setting at five in the afternoon this time of year.

"You know exactly what *we* are doing here...and you'd better hold on."

I grabbed onto the balcony railing. "You sure this is a good idea?"

He let out a soft chuckle. "This is a perfect idea."

The back of my robe lifted up. My skin pricked with goose bumps at the cool breeze that reached my bare skin. I heard the unmistakable sound of a belt buckle and a zipper.

Roman's warm hand splayed across my ass cheek, rubbing softly before he raised it and lowered it back down, giving it a *very* painful, stinging smack. My entire body lurched forward as he made contact.

My grip on the railing tightened.

"I warned you." His voice was stern, laced with heat. "You'd better hold on."

Lyndsay Marie

I leaned forward, bending at the waist and sticking my ass out. "Better?"

"Jesus Christ, Jameson. So much better."

He grabbed onto my hip with one hand and pushed against my lower back, urging me to arch my back even more. Then, he pressed the head of his dick to my dripping wet pussy, sliding it through my slick folds. I urged him on he lined himself up and slowly pushed the length of himself inside of me until he filled me completely.

I didn't even care anymore if someone looked up and saw us or if security had inadvertently caught us on one of the cameras or saw me bent over this balcony with my robe wide open in the front, exposing myself to the world. All that mattered in that moment was I was with Roman.

He grabbed onto both of my hips, pulling me backward into him as he thrust forward.

Over.

And over.

And over.

He claimed me from behind.

My orgasm built back up and buzzed through me like a bolt of lightning. I bit my bottom lip and held my breath to keep from letting out a scream that would catch the attention of anyone in the parking lot below.

Roman moved harder and faster, our bodies slapping together, until he growled, holding himself still as he came inside of me.

He eventually very slowly slid himself out and lifted me upright to a standing position. "You good, babe?"

"Uh, yeah." I turned around to face him. "Legs are a little wobbly, but it was worth it."

"Good. Now, let's get you inside for real this time and finish getting ready. There's still business to be done. Just make sure you wear panties." He winked.

I gave a half-hearted smile. The thought of what the rest of the night had to potentially hold killed my buzz. "Yeah. You're right. We've been out here a while. Let's go."

"Hey." Roman grabbed me. "Look at me. Everything is going to be fine. Okay?"

I wanted to believe him. I wanted to think that whatever went down, or however things turned out, he was right. "I—I know. It's going to be okay." I did not think things were going to be okay. But I didn't have time to worry about it now.

He leaned down and gave me the softest, lightest kiss on the lips. "I'd give you more, but I really will ruin this bang-up makeup job Lana did." He smiled.

I couldn't help but smile back. "Thanks. And that—" I tilted my head toward the railing behind me. "—was kinda hot."

"You're damned right it was. Just like our first time."

I sucked in a deep breath of cool, fresh air. When I blew it out, a cloud of fog formed between us. "Hopefully not our last."

Lyndsay Marie

TWENTY-SEVEN

Roman

Part of the plan was to keep my distance from Jameson so that she could mix and mingle, shake hands, throw on the charm, and flash her bright smile to win over the wallets of guests. She assured me there would be no ass-grabbing…by Chris or by me. Quite frankly, I was surprised he'd made an appearance—battered, bruised, and all.

I was getting sick of her *hands off* rules. The ones that applied to me, anyway.

While I wanted nothing more than to swoop her up into my arms and whisk her away from this place, there was still business to be conducted that hadn't been part of the original plan.

As we entered the event center, the room was already buzzing with energy. The room was filled with doctors, lawyers, men and women from the city council. The chief of police had shown up, as he should. Emerald Haze still had him and his entire department on payroll. Every who's who of what's what was there.

The turnout was twice the size of any event I'd ever seen hosted here. I guess people were really fucking curious as to what Jameson had been up to since taking over the family business. Most of the people here tonight would've never otherwise set foot in this place. I recognized a lot of familiar faces and repeat customers and just as many new ones, each of them with more money than sense.

As much as I hated that she would even attempt to host an event of this proportion, I knew how much it meant to her in the past, and even more so now for the sake of carrying on Elliott's legacy.

Unfortunately, it also meant she had to be at her most vulnerable.

I lost sight of her as she was swallowed up into a sea of jet-black tuxedos, glittery ball gowns, and everyone was wearing a fucking mask. Each time she disappeared, my body went into panic mode.

Eventually, she popped out of the crowd and made her way toward the stage.

I shoved my way through the mass of millionaires, not even giving a single flying fuck if I knocked into anyone.

She hiked up her dress to keep from tripping over the bottom of it and making her way up the stairs and onto the stage. My stomach tied into the biggest knot with anticipation.

The last thing in the world I wanted was for her to be standing front and center in a room with more than a

Lyndsay Marie

thousand people who would all have their eyes locked in on her.

I zeroed in on the guy from security standing off to the side of the stage, just behind the curtains and out of view of the crowd. Leon had brought in a team of men he'd put together. Some I knew, others I didn't but who Leon had worked with in the past. Each one stood their post at various places around the room, all the way from the perimeter below to the balcony above.

Only one spot left was currently unmanned—mine.

I jogged up the stairs to the side of the stage and got into place.

If you'd asked me a week ago if I saw myself back at Emerald Haze being paid to protect the heiress to one of Mississippi's largest organized crime establishments, I would have laughed in your face and said abso-fucking-lutely not. I would have thought you were more out of your mind than me.

Yet here we are.

I looked around and caught a glimpse of Ivan standing across the room, half in the shadows, half-washed in multicolored light. *Bastard*. He was half the fucking reason we were in this mess. Seeing him took me back to that night.

———◆———

"Roman!" Ivan called my name from across the kitchen.

"Yeah," I said, turning around toward the voice that made every muscle on my body tense at its sound.

He rounded the corner of a baker's rack stacked with industrial-sized stainless-steel pots and pans and baking sheets.

"You busy?" he asked as he swiped a handful of grapes out of a food storage bin sitting on top of the buffet before popping one into his mouth.

"I'm always busy."

"I understand that. Where you headed?"

"Out to the docks. We got a shipment on its way. It should be here any minute." I glanced up at the wall clock. "Soon."

"Well, I need you first. This shouldn't take a minute."

"That's like three minutes longer than I have right now. Tater will have my ass by then. We're expecting a boat to roll up any minute now."

He shrugged and dismissively swiped his hand in the air toward the back exit door that I was just about to go out of. "Fuck 'em. Tater can wait. This is more important."

I laughed. "Right. Nothing is more important than moving a load of cargo right now. Plus, have you seen how he responds to tardiness?"

Tater's idea of discipline involved anything from shooting at you while you zigzagged your way between pallets on the back dock, trying not to take a bullet to your ass, to having you strung up by your ankles and hung upside down over the railing with raw meat tied around your neck while you prayed a gator or gar wouldn't find you before he came back. I once saw him time tie a man up and throw him off the back of a barge and watched as he was dragged away down the Mississippi.

No fucking thank you.

"And have you seen how he responds to me?' Ivan asked. "I invented the consequences, and I trained him how to follow through. He takes his orders from me, so if I say I need you, he'll have no choice whether he likes it or not."

"Fair enough." Tater presented himself like a badass to everyone else, but when it came to Ivan, he was scared shitless. Hell, most of the men here were, sometimes myself included.

I glanced back up at the wall clock.

One minute.

Tater was gonna be all over my ass like white on rice, and I didn't trust Ivan enough to have my back. On the flip side, if I didn't show up to Ivan's office, *he* was gonna have my ass. Either way, I was fucked.

I sighed. "What's this about?" I couldn't think of one thing we had going on that took precedence over a new shipment of goods that would need to be moved out again just as fast as it had arrived.

"I've got a…job for you." He pulled his phone out, did something on it, then dropped it back into his pocket. "I'll meet you in my office," he said as he walked past me.

"Fuck," I breathed into my palms with a defeated moan, scrubbing my hands down my face.

"You'll be fine, kid," he called back as he exited the double doors on the far side of the kitchen. "I'll handle Tater."

"Boy, he can be a real prick sometimes, huh?"

The sound of a woman's voice caught me off guard. *I thought we were alone.*

"I—sorry, I didn't know anyone else was in here."

Josephine popped out from behind the bar of prepped food. Though I didn't need to see her to know who she was; I knew it was her just by the voice. She was the head of food and beverage…and probably a lot more than what she let on.

"He didn't either." She smiled. "I've been in this business longer than you've been alive. I know when and how to keep my mouth shut," she said with a wink.

I smiled back at her. "Good to know."

"You'd be amazed at the things you hear when you don't speak. You know how it is around here. People talk, but they really don't say anything." She started covering the open trays of food with lids. "Now, run along. Get out of my kitchen. I've got things to do, and unless you're going to grab a knife and start chopping, then you're just in my way."

"Yes, ma'am. Always bossy, never the boss," I joked with a smirk. Everyone knew she could probably pull rank over anyone in this business if she wanted to.

"I'll show you who's boss!" She threw a cherry tomato at me as I followed the same route as Ivan, veering off my original course. "Now, pick that up before someone slips and gets hurt."

Lyndsay Marie

I bent down and picked up the tomato, tossing it into the trash as I pushed through the doors. The space opened to an extension of the main casino floor, tucked into a dark, desolate corner. Other than a small food and beverage station, a handful of slot machines, and an emergency exit door that led to a stairwell, this side of the casino left a lot to be desired. It was where a handful of loners and regulars often played—the ones who started early and stayed well into the night.

I wound through the slots and pushed through the emergency exit. Then I hauled ass up the stairs, taking two at a time.

Ivan's office was on the second floor, halfway down a long, run-down hallway, located somewhere just above the kitchen. His office door had been left cracked open, awaiting my arrival. I knocked anyway.

"Come in," he said as I stepped into his tiny, suffocating office. "Close the door. Have a seat."

You'd think for a guy who'd been with this family doing business for as long as he had, he would have had a bigger, brighter office. One with a view of the parking lot, at least.

"So, what's up? What's so important that couldn't wait until later?" I asked as I dropped into the chair across from him.

He spun around in his decades-old wingback leather chair, turning his back to me, and popped the top off a decanter, pouring himself a drink. "Bourbon?"

"No. Thanks. I'm good." It wasn't even eleven in the morning.

I leaned back and crossed my legs, resting my ankle on my knee, and waited.

Impatiently.

This will only take a minute, yet he had time to offer me a drink.

He faced me. "I've got some new orders for you."

"Okay? Isn't that why you hired me?" That was what I'd been brought here to do all those years ago—take orders, help with the company's dirty work, perform petty tasks no one else wanted to do. Shit that kept everyone else from getting blood on their hands. Generally, I wasn't allowed to ask questions, and for the most part, I didn't.

"True," he said, taking a sip of his amber drink. He lit a cigarette and took a long, slow drag, then blew the smoke up into the air. I watched impatiently as the gray cloud reached the tiles of the drop ceiling, suffocating every pore in the dingy plaster. "You've been with us, what, almost five years now?"

"Six," I corrected him. "Almost six."

"Wow. Six already? That's a long time." He took another drag. "I'm impressed. You haven't wanted to leave yet, go back home?" he asked with another exhale of smoke.

Home. Ha. I left home because I couldn't get my shit together. This opportunity presented itself, and I took it without question.

I shrugged. "I mean, sure, I miss my brother, but you and I both know the road I was heading down. I probably wouldn't have lived this long had I stayed there."

"True. So, what you're saying is I kinda saved your life?"

Seriously? Where the fuck was he going? I didn't have time for this philosophical bullshit. I glanced down at my watch.

"Don't worry," he assured. "Tater knows you're here. I told him you'd be out when I was done with you first. That fucktard can wait."

"Where is this meeting going? Did you bring me in here to have a Hallmark moment? 'Cause we can do that out on the docks while I'm unloading."

"Patience has never been your thing, has it?" He shook his head and laughed. "Fine, I know you've got shit to do, so I'll get to it. I'm sending you back to Nashville."

"What?" He could not be serious right now. This had to be a joke. "Nashville? I'm sorry, wh—"

"You heard me. I'm sending you home." He smashed out his cigarette in a shit-green-colored glass ashtray that was probably twice as old as him, then flicked the crushed butt into a trash can full of smoked-up cigarettes.

"When?"

"Tomorrow."

"Tomorrow? Are you fucking serious right now? What about everything here?" Panic tore through me. I hadn't seen or spoken to a soul in Nashville, including my own brother, who'd worked his ass off trying to keep me out of trouble, since the day I'd left. Now, Ivan was about to send me packing back to an unfamiliar and very likely unwelcoming place. Never mind the new life I'd established here.

"I'll handle things on this end, no worries there."

"Why?"

"Because. I've got work for you there. Work you're better suited for."

I always knew this was a risk. A lot of men had come and gone in this industry. Most had been offed, but a very select few had been sent on to new assignments. My dumb ass had gotten comfortable, and here I was about to get a taste of this medicine.

"You've been an exemplary employee, Roman. You do what you're told when you're told. You don't ask questions, and you get shit done whe—"

"Then why get rid of me? Just like that?" I snapped my fingers. "Why now?"

"'Cause. You're the only person who I trust to follow through with the orders I'm about to give you and not fuck it all up."

"What the fuck, Ivan? I have spent every waking moment bending over backward for you and Elliott, learning the ins and outs of this business. I've done countless hours of shitty work because neither you nor anyone else wanted to do it. I've done nothing but protect you and Elliott and the rest of the crew. I have dedicated my life to you."

None of this was new information to him. I'd done nothing but work my ass off without question—ran drugs, moved priceless, stolen artwork, transported pallets of cash and weapons, disposed of people that wouldn't be missed—all to prove to him and Elliott I could. I was good at my job.

Did I miss home? Some days. Did that mean I wanted to go back, especially now? Absolutely fucking not.

He took another sip of his drink, and all I wanted to do was knock that glass into his teeth.

"Yes, you have, and your dedication is greatly appreciated."

"Prove it," I challenged him. "Prove your appreciation for me. Let me stay. I'm better here."

"I don't have to prove shit to you. I've already got a job lined up, and I'm sure you'll find it'll be…well worth your time."

At this point, *nothing* would be worth him shipping me away at the drop of a dime.

"How long?" I asked, holding on to a sliver of hope that this *job* would take just enough time for me to get in, get out, and come back here.

He shrugged. "I'm not sure yet. Until I need you again. Could be months, could be years. Depends."

"Jesus Christ," I mumbled under my breath.

"Sorry, kid. This is just the nature of this business."

Kid. I hated when he called me that, just because he had thirty-plus years on me.

"What about things here?"

"There's been a change in plans, but before we go any further, I need you to understand one thing. All of this stays right here in this room. Not one single word of this gets breathed to anyone else outside of these four walls. Got it?"

"Yeah, sure. Whatever you say." I guess I should be grateful he wasn't having me wiped off the Earth. I at least get to walk away with my life…for now.

"I mean it."

"I get it. Between us."

"No, no, no. I don't sense that you *get it*. When I say that everything I tell you stays here, I mean it stays between me and you." His tone changed. Something about the way he spoke did not sit right with me.

Not once in the time that I'd ever done work here had Ivan ever made me swear absolute secrecy, not to him, not to anyone. Keeping quiet and not running your mouth was one of those understood rules, regardless.

Besides, I'd learned who and who not to talk to over the years—I knew the ranks. Elliott was king shit. He made all the rules. Ivan took orders from Elliott, who then passed orders on to me or one of his other guys, depending on the job. Even still, Ivan was not in a position to make or give his own orders, which was exactly what this was, and I didn't like it.

"I got it. Just me and you."

"I fucking mean it, Roman. You and me. I better not find out you've talked to anyone. I know how some folks around here like ta run their mouths. Just fucking yipping and yapping like a buncha women at the hair salon. Don't be one of 'em. I will find out."

"Just you and me," I repeated. I let out a frustrated breath. "What if I don't agree to your proposition?"

He smirked. "Here's the deal, and you're probably not going to like this, but this isn't a proposition. These are orders. I'm not exactly giving you an option. Well, I guess that all depends on how you look at things."

I just stared at him, dumbfounded and seething inside. "What would my choices be if I were to see things differently?"

"Your options are take this assignment, follow through, start fresh, and you'll be set for life."

"Again, if I don't?"

He shrugged. "You disappear regardless."

"Is that a threat?" I'd spent a lot of years keeping this piece of shit alive. Now he wanted to make me disappear?

He popped his neck. *Mind if I help you?* "I don't make threats. I set boundaries."

I'd been around this place long enough to know that regardless of the time I'd put in here, I wasn't immune to the rules. I just didn't like that I'd somehow become the one in the hot seat…or that now I had to leave, no questions, no goodbyes.

I also knew I wasn't quite ready to sign my own death certificate. But I'd seen this play out before with other men who worked for Emerald Haze.

Fuck.

"Well, what's it gonna be, kid?" I always questioned whether or not I could trust him. This just tipped the scale and solidified my opinion. "I can tell you this." He took a long pull at his freshly lit cigarette and continued. "You're gonna be set for life. I admire you, you know. You're a smart kid, Roman."

"Then why me? Why not some other pissant working for Elliott."

"Because, Roman, you're the best man I got with the skills I need for this specific job."

Great. I had two choices: refuse his orders and risk dying now in this smoke-filled office or agree and probably die later but with benefits.

"Fine," I finally conceded. I had other shit to do at the moment. Sitting here wasn't one of them. It was time to buckle up and accept my fate. "Lay it on me."

He clapped his hands together. "I knew you'd make the right choice. Do you know how difficult it is to get rid of a body these days?"

"Very," I replied dryly. Had he forgotten everything I'd done for him over the years? "Can we wrap this up? Some of us have to work."

He cut his gaze at me. "Absolutely. Here's what I need from you." He continued to talk, raking over the details of this *job* that he needed me to do. Halfway through, I'd zoned out, only catching about every third word that fell through his lips due to the ringing in my ears. By the time he'd finished babbling, I was sick as fuck to my stomach, ready to put a bullet in my own skull.

"That's it," he said. "Tomorrow night. I need you at this address." He slid a scrap piece of paper across his desk to me. "Sharp. When I tell you don't be late, don't be early. This—" He tapped his fat, gold-ring-clad finger into the time written on the white scrap of paper below the address. "—is when you need to be there. Capiche?"

I bit into the inside of my lip to keep myself from arguing back. It wouldn't do any good. "Yeah. Capiche."

"Good. Now, let's get you back to work before Tater thinks he's going to rip *me* a new asshole for keeping you too long," he laughed as he stood up; I couldn't feel my own legs anymore. "Remember, you and me, nobody else."

He patted me on the shoulder. "We're gonna miss you around here."

"Yeah, I'm sure. I'm not going to miss a single goddamned soul within a five-hundred-mile radius of this casino."

He shook his head. "Yeah, sure, kid."

THE NEXT NIGHT

I killed the lights on my new Arc Vector—a parting gift from Ivan— as I rolled up to the address he'd given me at the exact time he'd instructed. He'd so graciously given me an all-electric motorcycle, one for its speed, and two, because it didn't have an engine and made no sounds. This thing had probably cost more than half the homes in Memphis.

His black Bugatti was parked a few hundred feet down the street and just around the corner at the edge of hole seven of a golf course, the front bumper barely visible from where I sat.

The neighborhood was quiet, peaceful, unknowing of what was about to take place—*the next* First 48. Houses in this part of town were fucking massive—antebellum style, with front porches bigger than any apartment I'd ever lived in, and had columns that soared two, sometimes three stories tall. Most of the yards were secured behind a brick and wrought iron wall, some with gated entry. *Not this one.*

Every professionally manicured lawn offered enough mature trees and land between them to keep nosey neighbors from knowing all of your business. Especially in the dark. And this time of night, most of these folks were well on their way to la-la land, dreaming about stocks and bonds and quarterly bonuses.

I sat on my bike, parked beside the curb beneath a magnolia tree that was probably as old as the city, rooted just at the edge of the property line. What few seconds I had left before go-time was spent trying to convince myself that this would all be worth it in the long haul. He had his reasons; I had mine.

The stage had been set—all I had to do was walk on, find my target, pull the trigger, get back on my bike, and follow the highway home. Go back to Nashville. Except this time with an entirely new life and a padded wallet. Simple enough.

Unfortunately, there were a lot of what-ifs involved. Like, what if I got caught? *I'm shit out of luck.* Though Ivan reassured me I wouldn't. Or what if this guy I was supposed to take out wasn't home? *He will be.* What if he wasn't where he was supposed to be? *And I get caught?* Again, Ivan had studied his every move. *He'll be there. Trust me.*

291

Lyndsay Marie

I pulled the collar of my leather jacket tighter up around my neck and took in a deep breath of cold air, reminding myself this could be my last. *Ready or not.*

Right on time, Ivan's car slowly rolled by. The driver's-side blacked-out window slid down as he came to a rolling stop. Without an exchanged word, I reached out and into his window, taking the gun from his barely outstretched hand. As he drove off, I tucked it into my waistband behind my back.

Brake lights flashed in my side mirror. Once. Twice. This was it, the moment I'd lost every wink of sleep over for the last thirty-something hours.

I rested my bike on its kickstand, swung my leg over, then made my way up the edge of the driveway to the side entry door. As per Ivan, I could see the shadowy outline of my target fumbling around the kitchen, probably tidying things up, getting ready to call it a night.

A part of me felt like I'd been set up, like this night was by design because it all felt way too easy. Another part of me thought maybe Ivan really just knew this guy well and had beef with him that he didn't want to handle himself, which wouldn't surprise me.

Either way, none of that mattered. My job was to pull the trigger, not ask questions. Not out loud, anyway.

I backed off and stood on a strip of grass that ran alongside the driveway, trying to stay lost in the shadows. I hid in the darkness, just beyond the beam of light that illuminated from the kitchen window.

I watched the large, shadowy figure move past the door. The kitchen light turned off. I was about to make my move until the side door flung open, and I almost shit my pants. My feet sunk down into the soft grass as I carefully and quietly took two steps backward, pressing my back flat against the wooden fence. Someone came out with a bag full of trash and tossed it into a can beside the door.

I didn't get a good look at him because, one, I was wearing my helmet, and two, I'd gotten out of the way as fast as fucking possible. I could only assume he was my target.

The door closed as the man went back inside. The porch light went off, shrouding the driveway in pitch-black darkness. I knew I had to move even faster now. Per Ivan, I had less than thirty seconds to unlock that door and get inside before the security alarm had been set for the night once the kitchen light had gone off.

He didn't account for the trash being taken out.

I secured my helmet firmly on my head and pulled the mirrored face shield up so I could see. As I stepped up to the door, I adjusted my leather gloves tighter onto my hands and got to work.

I'd picked a lot of locks in my time, long before this moment, so I was confident unlocking this door was going to be a walk in the park. A few slips of my tool, and *bingo*. The handle turned, and the door opened with ease. I carefully stepped inside the house and closed the door behind me.

The house was mostly dark, save for a few night-lights sprinkled throughout, shining a warm, soft glow in little pockets—the formal dining room, eat-in kitchen, and one on the far side in what I could only assume was the living room. My instructions were to enter through the side door, make my way around the front of the house near the front door—my exit point—and catch the target before he went to bed. If I stayed at the bottom of the staircase, I wouldn't have any issues spotting my target or making my exit.

Seeing as how things had already gone askew when my target had decided to take out the trash, I wasn't entirely confident that the rest of this assignment would go off without a single hitch. *Too late now*. I was already inside his house. I just fucking prayed that I wasn't the one who ended up shot for breaking and entering.

I held my breath as I rounded the corner into the living room. I stood silently in the shadows at the bottom of the stairs, waiting to make my next move. I watched my target as he appeared on the far side of the house, then as he started to make his way down a long hallway that led toward what I'd been told was his bedroom. His back was to me as he walked away, but there was a familiar feeling to him that I couldn't quite put my finger on.

I pulled my face shield down over my eyes as I reached for the gun I had tucked behind my back. It was already unlocked, loaded, and ready for action. Ivan said there wouldn't be time for safety. *He was right*. My window of opportunity was small and shrinking with each step my target took away from me. With an outstretched arm, I aimed my gun chest level at my target.

"Showtime," I finally spoke out loud before he disappeared into his bedroom.

When I said the words, the man stopped and turned around. "Excuse me?"

Bang.

One shot, no hesitation, no questions.

That was it. My job was done.

Except I didn't feel relief.

I felt…confused. And sadness. Anger. *So much anger.* All the wrong emotions washed over me.

And for the second time in my life, I wanted to kill Ivan. I didn't know exactly why I felt that way…yet.

I watched as my target clutched onto his chest, blood pooling over the front of his white cotton T-shirt, slowly running between his fingers and down his forearms.

Then recognition hit me like a bolt of fucking lightning as he fell to his knees.

I'd been set up to take out the only man I'd ever trusted and respected besides my own brother.

I'd just shot and killed Elliott.

I'd been set up.

I stood frozen solid in fear when I was supposed to be quietly slipping out through the front door to jump back on my bike, swinging past Ivan, who would be parked in the same spot as earlier, and swapping out my gun for a backpack full of cash, then heading east.

But I couldn't move.

All I could do was watch as one of the best men I'd ever known took his last breath on this Earth, all because of me.

Lyndsay Marie

As my brain tried to process the million and one thoughts running through it, the sound of a female's voice let out a blood-curdling scream, piercing through the static white noise. It was the scream of someone who should never have been in the house because I was assured my target would be alone.

Fuck. Fuck. Fuck.

I glanced up the stairs into the darkness just as the only woman I'd ever loved stopped midway, clutching onto the railing, screaming, staring down at her dad, who was now lying face down on the hallway floor.

————◆————

I stood tucked myself behind the stage curtain and scanned the crowd. So far, nothing seemed obviously out of the ordinary. We had a room full of smiling faces, lost in conversation, booming laughter, most everyone with a drink or plate of food in hand.

Jameson gently tapped the mic to grab the audience's attention.

"Um, hi. Good evening, everyone." The room fell silent as she began to speak. "You'll have to forgive me. I'm a bit nervous, well, for obvious reasons, and I didn't write down any notes."

She nervously glanced around the room. As she turned her head, she caught a glimpse of me out of the corner of her eye. Her shoulders relaxed as soon as she spotted me. She smiled softly.

I didn't return the gesture.

My gaze cut away from James and locked in on Ivan.

There's been a change in plans.

TWENTY-EIGHT

Jameson

I involuntarily smiled, inside and out, just seeing him watching over me, knowing he was right there and, in a way, had been all along. He was none the wiser he was the reason for my happiness. Roman was once my whole world and had become even more than that now, if that were even possible. Even considering all that we'd been through—the lies, the deceit—I fully understood the nature of this business. Of *his* business. Roman had chosen me first, time and time again.

That alone was all the reassurance I needed to know that we belonged together. And as soon as I was done giving my obligatory thank-you speech and walked off this stage, I was going to tell him exactly I felt about him, that I wanted him to stay here and be with me.

I just needed to make it out of here alive first.

I focused on bringing myself back to reality and continued speaking.

Sweat poured from every pore on my skin. From the blinding spotlights to the thought of being in the same room as Kane or one of his cronies, knowing that I was their target, I just knew I'd ruined this satin dress with perspiration.

"Thank you again," I began concluding my speech, "each and every one of you for being here tonight for the Haunted Hearts Gala, for me, and, most importantly, for my dad. He would have loved to have seen this turn out. Enjoy the rest of your night."

I welcomed Kelly to the podium and waved to the cheering crowd as I walked off the stage and down the steps. My heart pounded against my chest with anticipation of running to Roman.

As I slipped behind the thick, bloodred velvet curtain where he'd once stood not five minutes ago, a large hand reached out of the darkness and grabbed me by my arm above my elbow. He pushed me in front of him, shoving me to walk forward.

At first, I thought it was Roman trying to take me away from the party, but the grip was aggressive and tight—*way too tight.*

Then, I felt the barrel of his gun dig into my ribs. I swallowed down bile. *This is it.*

The chatter and laughter of the party grew exponentially softer as I was being dragged away, and Kelly took the stage to give her whole spiel on food and drinks and donations.

"Ouch. That hurts," I cried out, trying to pull away. But the guy's fingers were like a vise wrapped around my

Lyndsay Marie

arm. I tugged again a little harder but to no avail. "Get off me."

As I tried to turn and see the man who had my arm in a death grip, a fabric hood flew over my head from behind me.

He jerked me around, steering me away from the event center. The laughter and music faded into the distance as he took us through an emergency exit. I may not have been able to see in front of me, but I could see through the bottom of the hood. We made our way down a narrow, abandoned utilitarian hallway that led to an unused stairwell.

The emergency exit door slammed shut behind us, and all noise from the party ceased to exist.

Something plastic sounded like it had popped and broken, and within a few seconds, emergency strobe lights flashed, and fire alarms blared.

Idiot. Now they'll really find me.

He quickly walked me down the stairs two at a time. I stumbled once, twisting my ankle and losing a shoe in the process. His grip held tight though, and he tugged me back upright.

"I don't know who the fuck you are or what you want," I yelled over the blaring alarms, "but I assure you, we won't get far. My men are already looking for me. You just cost yourself your own life."

Everything happened so damned fast. I never even had the chance to see who'd taken me, and he still hadn't mumbled a single word. But he seemed to know exactly where we were going; he knew his way around my casino. That much I did know.

It was all I could do to maintain composure, knowing I wouldn't be here long. Roman and Ivan at the very least were already looking for me. My men were probably in a panic upstairs. They'd have this building locked down, and every square inch of this property searched from top to bottom in one sweep—not a single soul in or out until I was found.

He forced me down the last stairwell, a metal grate with peeling paint and rusted handrail. We'd finally reached the underbelly of the casino, the lowest point of the boat and subsequently my life at the moment.

I hated it down here. Not that I came down often—about once a year was my due diligence.

Single fluorescent bulbs hung sparsely from the ceiling that was lined with miles and miles of bundles of exposed cables and wires, all powering everything above us. The floor itself was covered in at least two inches of river water and another two inches of silt and mud below that.

We'd reached our final destination as he pushed the final door in front of me open with a loud, gritting creak.

This time, I fought back. I pulled and tugged and screamed and kicked as loud and hard as I could, trying to fight him off. It was a futile effort. This man was twice my weight and had probably ten times the strength. Nobody would hear me down here.

"You are not about to lock me in a cage on my own goddamned boat."

He'd taken me to the isolation room. For some, it was just a mythical place that only existed in fiction.. Those who claimed to have seen it believed. Those who didn't thought, no way, because surely no one with an ounce of humanity would lock another human being in a four-by-four concrete cell while they stood in four inches of muck and merk. Unfortunately for a few unlucky others, it had once been their reality.

Now, it was mine.

The cold barrel of his gun now pressed against my temple.

"Shut the fuck up, Jameson," he threatened under his breath, "or I swear to god I will fucking shoot you."

My heart sank as tears filled my eyes when he finally spoke. Recognition hit me like a freight train. There was no way this was happening to me right now. No fucking way.

"Roman?" My voice cracked. "Wha—what are you doing to me?"

"Exactly as I'm told to do. It's just a job, right?"

Just a job? This could not be happening to me. This was all just a nightmare, and I'd wake up any second. I'd wake up on the beach, sun-kissed skin with a margarita in one hand, good book in the other.

Stay calm. I'd never get out of this if I let him or my emotions get the best of me. Regardless of his intent, I was *not* going to die tonight.

I slowly inhaled a deep, head-clearing breath. "You don't have the balls," I challenged through gritted teeth. "You never have."

He jerked me against him. "I had enough to kill your dad." His voice was deep and laced with a threatening promise. "Don't tempt me now."

TWENTY-NINE
Roman

"Wh—what?" Her words had gone from strong and threatening to weak and forced.

"You heard me. I didn't stutter."

"No, that's not true," she whispered.

"What part don't you believe? I killed Elliott."

"I'm not going in there," she attempted to protest.

I flicked the safety off. "The fuck you aren't."

This was the last place anyone wanted to go. Those who'd heard about it never wanted to see to believe; those who'd experienced it wished they hadn't.

It was a makeshift solitary confinement space where people were kept if they fucked up or got out of line. Some made it out; few did not. There was no overhead light, no window, no bed or seating. Just three walls, a cold, flooded floor, and a thick metal door with a cutout just big enough for airflow, small enough the person inside couldn't fit through it. Once the door was closed, the only way to get out was from the outside, and if the lights on the other side were shut off, the entire space went pitch-black.

I pushed her forward into the room. She lost balance, stumbling over her own feet, falling to the ground and landing with a splash.

"Why? Why are you doing this to me?" She tried to clamor to her feet but lost balance again, landing on her hands and knees.

"It's for your own good." Before she could try to stand up and make a run for it, I leveled my arm with the gun still in my hand, pointing it straight at her.

She fell on her ass and scurried backward, pressing herself against the wall.

It's a shame. That dress was so pretty on her.

I froze for a brief moment, just like before, second-guessing, doubting what I was about to do.

But I had to remind myself this was just a job. *Don't take it personally.*

I gave her one last look. Her eyes were tired and tearful in the dim lighting, silently begging me not to hurt her. I didn't *want* to do this—I had to. There was no other way.

She opened her mouth to make one final plea for her life.

Just before I slammed the door shut, I pulled the trigger.

THIRTY
Jameson

Loving Roman was like playing a game of trust fall—the game where you blindly fall backward on a hope and a prayer that your friend would catch you. You trust them not to let you hit the floor flat on your back.

Roman was that friend standing behind me, and I was the one letting go.

Just fall. I've got you.

Hesitantly, as the rules go, you start to lean back. Further and further, until eventually you reach the point of no return, trusting there's someone there to catch you before you hit the ground.

Except when I leaned back, I kept falling.

And falling.

And falling.

Down into a dark and lonely abyss. There was nobody there, no arms to catch me, no one to save me.

Trusting him again felt like I'd taken a swan dive off the top of the Empire State Building in complete free fall—no safety net, no parachute. Just me and my body versus gravity.

And I'd just landed face down on the sidewalk below.

THIRTY-ONE

Roman

Saying those words out loud, *I killed Elliott*, was liberating. I'd long wanted to get that off my chest, and damn did it feel like the weight of the world had been lifted off my shoulders.

Jameson, on the other hand, didn't agree. Her body went limp in my grasp when I'd finally confessed to her that I was the one who had killed her dad, her only living parent. The guilt and anger and pain that she must have felt coursing through her body all at once at my admission, knowing she'd been sleeping with the enemy all along, fucking gutted me.

I knew better. I'd warned her from the very beginning this was a bad idea, me and her, that we had no business being together.

Fuck.

Everything was finally coming together though. Soon enough, she'd understand. We all would. Right now, there were still a few loose ends that needed to be tied up.

I made my way back up to the ballroom. The place had mostly cleared out—a few people were still pushing their way toward the main entrance. Our own security had taken off, save for a few who were sweeping the room.

Several chairs had been tipped over. Wine flutes, cups, and plates had been dropped in place; other various pieces of trash and remnants from a good time littered the floor.

I hung back in a dark corner at the top of the hull stairs. The last thing I needed was for anyone to see or recognize me and wonder why I hadn't left yet.

"Where the fuck is he," I mumbled to myself as I scanned the massive room. I knew that piece of shit had to be around here somewhere. This was the singular moment of his career that would launch Kane to the top. He'd be the last man standing.

Except he wouldn't because he couldn't get to James anymore, and that was the one missing piece he needed to win this war. He'd have to settle for me in the meantime.

With my gun in a tight grip, pointed to the floor yet still very ready to fire at a moment's notice, I walked out to the middle of the massive empty room, exposing myself out in the open. Emergency lights flashed from every corner, and alarms blared with an ear-assaulting echo.

"Come on out, you piece of shit," I called out loud. "I know you're here."

He'd better have fucking been here, or this was a whole lot of planning and organizing for nothing.

I stood in the middle of the room, making myself a wide-open target. It was a huge risk 'cause if Kane had decent aim and if he wanted to, he could take me out with a single shot, right here, right now.

"You clean up well for hired help," I heard Kane's voice come from behind me.

I raised my gun as I turned around, coming face-to-face with the man of the hour.

"I see you dressed for the event yourself."

Kane brushed his hands down the front of his suit at invisible lint, then fumbled with the buttons on his sleeve. "Wouldn't miss it for the world."

"Bold of you to brave this alone."

His fumbling hand stilled and cut his eyes up at me. "Who says I'm here alone?"

"If it were me trying to take down the leader of an empire," I said, ignoring his question, "I would've at least come with some kind of backup."

River had done extensive research on Kane over the last twenty-four hours. He'd already warned me there would be someone else, but River would have my back should shit hit the fan. There was no way Kane would god own without a fight, so a mess would surely ensue.

"Speaking of empire, where is the lady of the night? I was looking forward to seeing her up close in that ball gown."

This motherfucker.

I steadied my aim, maintaining clear and precise focus on my target. One slight move out of line was all it would take to end him, and I would have had I known where the other guy was hiding. I needed him out in the open. Kane and his accomplice weren't even my biggest problems. Right now, I couldn't hear shit over the squelching of the alarms to know if someone *was* coming up behind me, and I couldn't turn my back on Kane. I'd just have to wait and find out the hard way.

"First, you lose your boats; now, you lose your target. Damn, Kane, seems like you're good at misplacing some pretty important shit for someone who runs a multibillion-dollar-a-year business."

He let out a barely audible soft chuckle. "You're quite entertaining, you know that?"

"Why didn't you take her out when you had the chance?"

He grinned. "A magician never reveals his secrets."

There was no way he had any other plan. Even if he did, he couldn't get to her now. Nothing else mattered.

"Keep your secrets. You'll never get to her."

"I beg to differ."

Just then, something hard pressed to the back of my head. *Fucking alarms.*

"Classic move," I said to Kane, who stood as casually as could be, like he had other shit to do and this was infringing on his time.

"You didn't think I was going to get any blood on my hands, did you?"

Lyndsay Marie

I'd never taken Kane for a complete idiot, but he probably never planned on my being here. This was single-handedly the moment I'd been waiting for.

"Not mine."

Without thinking, as if on autopilot, I tossed my gun down to the floor toward Kane. Then, in one calculated move, I reached behind my head, grabbed the guy by the wrist, and pulled him forward at the same time I ducked and twisted his arm behind his back.

My gun went off, and the guy in front of me went limp. *Too fucking predictable.*

I pulled his gun from his dead hand as his body dropped to the floor and leveled it at Kane.

My own gun was now pointed directly at me.

"You're good," he mused. "Seems like I may have underestimated you."

I cocked the dead guy's gun. This shit was getting old and needed to end.

Just as I was about to pull the trigger, an explosion went off somewhere in the distance. The floor shook beneath our feet. *What the fuck, River?*

I made the rookie mistake of taking my eyes off Kane for 0.5 seconds. Just long enough for him to launch himself at me, taking me to the floor with a hit to the ribs. He landed on top of me, squishing the breath out of my chest. My gun went flying from my hand.

Well, shit.

No worries. I wasn't about to get my ass beat by a man who had probably twenty years on me.

We wrestled around, tossing punches, taking hits from each other, until I was able to get my own gun back from him. I managed to shove him off me and onto his side, but he got up and came back for more. I took my shot as he lurched forward, but he managed to avoid my bullet. *Fuck.*

Seems like I'd been the one to underestimate him.

Where the fuck was River? He was supposed to be my damned backup here.

As Kane knocked into me, I planted my feet into the floor to keep my balance but fell as searing pain shot through me.

"What the hell?" I cursed to myself as I landed on my back.

As I lay there, Kane hovered over me, bloody knife in his hand. "Never bring a gun to a knife fight or whatever the hell it is they say," he smirked.

I grabbed onto my side. That motherfucker stabbed me. *Shit*, I did not see that coming. *Who's the rookie now?*

"Christ, what kind of knife did you use? That hurt like a bitch," I said between painful breaths. This wasn't my first time being stabbed...or second or third. Just the first time it damn near debilitated me.

Kane braced himself on a knee as he bent down and hovered over me. "Pussy. It's not even that big."

As if shit weren't bad enough, not having a gun, now subdued by the pain shooting through my side, Kane shoved the tip of my gun into the knife wound.

"Ahh. Fuck," I hissed through gritted teeth.

"Not so tough, are we? And to think, someone thought you'd be the end to all of this."

As he stood up, another shot rang out over the still loud-as-fuck fire alarms. *River*. Thank fuck.

Kane froze mid-air, a look of shock on his face. He fell down to the floor, half-slumped on top of me.

"It's about time, asshole," I said as I shoved Kane's now lifeless body and haphazardly pushed him onto the floor by my side.

"You're welcome."

I rolled over and attempted to stand upright. I hunched over on my knees, gripping my side. "Nice shot."

Josephine half shrugged. "Ain't missed one yet."

"Yeah, well, you didn't have to do that."

"It was an easy decision. He was a shitty nephew."

"Yeah. Well thanks for only ever throwing a tomato at me."

"It's never too late." She smiled.

"Noted. Now, get out of here. Go out of the main entrance to the parking lot. I'll be right there."

"What about you? You can't even stand up."

"Don't worry about me. I'll be fine. I'm gonna do one more sweep of the place, make sure there's no stragglers or people hiding out in the bathroom."

She shook her head. "Sounds like that's their problem for not leaving, but if you insist."

"Speaking of, why didn't you leave when the alarms went off?"

"'Cause nobody tells me what to do."

Josephine left, and I forced myself to stand upright. "Walk it off. Don't be a bitch," I said to myself.

Fucking Christ. Judging by the size of the knife Kane had used and the force he'd shoved it into me, there was no way I didn't have some kind of internal damage.

I swiped up my gun and started limping my way around the event center. I called out for River as I shuffled along, but he didn't respond.

Just as I was getting ready to make my way toward the main entrance, another explosion went off. This time, the chandeliers shook, and plaster rained down in pieces from the ceiling.

A third explosion went off, then a fourth. They were coming more frequently and louder than the one before. This time, the pillars near the exit to the casino, aka my escape, fell over, blocking the doors. Then the lights went out.

"Fuck, River. The hell are you doing"

The only other way out was through a service hall that led to the kitchen and out to the docks. It wasn't an ideal getaway plan, but it was my only option.

Sink or swim. Those were literally my only two options at this point—literally. Sink with the boat or swim with the gar.

I made it to the docks just as a series of more explosions went off. I jumped over the guardrail to get to the rusted ladder hanging over the side and almost threw up from the pain.

Lyndsay Marie

Fuck it.

I didn't make it this far to give up now.

As I lowered myself down into the cool, murky water, an unexpected clanging noise forced me to stop. I froze in place, already knee-deep in water, with a death grip on the ladder rung. I looked up in the direction of the noise. A push broom had been knocked over.

"What in the hell are you doing out here?"

THIRTY-TWO

Stuck in the hull of my own boat. Of all the places to be.

Cussing.

Screaming.

Kicking at cold, muddy water. *I knew I should have had this shit drained out when maintenance had mentioned to me that it needed to be done.* It wasn't exactly at the top of my priority list—ever.

That motherfucker shot me. He actually fucking shot me! "You've got piss-poor aim, you piece of shit," I screamed through the tiny little hole in the door at no one because no one else was down here but me. They wouldn't even hear me if I wanted them to.

I felt the spot where I'd been hit. There was nothing there but a spot of torn fabric. "Did he fire a blank?"

It was a damned good thing one of Leon's security members had Kevlar sewn into my dress. No one had even thought of it, myself included.

I was so confused…and hurt. Emotionally and physically. The spot where I'd been hit on the ribs was tender and probably starting to bruise.

This was literal hell. There was no way out.

The room Roman piece-of-fucking-traitorous-shit Stone had locked me inside of was the equivalent of a jail cell in the bottom of a submarine, and the only way out was from the outside.

And now, the goddamned fire alarms were going off upstairs.

"I swear to god," I screamed out loud, banging my fists on the door, "if I ever get out of here, I'm going to choke the life out of you with my bare fucking hands."

Why? *Why*? I trusted him! I left my life in his hands, and *this* was what I got?

And Ivan? Oh, that motherfucker. *He* did this, too. He was just as guilty as anyone. "I know a guy," I mocked him. "I'm killing both of them."

As I stood there in total darkness and silence, the only noise came from my own mouth…and then it hit me all at once. Roman had just admitted to killing my dad.

Despite his admission, I still didn't want to believe him. But what he said had started making sense. I wasn't supposed to be home. I was in Aspen on a last-minute vacation. My dad had called me the day after I arrived; he said he needed me back home for emergency family business. Since everything was handled in person, I didn't question him. I hopped on the next flight out and came home.

What had started out as just another normal night had quickly turned into a series of total chaos that was a mere blur now.

I remember talking to my dad in his office. We'd discussed a recent shipment of goods that had come through his port—a shipment that was an absolute no-no for him—the night that I'd left for Colorado. He needed to act fast, so he'd made the decision to reroute that shipment to the proper authorities, but we all knew once he did, it would start an all-out war.

He was right.

We agreed to regroup in the morning at his office and devise a game plan. I got ready for bed and turned in for the night first. It wasn't two hours later that I was woken up to the very familiar sound of a gunshot. I flew out of bed and ran downstairs toward my dad's bedroom.

I stopped dead in my tracks halfway down the stairs when I saw him. My dad first, then the intruder.

It was too dark to make out any real details of the other guy. I just remembered him being a tall, shadowy figure standing between the bottom of the stairs and the front door wearing a…bike helmet.

Oh. My. God.

He did it.

It was him.

Lyndsay Marie

This was why Roman didn't want to tell me where he'd been. Who knew if he was even telling me the truth that he'd been in Nashville this whole time.

Roman was so full of shit.

I sank to the floor, now completely barefoot, still in a full-length ball gown, and sat down in the water in defeat. Confused as I was, things had slowly started to come together and make some sense. Well, everything except for why. And Ivan's involvement. He *had* to know something. I wondered if he'd had my dad killed? What I didn't get was how my dad was the one who'd sent Roman away. Hell, maybe that was a lie to protect Ivan.

"It's complicated," I mocked Roman to myself. "I bet it is, asshole."

This was absolute horse shit. There was no way out. The room Roman piece-of-fucking-traitorous-shit Stone had locked me inside of was the equivalent of a jail cell in the bottom of a submarine. The walls were metal, the door locked from the outside. Never in a million years did I think I would be the one stuck in the hull of my own boat.

As I sat there, an explosion went off in the distance, causing the floor and walls to vibrate.

"Roman!" I stood up and threw myself into the door. It didn't budge. "Roman! Ivan? Please. I'm down here. Get me out!"

I grabbed the bars covering the little window and shook the door. It was useless. That room had been designed for permanence.

Another explosion went off upstairs, this one a hell of a lot closer than I was comfortable with. Loose dirt and debris fell from the ceiling.

"Oh my god," I whined on the verge of tears. "Help!" I banged against the metal door until my hands stung.

I blew out a defeated breath, trying to collect my thoughts. The old storage room door at the other end of the room slowly opened with a deafening screeching sound.

I slapped my hand over my mouth to stop myself from yelling for help again because if someone had just opened that door, it meant that they'd been down here with me the entire time.

They'd heard me all along.

Oh shit. Fuck. Someone's out there. Don't panic.

I held my breath, completely frozen.

I couldn't move. There was nowhere for me to go. Even if I could have, they would hear and find me locked inside of here.

Another series of explosions went off, this time each one closer and closer above my head. The last one was loud enough to ripple the water around my ankles and kill the power in an already barely lit space. The space went pitch-black.

Please don't find me. Please don't find me.

Whoever it was that was out there was going to have to speak first and find me. Whether by explosion or the hands of someone else, I was not ready to die. Not tonight.

Lyndsay Marie

My heart pounded against my chest as the sound of feet shuffling, splashing water, grew louder and louder, closer to me.

"Jameson," a voice whispered into the darkness.

The latch on the door in front of me released with a loud scratching sound as the handle was turned upward.

I scurried backward away from the opening door, water sloshing around me, and pressed my back to the wall.

That voice. This had to be a joke. A sick and twisted joke. Bile rose up from my throat; I swallowed down the burning liquid.

"James—Jameson, say something."

No.

No, no, no.

I couldn't. I didn't want to. That voice—*his* voice—was like a ghost from my past that had come back to haunt me.

"Maggie-J, come on. I need to get you out of here, and I can't see."

Maggie-J. He called me by my nickname, one that only he'd ever used. It was a name he'd given me when I was just a kid. He'd hired someone named Jameson, and anytime someone said his name, I answered them. It confused me, so my dad started calling me a mixed-up combination of my first and middle name—Jameson Magnolia.

"Say something," he pleaded. "Please."

What difference would it make now? I'd already spent the past depressed in constant fight or flight mode,

322

then dragged down into the literal pits of hell with a gun pressed to my head by the only man I had ever trusted and loved. If this was how it ended, by my speaking up, then so be it. *Let's just get this shit over with.*

I swallowed down a massive lump that had formed in my throat before forcing out the only word my mind could form.

"Dad?"

THIRTY-THREE

Jameson

He was alive?

He was alive! My dad hadn't been dead this entire time? I'd never been more relieved and confused and hurt at the same time. So many emotions and questions ran through me, even more than before.

He reached out into the dark and grabbed me by the hand and pulled me out of the isolation room.

"Stop!" I tried pulling away from him, but he gripped onto me tighter.

"We're running out of time."

"I'm not going with you." I tugged again. "Not until you tell me what's going on!"

"Later. Right now, you're going to have to trust me. Please come on. We don't have a lot of time—actually, we don't have any.

He pulled me by the arm, practically dragging me. "Can you at least slow down? I can't see shit." We were sprinting through ankle-deep water, slipping and sliding in thick, silky mud beneath our feet.

I lost my footing and fell at one point, but he lifted me back up.

"Almost there."

I hadn't the slightest clue where he thought he was taking me because the direction we were heading led right into a storage room at the dead end of the hull. I almost didn't want to trust him, and a part of me didn't.

I heard the metal grating as the storage room door shut behind me. "Dad, what's going on? We can't get out this way."

"Yes, we can." I heard the click of a button, and a tiny flashlight came on, illuminating the small room. My dad's face came into view.

"It's you," I whispered.

He smiled. "Yup. It's me."

I threw myself into him in a hug. His arms wrapped tightly around me, squeezing extra hard. "As much as I need this, this actually hurts like a bitch. But I think you're right. Neither of us is gonna be left if I don't get us out of here."

I pulled away. "Okay. Okay, but how?"

He walked over to the back wall and pushed on it. It swung inward, revealing a dark space. He held out his hand. "Come. Let's go."

"I—what in the world?"

Lyndsay Marie

I took his hand, hiked my dress up with the other, and stepped over the bottom of the doorway. The space was a long, narrow hallway barely wide enough for one person and zero lighting that ran what felt like the length of the entire barge.

More explosions went off above us.

"James, we need to run. Now."

"Okay, Dad. Let's go."

My dad had never steered me wrong, with the exception of the last twelve months, but given my current circumstances, I was left with no choice but to trust him. Considering I had zero idea where I was or where we were heading or that this hallway existed, and now it sounded like my casino was under attack from the inside, all I could do was let go.

After running for what felt like forever, we made it to the end. "A ladder? You want me to climb a ladder?"

"It's either that or sink. You pick."

I blew a breath at my wet, dirty, disheveled hair that had fallen across my face. "Fuck it," I said as I gripped onto the sides of the ladder and stepped up on the first metal rung. "Don't let me fall."

He flashed the light at me. "Then don't fall…and whatever you do, don't stop."

I looked up and could see a literal light at the end of a tunnel because this skinny metal ladder had been welded inside the walls of an actual tunnel that soared straight upward. Eventually, I reached the top and was able to pull myself out. My dad climbed out right behind me.

"Dad, where in the hell are we?"

I stood up and looked around. We were at the far other end of the property on the opposite end of the event center. It looked like we'd just climbed out of a manhole cover in the grass.

"Not far enough away. We need to be out there." He pointed toward the parking lot that was now full of partygoers, staff members, and a few emergency vehicles.

We made our way out to the crowd, looking for anyone we'd recognize.

Ivan spotted us first. "Shit, I didn't think y'all were gonna make it."

"I didn't either," Dad told him as he wrapped his arm cautiously around me.

"Well, glad you're here. People are already talking, whispering and shit. I don't know what to tell them."

"I'll handle it." Dad faced me. "You okay?"

I grabbed on to my side where I'd been hit with a blank. "Yeah, I think so. It'll heal."

"I know that was a lot, and we have a lot to talk about."

I didn't know what to say. Less than a year ago, I'd held a funeral for my dad. I mourned over him. I fought for him. Hell, I tried to kill someone who I thought was the reason for his death, and he wasn't even the right guy?

I still didn't know my ass from a hole in the ground and was left with more questions than answers at the moment. Only one question stuck out the most. "Where have you been?"

"Hiding." He sighed. "You remember the night I—?"

"How could I forget?" I cut him off. I knew exactly what night he was referring to. "I watched my dad die in front of me."

"And I'm sorry for that. But Kane needed to be stopped."

Dad had already caught him moving people once years and years ago, before I was even born. Back then, they'd come to some kind of civil agreement that Dad wouldn't interfere with Kane's transactions with the assurance that Kane wouldn't move any more people.

While my dad ran a business in an industry that practically thrived on human sacrifice to a certain degree, those lives were here voluntarily. They knew the rules, the stakes, and the consequences.

Trafficking victims were just that—victims. They didn't ask for what they'd gone through.

I guess once my dad learned that Kane had gotten back on his bullshit, he wasn't having any of it anymore.

"This still doesn't make any sense."

"I know, and it will. That night, I randomly picked off one of Kane's boats, you know, make sure he was behaving. He wasn't. I'd hit the jackpot and chosen the right one. When we cleared it, we found women and children. I'd had enough of this shit. So I made a few phone calls to my connections and called in a few favors with some authorities in very high places. Our operation was born almost overnight. The problem was I was only given twelve months to make it happen, start to finish, otherwise I'd be pulled from our ops, and all the higher-ups within every three-letter agency involved would take over."

"Oh my god, Dad. I don't even know what to say."

"I know," he continued. "The long and short of it is I've been under in my own self-made witness protection program working day in and day out to get to the source of this ring and bust it up or, at the very least, stop it on Kane's end. It took longer than expected when he disappeared a few months in, and his boats stopped moving. I figured he was onto us. Turns out he'd gone on a vacation to Italy for six months. He just got back last month, and we kicked everything into high gear."

My heart sank. I thought back to around that time Kane came back from his vacation. That was when we found one of our security guards dead on his golf cart.

"That's when he killed Briggs. Was that because of you?" He looked at me but didn't answer. "Dad…"

"I'm sorry, Maggie-J, but we did what had to be done. Not letting a single one of his transactions slip by unsearched was our number one priority."

"I understand." Kind of. I knew my dad had good intentions, but what the fuck? "What about that guy? The one that came to see me?"

He sighed. "Y'all showed up at the house that night, and I panicked. I didn't need y'all nosing around again and blowing my cover. You know I don't like to play dirty unless I have to. He used to be one of Kane's. Ivan knew Kane had gotten rid of him, so he hunted him down, used him."

My stomach dropped. "I guess, but was it necessary to fake your own death? That seems a little extreme and flat-out wrong. I feel like you could've come up with a better plan."

"I know, Maggie-J. I'm sorry. If we wanted everything to play out according to the deal we'd worked up, I needed to disappear and not just go under. Kane had to think I'd fucked with the wrong person or pissed off someone else and they took care of me, which saved him the trouble. As soon as he got back and his boats started moving again, we searched each and every one that passed, and when we found what we were looking for, we took it."

"He thought it was me, didn't he? He thought I was the one who had interfered with his shipments."

"Yup," Ivan joined in. "We hadn't accounted for that just yet, but we knew then shit was about to hit the fan because that wasn't part of the original plan. We had to think fast and act even faster. That's when Elliott called me and said I needed to start working on convincing you to let me get some outside help."

"Roman?" I asked, my words barely a whisper.

I glanced around. There were even fewer people here now, and not one of them Roman. *Where the hell is he?*

"He was the only person besides Ivan that I knew I could trust with you...with everything."

Holy shit. My dad only did what he thought he had to do to protect me and entire lives of people he didn't know.

"I'm really sorry I dragged you through all of this, but it needed to be done to stop Kane permanently. I knew we could do it, and a hell of a lot faster than anyone else."

"So you used him? You took advantage of him this entire time? What if something had actually happened to him?"

"That was just a risk we had to take. He knew well what he was getting into when Ivan called him back. It's his job."

I couldn't believe it—any of it. Even though I was beyond grateful for my dad to be alive, grateful that I had Roman back and *he* was alive…I think.

"Y'all let me think he was *dead*! I thought—fuck, I need to sit down."

My dad walked me over to a curb. The tightness of the corset of the dress squeezed my chest as I carefully sat down.

"So what happens next? I mean, this can't just be the end as if none of this happened?"

Dad smirked. "I told you—I called in a few favors that were owed to me. We worked out a deal. Clean slate for everyone."

That wasn't surprising. My dad had friends and connections in *very* high places. It was how he'd managed to keep Emerald Haze open, and I'm not talking the casino side of the business.

"Josephine!" I spotted her across the parking lot at the edge of the crowd, looking as lost as the rest of us. I got up and ran toward her. "Josephine! Where's Roman? Have you seen him?"

"Yeah, he's still inside."

"Inside? What do you mean he's still inside? Why isn't he out here yet?"

"Don't know. He said he was gonna do one last sweep, make sure everyone is out."

"What? No! Have you heard those explosions?"

We looked up at the casino. Dark smoke billowed from the roof of the event center, getting lost in an even darker sky.

"Yes, ma'am. I told him I didn't like—"

Her words were cut short as a series of even more explosions went off, one after the other. The ground shook as the entire event center side of the casino blew clean off its foundation and separated from the building.

Josephine wrapped her arms around me, and we ducked down as ash and pieces of the building rained down on us.

Our eyes locked. We had the exact same thought.

Even more fire truck and emergency vehicle sirens blared in the distance. The entire parking lot had been blocked off by yellow tape and police officers on foot creating a barricade. Most of the patrons had been cleared out, save for a few who were being interviewed by police.

Josephine and I held on to each other as we stood and watched a third of the building tilt at an angle, then finally break off from the main building.

"Shit."

"Shit is right," Josephine echoed.

My dad walked up from behind and wrapped his arm around me. "Damn. That's gonna hurt."

"Dad! Really?"

"What?"

"What? We still don't have Roma—" As I said his name, I spotted him. He was limping his way across the parking lot on the other side of the building from the explosion.

"Roman!" I screamed his name as I took off running toward him as fast as I could with bare feet and a shredded Valentino ball gown that had literally been dragged through the mud and across asphalt.

"Babe" was all he mustered as I threw myself into his arms. "Wait, wait—hold on. Fuck," he hissed.

He winced as I pulled back, looking him over. "What is it? What's wrong? Are you hurt?"

"Just a little."

"Where?"

He pulled the front of his jacket to the side. The entire side of his white button-down shirt was soaked in bright red blood.

"Oh, god. Roman! You're bleeding!"

"I'll be fine. Here, take this." He reached into the inside pocket of his jacket and pulled out a kitten. He handed it to me.

"Where in the hell did you get this thing?"

Lyndsay Marie

"It's a long story." He put his arm over my shoulders on his good side and squeezed me into him. "Fuck, James, you stink."

I held up the fluffy orange-and-white, blue-eyed kitten and nuzzled my nose against its cold, wet one. The kitten let out a high-pitched meow.

"Comes with the territory."

THIRTY-FOUR

Roman

This had no doubt been the longest night in my entire career. Scratch that—my entire fucking life. I'd been close to fatally stabbed by someone weaker than me, damn near blown up by my own brother, who I'd yet to see. I'd kidnapped my girlfriend at gunpoint and shot her. Now, I had a fuck ton of explaining to do.

"I need to sit down."

"Let me help you." Jameson limped along beside me.

We walked over to where most of the crew had gathered. I was relieved to see Josephine had made it out because I just knew she was going to wait for me at the main entrance.

"Have you seen River?" I asked Elliott since he was the only person besides myself who knew that he was even here.

So far, the only people I'd seen were Jameson, Elliott, Ivan, Josephine, Leon, and a few others from security. Kelly and Chris weren't far away.

"River?" Jameson asked as she sat down beside me with her new furry friend curled up in her arms. "Your brother?"

"The one and only." I carefully shrugged out of my suit jacket, balled it up, and pressed it into my side. "Fuck, this hurts like a bitch."

"Haven't seen him yet," Elliott answered. "Glad you're okay. Well, mostly."

"Thanks."

Jameson stared down at my blood-soaked shirt. "You need to go to the hospital and get checked out."

"Yeah, I will…eventually." I wasn't worried about me.

EMS would be here until the last person had been checked out. What worried me was that no one had seen River, and I knew he didn't up and leave.

"I'm a little heartbroken y'all went behind my back and devised your own scheme, but it probably saved me an ulcer or two," Ivan said as he lit up what was probably his tenth cigarette.

"Yeah, you're welcome," I told him. "But I knew after we talked the other day that shit you had planned wasn't going to work. Not with me involved."

The day I'd walked out on Ivan talking on the phone, I knew there was more to the story, and he was gonna start spilling shit. If he wanted me to be his puppet, the very least he could do was tell me what the fuck was going on.

He laid it all out on the table.

Last year, when Elliott found out that Kane was still running people, he'd had enough. Elliott devised a plan and called in some owed favors. In order to do what had to be done, he needed to disappear. So he faked his own death. That was where I came into play. Ivan hired me to take out a hit on someone that he'd told me at the time was interfering with the family business. He'd just left out *who* it was that he wanted taken out—and it made no difference to me at the time—because he knew that if he'd told me about any of what his and Elliott's plans were, I never would have gone along with it. Not knowing Jameson was involved.

The night that I rolled up to Magnolia Estate, I still had no idea it was Elliott's house. I'd never been. All I was given was an address and time, along with a new bike and backpack full of cash, to disappear.

I carried on just like I'd been instructed to do— break into the side door, find my target on his way to bed, single shot to the chest would do just fine. Except my target hadn't been alone as I was told he would be.

Jameson was there. She'd been strategically called home early from her vacation due to needing help with the business, something she'd never questioned. What they'd needed was for her to already be home, witness her father's death, and take over the family business that night. Otherwise, she might never have returned home.

Lyndsay Marie

It's just a job. Ivan had assured me that was all this was—a job. I usually never questioned him or his weird requests, not until it involved my own disappearance. He told me once I completed the hit, I was to get on my new bike and head to another address he'd given me. *Don't call me; I'll call you.*

I'd been lying low in Nashville for the last year as though I'd never existed.

Getting the fuck out of Dodge wasn't the problem; it was seeing Elliott's face in the dim lighting from the night-light when I spoke the word "showtime," the code word Ivan told me needed to be the last thing our victim heard before I pulled the trigger on him.

His life or yours. That was Ivan's promise to me. I chose him.

Then I heard her...that scream. I knew I'd fucked up.

I'd lived with the pain and grief of that night for the longest time. Hell, I almost took my own life at one point because of it, but I couldn't. Not knowing that Jameson would still be out there and possibly need me one day. Whether she'd thought I was dead or alive at the time didn't matter. I'd still have been here for her.

Thank fuck I'd held out as long as I did because once Kane got back from Italy, he immediately started moving people again. Elliott knew his window of opportunity to end it was really fucking small. Initially, Elliott and Ivan had planned on working with their team of feds to invade his property and take him down, but when the first boat disappeared, Kane immediately jumped all over Jameson's ass and went after her and her people. They had to switch things up.

That's where I came in...or back.

Knowing Kane loved to make a spectacle of every damned thing he did, they betted on him coming after James at her own fundraiser. Since I was still on payroll, Ivan called me back to Mississippi, knowing once I'd made it to the property and gotten all the details of my *job*, that I'd be more than willing to risk my life.

After learning everything from Ivan, I knew we couldn't take Kane on our own. Elliott and Ivan were way over their heads, even with the outside help they'd had. The only problem was I still didn't know how much I could trust Ivan since he'd already schemed behind my back and set me up once before. So I called in my brother, River, for reinforcements. I had the brawn; he had the brains. River was the intelligence guy and a chameleon of sorts. I knew if I couldn't get through this with his help, then it would never happen.

As soon as he got here, I had him do a deep dive into Elliott. *Find him* was all I asked. Lo and behold, he did...hiding out inside his own damned house—the one James and I had staked out because I just *knew* something was amiss with that place.

Turned out I was right.

The problem then became how to get to Elliott without anyone else knowing. But I put my faith into River that he could do it, and he did. I didn't ask.

The new plan: let Ivan and Elliott's original operation continue as normal, or at least let them think that was what was happening. The reality was only River, Elliott, and I knew the new plan. I didn't want anyone else to find out because it was the best way to keep James safe. I didn't want her standing front and center on her own stage like a sitting duck, knowing that at any moment, Kane or one of his men could end her. Elliott agreed for obvious reasons.

River went undercover in I didn't even know how many roles at Emerald Haze over the span of two days, but he did. He pulled it off. One of Leon's security being one of them. He'd made sure that her dress had been reinforced with layers of Kevlar during a last-minute alteration, and assured her that it would be in her best interest not to tell anyone. Not even me.

Except I did know.

Once she took center stage, I knew we only had about three to five minutes of vulnerability, and if she made it off there safely, then we'd continue with my plan and not allow her to make it to the closing speech. Which was exactly where we'd anticipated Kane finishing the job.

I grabbed her as she came down the side steps and hauled her to the hull. I had just a few minutes to get her down there before Ivan or Leon and his men went on a manhunt looking for her.

Elliott had told River about an escape route he'd created down there, one of several on the property—some of which he'd been using to sneak into and out of his own office that James had been using. She didn't have a damned clue he'd even been in and out of there. Turns out she wasn't entirely crazy; her dad had been in and out of there on occasion, accessing things he needed but couldn't just up and take with him. Said he'd almost got caught by her once. That shit had me laughing.

Once I had her in isolation, locked up and safe, I had to do something to get her to shut up. She was going to draw unwanted attention to us, and I didn't need anyone finding us down there, fucking up our entire plan.

So, I shot her.

I did it for a few reasons. One, if I'd shot at her, I'd have risked the bullet ricocheting off the wall and actually hitting her somewhere she was unprotected. Two, I knew doing it would stun her into silence, even for a brief moment, and not leave her with any permanent physical damage. Three, it gave Elliott the signal that she was in place, and I was heading back up, and he needed to get her the hell out of there.

Shooting the love of my life was not something I was comfortable doing, but River had assured me repeatedly that she would be fine if she didn't move and I didn't miss.

No pressure.

The plan worked. She got quiet from the shock of it all.

Then she got loud.

Really fucking loud.

I heard her screaming at me from all the way to the top of the stairs.

I left her down there with Elliott, who would then get her out another way. I knew she'd have a million

341

questions, none of which I could even answer at the time, but she'd at least have her dad back.

As I made it to the exit to head back into the ballroom, I pulled the fire alarm. That was only one way I knew to get the entire place evacuated as quickly as possible. It was also River's cue that James was in place and he could start working on things on his end.

Elliott had documents and a hard drive that, if in the wrong hands, would end his entire business despite having law enforcement and city leaders in his back pocket, and he hadn't had the chance to get them from his office. Not to mention the files that River inadvertently accessed during his search for Elliott that were, no doubt, not meant for anyone else's eyes. Even more obscure than the ones I had access to. So we agreed to blow the place up and get rid of as much of the evidence as possible since Elliott / Jameson's office sat just above the convention center. We all knew after this night there was no way the rest of the force wouldn't get involved and launch a full-blown investigation on Emerald Haze. They'd raid the place, taking every single shred of dust as evidence, and we didn't have time to do a sweep.

"I'm still mad at you," Jameson said to me. Her hair was a tangled mess, half-up, half-down, and one hundred percent looked like it'd been combed with a stick of lit dynamite. Despite her wild hair, smudged makeup, and mud-covered face and arms, torn dress, she still looked just as beautiful as ever.

"Me?" I asked in a sarcastic, shocked tone. "What'd I do?"

She reared her head back. "You shot me, for starters! Was that necessary?"

I sighed. "Okay, fair enough, but that wasn't just my idea."

"So what? What if you'd missed? You'd feel like shit right now. I feel like shit now, no thanks to you!"

"First of all, I have excellent marksmanship. Second, I'm really, really sorry. Regardless." I leaned over as best I could despite the burning pain in my side and kissed her temple. "But it won't happen again. Promise."

"I appreciate that. But how did you know Kane would for sure be here?"

"We honestly didn't. Not for a fact, but given Kane's track record and River's investigation skills, we rolled the dice. We were right. Plus, River spotted him at the fundraiser. That was all the green light I needed."

She sunk back, leaning against the light pole. "How did he even get in?"

I just gave her a look. "You picked a masquerade ball as a theme. That and we let him."

"Anyone looking for me?" River finally showed up.

"Where the fuck have you been?"

He grinned. "Accidentally blew up my escape route. I had to devise a new plan. Then—" He reached into his shirt and pulled out...a kitten? "—I found this thing walking along the back of the event center. I couldn't leave him there knowing it was about to cease to exist."

Lyndsay Marie

"Oh my god!" Jameson practically cried. Hell, she probably needed to after the night she'd just had. "Another one?" She held up the kitten she already had in her hands.

"Cute. Here." River bent down and handed her the second kitten. "Have another one. Hey," River said to me, "you're bleeding…a *lot*."

"No shit, Captain Obvious. Where the hell were you back there? I almost got my ass whooped, and I most definitely got stabbed. That squirrely motherfucker could have killed me."

"Oh, shit. Sorry, baby bro. I had some technical difficulties. You want me to grab a medic?"

"No. I'm fine. I'll see one in a minute."

"*You* blew up my—my dad's casino?" James practically screeched.

He shrugged. "Had to. But I had a slight wiring issue in the beginning."

We all looked at the building as it fell half off its foundation.

"Yeah, well, one of your bombs went off at the time you were supposed to be having my back."

"Faulty circuit."

"So, I almost died because of a faulty circuit?"

"I mean, I'm usually the guy behind the screen, not the one in the field putting shit together." He mouthed the word *sorry* just as Chris and Kelly walked up.

"Kitties!" Kelly squealed, taking a seat next to Jameson and grabbing one of the kittens.

"Everyone okay?" Chris asked.

Secretly, I'd hoped he hadn't made it out.

We all gave a half-assed collective "yeah, we're good, I'm okay, glad it's over" answer.

I carefully stood up so I could be at eye level with everyone else.

"You got a mean hook on you," Chris said to me.

"Indeed. I guess I should officially apologize for that?"

He shrugged. "It's all good."

"You're not gonna press charges, are you?" I knew he wouldn't; *he* knew he wouldn't.

He laughed. "Nah. We'll just call it even."

I didn't laugh. Instead, I asked if I could have a word with him away from the group. "So, is sleeping with your boss part of your job description?" I asked when we were out of earshot from everyone else.

He flicked his gaze to the crowd behind me. "No, but can we keep that between us?"

"If you disappear on your own."

"Deal."

We shook hands, and then he waved bye to everyone. I knew that would be the last time I'd see him. I didn't technically have the power to fire him, but I didn't think he gave a shit at that point.

I rejoined what few people we had left in our group.

Jameson came over and stood beside me. "What were the two of you talking about?"

"Nothing much. Just saying our goodbyes."

"Is he leaving?"

"Yeah...for good."

She jerked her head back. "For good? Why?"

"Because I told him to."

"Roman! That's my GM! You can't just fire my people."

"Yeah, I can. It just means you'll be demoted into his position now that Elliott's back. I'm sure he'll want to take over."

"We'll see." She shook her head, then pointed at my brother, who, not surprisingly, had found his way to Kelly. "Looks like those two are getting cozy."

I rolled my eyes. "Typical."

"Well, I'm glad I finally got to meet the man, myth, and legend. I've only ever heard you talk about him occasionally in passing. I was beginning to think he wasn't real."

"There's a lot you don't know about me yet, but you're about to find out."

"Like what?"

"Like the fact that I want to make you my wife." I reached into my front pocket and pulled out the ring that I had been fighting for my life not to lose. I didn't have some fancy speech prepared or some crazy romantic proposal planned out—though anything would have been better than this.

But this? This was us.

Jameson's eyes went as wide as a deer in headlights when I grabbed her hand and slipped the ring onto her finger.

She looked down at her hand with tears in her eyes. "It's—this is my mom's ring. How did you...?"

I smiled. "I have my connections."

Elliott stood off to the side just behind with Josephine who was grinning from ear to ear, clutching onto his arm for dear life.

"You can't be serious. Do you really think we need to get married? We've never even talked about it."

"Here's the deal, Jameson. If you want me in your life, to start over, you're going to have to marry me. Be my wife."

"Why? So you can hold that title over my head and spend the rest of your life telling me what to do? I don't think—"

"No. Because I fucking love you. There isn't a single soul on this Earth who I'd rather tolerate on a daily basis, no one who knows more about me or who I'd rather spend the rest of my life with, however long that might be. Plus, I think we both know by now I can't tell you what to do."

Tears finally fell down her cheeks, washing away that dust and dirt in long streaks. "What happens if I say no?"

I blew out a slow and controlled breath because my side was on fucking fire. I was also nervous as hell she was going to say no.

Lyndsay Marie

"Then I guess I leave. Start a new life again." The thought of that was comical, but the thought of her declining my proposal gutted me.

"Really? You'd leave?"

"Not if you say yes."

She looked up at me. Her tear-filled eyes searched mine. There was doubt, fear, love.

Fuck, say something.

"Okay," she finally breathed. "Yes."

The End.

Trust Fall

Lyndsay Marie

thank ♥ you

Dear Reader,

Holy Moly, it's done…and thank YOU! Seriously. Thank you. Thanks for sticking with me through this process, reaching out and checking up on me! Thanks for reading and recommending my books. All of it means the world to me. I'll see you in the next one.

Huge shoutout to my editor, Sandy! She's the real rockstar here. And my cover artist, Staci. Thanks for bringing my ideas to life!

If you want to read my other books or keep up with new releases, check out my website—

Author Lyndsay Marie
www.AuthorLyndsayMarie.com

or visit me on Amazon
https://www.amazon.com/author/lyndsaymarie

www.ingramcontent.com/pod-product-compliance
Lightning Source LLC
Chambersburg PA
CBHW050513110726
47899CB00005B/1441